DARK SEPTEMBER

INGER WOLF

PEOPLE'S PRESS

Dark September is translated from Danish after *Sort Sensommer* by Mark
Kline markwkline@gmail.com.

Cover: Juan Padron,
https://juanjjpadron.wixsite.com/juanpadron

ISBN-13: 978-87-7180-901-5
ISBN-10: 87-7180-901-5

People'sPress
Vester Farimagsgade 41, 1606 København V

Chapter One

SUNDAY, September 21

THE WHITE POISONOUS plant lay fanned out over the woman's exposed breast. In the dawning light, dew still sparkled on the thin red-speckled stalks nodding in the light breeze. A nearby brown Irish setter raised his snout from a pile of dead leaves and sniffed at the various forest scents, one of which was unfamiliar. He checked it out cautiously. The naked woman lay in the clearing that formed a natural boundary between the tall beeches and a small dense cluster of ever-greens. She faced the sky with arms and legs spread out on a bed of fallen leaves, ferns, mushrooms, and impatiens that had finished bloom-ing. She might have been daydreaming. The setter sniffed along the woman's stomach, then it froze when its owner called in the distance. First questioningly, then insistently. The dog looked at the trail and back at the woman, then it began to bark.

THE CLEARING in front of Lieutenant Detective Daniel Trokic was covered with a chilly dew. For one of the first times that fall, filmy clouds of breath hung in the morning air. He'd driven his Peugeot past the red barrier that normally separated the quiet forest from the noise of traffic and civilization. Rammstein's muted metallic rhythms seeped out through his open windows into the mist. No one gave him dirty looks about the music when he stepped under the barrier tape and greeted them. Maybe they hadn't heard it, or maybe it seemed fitting. Trokic sensed this place had been in harmony until now. Like some strange omen, he had dreamt about the forest and a blanket of ash-gray rabbits, a troubling, recurring dream that had been interrupted by a call from the dispatcher. The forensic pathologist, Torben Bach, wore plastic gloves and shoe covers, as did the two techs who had photographed and measured the area.

"Who is she?" Trokic asked.

"We don't know," one of the techs said. "No ID on her."

The young woman beside Trokic lay on her back, her blonde hair unfurled around her face. Her eyes, one brown and one blue, were blank and bloodless as if they were covered with a fine milky-white net. They stared at a point in the silent forest. Her mouth was frozen into the shape of a final breath. He wished he could cover her with a blanket.

What stuck out most about the woman, though, was the handful of whitish flowers arranged on her breast. Not enough for a bouquet. Artful yet grotesque. A bride? Was that what she was supposed to look like?

Bach nodded at Trokic. Carefully, he lifted the hair from the woman's throat and pushed aside a stray toad to show him the fatal wound. The deep cut started at her left ear and continued down to her sternum, exposing bone and musculature underneath her clear skin. Dried reddish-black blood was caked in her hair and on her body. Also, part of her upper arm was torn up, an open, lacerated wound, with several gaping bite marks on her left breast and under her ribs. Trokic guessed some small forest animal had been disturbed during its meal.

"Who found her?" Trokic said.

Bach's gray eyes had clouded over from the sight in front of him. "Leif Korning, he walks dogs around here. They took him to the station."

Trokic glanced around the dense forest surrounding them. According to the map, a trail, Løkpåts Vej, was nearby. They were six kilometers from the center of town, in an old-growth section of gnarled trees. It was pitch-dark at night out here, and far from the nearest house, the old forest manager residence fifteen minutes' walk to the northwest. Evergreens and cobweb-filled brambles stood to his right. The broad trail and the beech forest lay behind him, with a small heart-shaped green pond surrounded by a meadow not far off.

His temples ached. He'd been up late last night watching a Zrinko Ogresta film, with a bottle of red wine for company; it wasn't even eight-thirty yet, and he was still feeling the effects.

While the pathologist took the temperature of the dead woman's ear, the youngest tech walked over. He was wearing big boots, and his longish hair had been tucked under his hood. "She would've been hidden better over in the bushes."

"Or in the lake," Trokic said. "A damn psycho," he added, mumbling now.

Trokic was grateful for his warm, blue thermal coat. It was old and out of fashion, but at least he wasn't cold. "What's that plant on top of her, do you know?"

"It looks like ground elder," the tech said. "It's all over around my house, the only way to get rid of the shit is chemical warfare."

The pathologist shook his head and wiped his nose. "It's not blooming anymore. Nothing's blooming anymore."

"How long has she been dead?" Trokic said.

"My guess is since early yesterday evening."

"That sounds about right. There must be a lot of joggers and mountain bikers out here in the daytime; they would've seen her if it had happened earlier. There's probably not many around after dark."

"And even if they were, they wouldn't have noticed her this far from the trail," the tech said. "It gets dark earlier in here too, all the shadows falling, all that. It's tough finding your way around in here, early evening."

"We found traces of something that looks like semen," Bach said, pointing to her stomach. It was barely visible. He and Trokic looked at each other. "Maybe the rapist from the Botanical Gardens has new hunting grounds?"

Trokic frowned. "It's not impossible."

"Must have been tiring though, hiding in here, waiting to ambush someone."

"Yeah, but somebody was screwed up enough to do it," Trokic mumbled. "Any other signs of sexual assault? Besides the fact that she's naked?"

"No. Apart from the bite marks, it doesn't look like she's been touched. But let's see when we get her in."

Trokic took another look at the woman. She had no make-up on, no jewelry; only her toenails had nail polish, pink. Uneven. She'd been pretty.

They heard the crunch of gravel and dirt from the trail, and a moment later a man appeared, a bit out of breath. Obviously, he'd been in a hurry, from the sight of striped pajamas sticking out from underneath his blue sweater.

"What the hell?" he said. "How'd you drive in here? I couldn't find that damn parking area you talked about; I've been walking around at least fifteen minutes."

He swiped angrily at his sweaty temples with a handkerchief. Trokic walked down the striped barrier tape to greet his boss.

"Do we have an ID?" Captain Agersund said, nodding at the woman.

Trokic shook his head. "Did you bring coffee?"

"I just got out of bed," Agersund explained. One of the men behind them groaned. "Has anyone been reported missing the past few days?"

"Only a woman from the north part of town, according to the duty officer. And she returned this morning; otherwise, no one who fits the description."

"She doesn't look good. What are those flowers?" Agersund squinted and studied them for a moment. "Hard to see from here, it could be chervil or fool's parsley…"

"I'm sure the techs have taken plenty of photos," Trokic said.

"What about the weapon?"

"Nothing yet."

Trokic had requested two police dogs. A good nose or two was invaluable in this rolling forest terrain, and in all likelihood, they were looking for a sharp knife and bloody clothing. Agersund turned to the pathologist. "What else do you have?"

Bach repeated what Trokic had earlier heard him speak into the Dictaphone. The woman was in her twenties. Cause of death most likely her cut throat. Her leg muscles bulged under pale skin; she seemed to be in good physical shape. And a delicate web of silver lines on her stomach could mean she'd been pregnant at some time.

"Was she killed here?"

Bach nodded. "It's almost certain she's only been moved a few meters. Livor mortis is evident on her back, and there's a partial trail of blood through the underbrush."

A tech joined them. "Right over there, see?" He pointed to an old beech close to the trail. "I think that's where she was killed. There's more blood there than anywhere else, and the leaves are scattered around. And some of the mushrooms have been stepped on. Someone dragged her over here by the hair or arms, you can see faint signs of it. I think her clothes were taken off where she's lying; otherwise, there would have been a lot more blood on her body."

"So, the sexual act happened after death?" Agersund asked.

"It's just my opinion."

A crease appeared on Agersund's forehead. "I'd believe anything, the way she looks."

He turned to Trokic. "Where's the media? They all sleeping in late, or what?"

"They probably can't find their way out here, either."

Agersund shook his head. "Here we go again. We're undermanned. It's bad enough to start with, those shitheads taking about a fourth of us for their summit meeting. All right...let's get an idea of where we're at here. I want you to head up the investigation; I'm assigning Lisa and Jasper to you."

Trokic stared at his boss. "Lisa Kornelius?"

"Yeah. So?" He stared back at Trokic.

"It's just…" Trokic looked down at the ground. "I heard she's in Copenhagen this weekend."

"What?!" Agersund frowned at the people around him working as he picked at something lodged between his front teeth. "Call her then, fill her in. When are you finished?" he asked the techs.

They both shook their heads. It was going to take several more hours.

Trokic studied the woman's elegant face, her pale forehead. What had she been thinking?

Chapter Two

TROKIC FOLLOWED one of the trails leading away from the clearing. As so often before, he was taken in by the mystery of a crime scene. The intensity of events. And why there? Often, it wasn't a coincidence.

It had been more like southern Europe that summer, the heat, the odors. Evenings so quiet that he could hear the frogs and crickets from the porch of his small house in town. But autumn was gaining the upper hand. On his right, acorns were thick under an oak tree, and the dying grass beside the trail smelled strong and sweet. There was something else, though. Even in daylight, the forest was murkier than he would have expected. He strode up the trail, checking both sides every step of the way. A strolling couple appeared ahead of him. He spoke to them for a moment then let them pass. Tourists from a nearby hotel.

He walked around a bend and noticed a young woman approaching. A playful golden retriever ran circles around her. "Europa!" she called out when the dog galloped towards him. The woman caught up to it and fastened a leash to its collar.

"She's still young, still learning," she said. Abruptly, she stood up. "You're from the police?"

"Yes."

Trokic still imagined himself to be an average thirty-eight-year-old man who people thought of as an accountant or office worker or whatever. It surprised him whenever someone pegged him as a policeman, maybe because he didn't identify all that well with the rest of the police force. Suddenly, he was aware of the look of his warm thermal coat. He showed her his badge.

"Tro-kick?"

"Tro-kitch," he said.

"I walked by where you sealed off earlier," she explained. "Did something serious happen?"

Her blonde hair was pulled back in a thin ponytail. She didn't seem to be wearing any makeup, yet it was hard to avoid her dark blue eyes. "Yes."

He wondered how many women would be walking around in the forest, once the news about the sexual assault and murder came out. He noticed a few pale spots on the woman's slightly reddened throat in the cool air. "Do you walk your dog a lot here?"

"Once a day, when I have time."

"What about yesterday?"

"I was here in the morning."

"Okay. You don't happen to know anyone else who comes out here, someone who knows the area and might have seen something?"

She hesitated, perhaps considering what to say. "I know a few. A lot of people run out here. In fact, I was in a group from the university who ran together, every Thursday evening, but it didn't last. Most of them are serious about running, though; they still come out here. Just at different times."

"Could you give me the names of all the people you know who run in the forest? We need to speak to as many of them as possible."

"I'm reasonably certain I have a list of everyone in the group. I can find it for you, it's at home."

She looked up and frowned at him. Trokic petted the dog, who kept nudging her pink wet snout against his leg. Her tail, hind legs, and chest were covered with long, wavy, well-brushed fur.

"Can you send it to me? Or call?"

She thought for a moment. "I'll be home in an hour. I'll find it then."

The past months had been strange. The media called it the bloodiest summer in memory. Traffic deaths had been at a record level, and there had been an extraordinary amount of violence. And now this. It was as if everything was falling apart, all this black, disgusting hate bubbling up to the surface. And it seemed to be getting worse. They'd been swamped with work.

"Be careful. Stay on the trails and keep your dog close. Believe me, it's important to be cautious."

"Of course."

He thanked her for the information and gave her his card. She wrote down her name, address, and phone number for him. Finally, he walked back to the pond and sealed-off area.

After signing in the techs' log book again, he was allowed to pass the barrier tape for the second time that day. When the many pieces of the investigation puzzle were laid out, the physical evidence he, the techs, and the forensic pathologist gathered was often the most reliable. They called this tangible evidence "the silent witnesses." People, on the other hand, lied and led them astray.

The pond was greenish-brown from fallen leaves and

food thrown out to ducks. He knew the area close by might be soggy, yet despite being careful, his yellow sneakers were soon soaked. The cold water slowly seeped up his pant legs. He swore loudly. A duck flew up out of the reeds when he reached the far end of the pond. It was a natural waterhole, about forty yards in diameter. If the murder weapon and her clothes didn't show up around the crime scene, they would have to call in divers to search the dark water, a time-consuming job.

He checked the ground for footprints, even though he knew one of the techs had already gone over the area. He noticed a small patch of a plant similar to what they'd found on the woman and walked over to take a look. His gut told him it was the same plant, even though it had tiny seeds; its flowers were wilted but not yet dry. Despite this tiny victory, the question was: why did the killer choose those specific flowers? Did it have to do with some sort of ritual? He picked a few, put them in a plastic bag, and washed his fingers in the pond.

Finally, he stood in the stillness, gazing at the calm water. His eyes followed the many spider webs. Something glinted down in the grass. Instinctively, he grabbed it and held it up to the light. A silver necklace. A few strands of blond hair were stuck to the chain. Someone had been here. He took a DNA kit out of his pocket and dropped the chain in the paper bag.

TROKIC'S PHONE RANG. He walked over to his car, sat down inside, and lit a cigarette. Smoking wasn't allowed at the crime scene. The call was from the station. He listened intently while watching his colleagues through the car window. Two minutes later, he joined them.

"We might have an ID on her," he told Agersund. "A

neighbor of a single mother called from an apartment building not far away. A child's been screaming in the mother's apartment for several hours, and nobody answers the door when the neighbor rings the doorbell. He says he's looked in all the windows and can't see anything. He got worried about the young boy, so he called. It's only a five-minute drive. Jasper's on his way; I'll meet him there."

He might know who she was very soon.

Chapter Three

EVEN IN THE light morning mist, the apartment building looked clean, and the sand-colored walls contrasted beautifully against the background of the forest. Trokic and Detective Jasper Taurup heard the hollow sound the moment they stepped inside the hall. A low whimper that occasionally turned into sobbing. They rang the doorbell of the first-floor apartment with a name printed on the door: Anna Kiehl. The neighbor, a white-haired man, opened his door and stuck his head out.

"Police," Trokic said. "Are you the one who called us?"

"Yeah, he's been screaming for hours, right up until now."

Trokic rang the doorbell again. "How old is the boy?"

"I think he's three. Peter's his name."

"And you don't have an extra key, or know where to get one?"

"No, otherwise I'd have gone in myself."

A three-year-old could hardly unlock that type of door, Trokic thought. He let the doorbell ring twice more, then Jasper readied himself to kick the door in.

"Stop," Trokic said. "Bring the toolbox in from the car. You can't break a door like this, and we can't wait for a locksmith."

The neighbor hadn't budged an inch. "And you don't want to scare the wits out of the boy."

"Christ," Jasper said, visibly shaken at the thought of the abandoned child. He ran out to the car and returned with the tools, and a half minute later, the door swung open.

It was quiet when Trokic stepped into the apartment. His partner bit his lip and rubbed his arm as if he were freezing.

"Peter," Trokic said, his voice calm; the child must be frightened if he'd really been left alone. No answer. Trokic walked into the kitchen and looked around. The faint odor of cleanser hung in the air. Ammonia and flowers. Everything seemed to be in its place. He walked on into the light-green living room; reproductions of Asger Jorn and Kurt Trampedach hung on the walls. On the coffee table lay an anthology of Modernism, two thick volumes about Renaissance artists, and a children's book with a dragon on the front. The books were worn.

Trokic called out the child's name again, this time louder, as he systematically checked the few rooms. They were empty and quiet. A digital alarm clock blinked in the bedroom—four zeroes, as if time no longer existed. There was no sign of anyone having slept in the bed, and the open Venetian blinds allowed the dust-free columns of sunlight to stream in. Finally, he reached the child's bedroom and glanced around, but the boy was nowhere in sight. He knelt down and looked under the bed, lifted up the comforter with its red and green animal figures. Nothing. The closet door to the right of the window stood open a crack. Slowly, he opened it and looked inside.

A little boy with blond hair sticking up stared at a point on the wall behind Trokic. His eyes were green, and he wore a pair of purple Harry Potter pajamas. He sat huddled in a corner, his arms hugging his knees.

Trokic sighed in relief. "Hi, Peter."

The boy didn't react. Trokic wasn't confident around young children, and he hesitated, uncertain of what to say. What if he frightened and upset the boy even more? He returned to the living room.

"I found him in the closet, but he doesn't want to come out."

"I'll take care of him," Jasper said. "Take a look...is it her?" He pointed to the television then walked into the bedroom.

Trokic put on a plastic glove and carefully picked the photo up from the back to avoid adding his fingerprints to it. Her hair was shorter, she had more of a suntan, and she was wearing turquoise eyeshadow, but he was certain: this was the woman in the forest. One blue and one brown eye. Anna Kiehl, if the name on the door was correct. A small mouth, a hint of a guarded smile. As if she were wondering about something the photographer had said. Her eyes looked directly at him. Lively, a bit curious. Surrounded by dark eyebrows and eyelids.

"It's her," he mumbled.

At last, Trokic looked up and glanced around the living room. Jasper was speaking softly to the boy in the bedroom. Not that his partner had any special qualifications for handling a child in a crisis situation. He was simply better at it than Trokic. And back when they'd realized that (it had only taken a single incident for them to know), Jasper had taken over that particular task. It was never easy to inform someone of a death, but in this case, someone in the boy's immediate family would have to tell him. The important thing now was that until his father or a grandparent arrived, someone had to take care of him and show the appropriate respect for a child whose home suddenly had been taken over by the police.

"What are you doing here? Has something happened?"

Trokic started. The voice was thick and husky as if its owner had just woken up from a long sleep.

Chapter Four

DETECTIVE LISA KORNELIUS had just thrown her dingy traveling clothes in a big pile on the floor of her apartment. She walked around naked, looking for her cigarettes as she listened to the messages on her cell phone. Trokic explained in detail the circumstances of the case to which she'd been assigned by Agersund. And now she had to report directly to *him*.

Lisa had requested—had earned—a transfer to Homicide. She'd wanted out of her area of expertise, IT work that included cases involving pedophiles and child porn on the net. But knowing that Trokic would be heading up the investigation dampened her enthusiasm considerably. Their paths had crossed on cases a few times, and somehow, though he tried to be friendly, he always managed to make her feel like a trainee who was in the way. She didn't feel that the five years difference in their ages, or for that matter, his experience, justified his attitude. She'd seen just as much shit as he had, if that's what it came down to. Just a different type of shit. His Croatian roots, and the fact that he lived alone and never talked about anything other than work didn't help her understand him. In short, as things stood now, he was low on the list of her favorite colleagues.

She glanced through the mail she'd brought in from her postbox and stopped at the sight of a window envelope. "No more unpleasant surprises," she mumbled to herself. She shuddered and tossed the whole pile onto the kitchen table.

After at last finding a pack of cigarettes, she recalled her promise to herself to not smoke at home. But what the heck. She grabbed a thin silk kimono from the chair, draped it around her slender body, and opened one of the small windows for some air in the crowded apartment. A marble-like mist lay over the city's jumble of asymmetrical roofs. The city seemed deserted. Subdued even, melancholy.

A woman her age had been killed in the forest. Trokic wanted her to be at the autopsy. She took a drag on her cigarette and tried to prepare herself, though she knew that was impossible. True, she had witnessed two autopsies while in police school, but she had the feeling this would be different.

She peered at the bird in a wooden cage in the corner and said, "Tell me if you're cold." The large macaw, Flossy Bent P., came from an ex-boyfriend studying Spanish who dumped her to go trekking in South America. She'd done her best to get rid of the red-green bird, not least because it croaked out "That's swell," one of *his* favorite expressions, several times a day. Finally, she'd given up; apparently, the bird was meant to be a part of her messy apartment the rest of its days.

She listened to the message on her phone once more, this time taking notes in a small, leather-bound notebook. After delaying as long as possible, she took a quick shower before heading for the station. The autopsy would be performed as soon as possible, Trokic had said, and she had to be there. Whether she wanted to or not.

Chapter Five

A PALE WOMAN around sixty wobbled into sight. She was wearing a frayed pink dressing gown with white stars, and Trokic caught a faint whiff of alcohol and bacon. But on Sunday mornings, you could smell like practically anything, he had to admit. She reminded him of something he'd seen in an American film. A former diva who had given up on making an impression. Her sunken eyes were still bright blue, contrasting starkly against skin that had seen too much sun. Or maybe too much of everything.

"Police," Trokic said. "And you are?"

"I live upstairs. My name is Ursula Skousen. Where's Anna? And Peter?"

She glanced around the room as if she'd never seen it before. Or at least as if it looked different than usual. She sounded apprehensive, though she likely already had an inkling of the situation, given the empty apartment and the somber faces around her.

"Not here," Trokic said, trying to keep his voice neutral.

"What *happened*?" Her hand flew up to her throat, which startled Trokic.

While his colleague continued to coax the boy out of the closet, he led Fru Skousen out to the end of the hallway.

"It can't be true," she said after he briefly explained about the woman in the forest. He emphasized that a final identification needed to be made before they could be absolutely certain it was Anna Kiehl. He didn't mention who would identify her; sometimes it was best not to say too much in the beginning. She looked terrified.

"I'm afraid it is."

"How's poor little Peter? And where is he?"

"We're taking care of him until the family has been contacted. When was the last time you saw Anna?"

"Yesterday evening. After dinner. Before she went out on her run. I looked after Peter; I do that often when she needs to study."

"She's a student?"

"At the university, yes. Anthropology. She's very talented. And that girl's a hard worker."

"What about later on in the evening?"

She hesitated, then a guilty expression passed over her face. "It was Saturday last night, you know. I wanted to see a program. She doesn't have a TV, so when Peter fell asleep and she hadn't come back from her run yet, I took the baby alarm upstairs with me and watched the program. He was sleeping like an angel."

"So, the last time you saw her was…after dinner. What time was that?"

"It was just after the program with that crazy Englishman started, that's when I went down."

Trokic squinted in concentration. "Mr. Bean? That would've been at seven."

He'd also watched the program while eating spicy Turkish sausage with glazed cabbage at the dinner table.

19

Thinking about it, his stomach growled; he hadn't had time for breakfast that morning.

"If you say so."

"You didn't worry when she didn't get back from her run?"

Fru Skousen looked puzzled. "But she did. I heard her later, so I shut the alarm off."

Trokic gave her a skeptical look.

"She came back," she said, her voice now firm. "I heard her rummaging about, and I can see she's picked things up around here for once." Trokic let that hang in the air for a moment. That and the scent of alcohol.

"What about boyfriends?" he asked. "Guests? Did you notice anyone visiting her yesterday?"

"No, no one. She was always saying that her studies took all her time. A few people stopped by once in a while, but I don't know who they were."

"Right now, it's very important to us." He didn't mention the sexual angle. "If you happen to think of someone, we'd like to know."

He stopped to gather his thoughts. He had to get rid of this headache. The station would be in total chaos, and he wouldn't be getting any sleep for a long time. He pressed a few fingers against a spot on his neck to help him concentrate on the woman in front of him.

She sat down on the steps and looked at him with an inscrutable expression. It was soaking in for her, he thought. The realization that Anna might not have returned.

"Does she usually run?"

"Yes. Always the same route. I know because the dear girl told me that she was trying to improve her time. It's about five kilometers long. Three times a week. Tuesday, Thursday, and Saturday."

"The same route? You're sure of that?"

"Yes. Tuesdays and Thursdays, he's in daycare, but once in a while, I look after him on Saturday. It never takes long. And I'm supposed to call her if there's any problem."

"Call? While she's running?"

"Yes, I don't like not being able to get ahold of her, in case something happens to Peter. So, she always has her cell phone with her. I'm not all that young anymore."

Trokic frowned and made a note. They hadn't found her phone yet. "So, there was nothing at all out of the ordinary yesterday before she went out on her usual run?"

"Everything was perfectly normal."

"Did she sound different in any way?"

"No. I told her it would be dark soon, but she said it wasn't a problem, she could run her route blindfolded."

She shook her head. He looked into her small eyes; despite the shock she must have been feeling, the situation seemed to be exciting to her in some way, arousing even. Trokic wanted to shake her.

"I told her there could be godawful types around. Flashers and such. You'd never catch me running around in that forest alone."

"But you didn't sense anything unusual when she left?"

Fru Skousen pulled down the sleeves of her robe. "No. Peter was already asleep, and I read a magazine until I went back upstairs. I didn't hear him again."

Trokic grimaced. He had the feeling she'd fallen asleep in front of the television and therefore couldn't provide more information about yesterday evening. He doubted she'd heard Anna Kiehl return. She had bags under her eyes, and she pulled her robe tighter as he stared at her.

"We'll need a complete statement from you, and I'm afraid I'm going to have to ask you to identify her."

She looked shocked as if a thriller had leaped out of the TV and into the room. "Identify her?" She tasted the words.

"Yes. We don't want to contact her parents before we're absolutely sure, and there are a number of other things I want to hear more about. Like the route she ran, her habits, things like that. Detective Taurup can drive you to the station if you'd like."

"You seem very certain it's her," she said. "It could be someone else. Maybe she's just out buying bread for breakfast. Maybe she met someone she knew, maybe she's...I don't know what, I just can't imagine..."

He remembered her strange eyes. "Anna has one blue and one brown eye, doesn't she?"

Fru Skousen slumped.

BACK IN THE boy's bedroom, his colleague was sitting on the bed. The blond-haired boy lay stiff as a board, staring straight up at the ceiling. Trokic swallowed at the sight of him, so tiny and fragile. He closely resembled his mother.

"I called for a doctor," Jasper said quietly. "I think the boy's in shock."

Chapter Six

POLICE HEADQUARTERS WAS LOCATED in several buildings surrounding a square courtyard. The Criminal Investigations Division occupied the fourth floor in one of the newer, less attractive buildings. Trokic's office, which also served as a small meeting room, looked out on the courtyard. Meager sunlight, even now late in the morning, made the office gloomy and stuffy during winter, the worst time of year for him. When full sunlight seemed so far away. Often, he found himself planning trips to his other homeland, knowing well that Zagreb wasn't much warmer because of its inland climate. It just seemed warmer. As if the sun could break through any second and warm everything up. In Denmark, everything was damp and cold through and through, with no hope of relief.

Agersund's ample body overflowed the chair across from him, and his gruff voice echoed through the room. "So, the neighbor and her parents identified her. That was quick. Where's the boy now?"

They'd been working together for seven years, starting when Trokic had started at Homicide. He would have liked to describe their relationship as collegial, characterized by mutual respect and cordiality. But the fact was that the captain reminded him of the ants that invaded his kitchen every summer: they got into everything that smelled of sugar, and they were impossible to get rid of.

"He's with her parents. A doctor and a psychologist took care of him. We were really worried; he was completely apathetic when they carried him out of the apartment."

Agersund's short gray hair stood straight up as if at attention. Before long, he would be darting around like a lizard on a stone wall. "Damn tough for him. I've already taken the first call from the press. Probably listening in on a police scanner. He started yapping about the rapist from the Botanical Gardens. Damn, I was hoping this wouldn't get out; the media will be on it like flies on shit."

This wasn't a new problem. Sometimes the press beat them to the crime scene. Many reporters called in several times a day to hear what was going on, and it was the dispatcher's job to handle it. They had ways to limit the media's access to their communication. By encrypting sensitive information when possible, for example. Or by using cell phones. But it didn't always work, and public knowledge of a case in its early stages often did serious harm. Not only to the investigation but also to the persons involved. Agersund knew how to handle the press. Every day during a major case, he fed the reporters a tasty morsel they could turn into a headline, which essentially was what they were after. That kept them off the backs of the police.

Trokic looked over at the big whiteboard on the wall, at the photo of the naked young woman and the flowers. There were photos of the woman from every angle, showing her tangled hair, her pleasant-featured but lifeless face, the open wound on her neck. Trokic had also put up a map of the forest and made his own sketch of the chaotic crime scene he would be spending a lot of time analyzing. Crime scenes like this were a rare sight, simply because such cases were rare.

He scratched his cheek. "They say the dogs tracked a scent down to the rest area, too. The killer might have arrived in a car."

"That could be anybody," Agersund said.

Trokic absentmindedly ran a hand through his black hair as pieces of the puzzle whirled around in his head. Too few pieces, he realized, to know what the picture would be in the end. He drummed his fingers on the desk. He had to get out of there. Get going.

Detective Taurup stood in the doorway. His boyish body seemed even thinner in his blue windbreaker. Like Trokic, he hadn't shaved that morning, though in Trokic's case it made little difference, as his five o'clock shadow always showed up early.

"What's going on?" Trokic said. "Do we have a report from the first responding officers?"

"Yup. Leif Korning, the guy who found her, has been cleared. His alibi checked out."

"That's what I figured. The guy's half blind, I hear. He couldn't possibly be involved."

"Hey, are you okay, Daniel? You look a little rough around—"

"I'm fine." Trokic ignored the "rough around" bit. He still had a headache.

"I want that murder weapon and the cell phone," Agersund said. "And her clothes. We might have to take a closer look at that pond, get some divers down in there. However, part of the forest is a preserve. Before you know it, we'll be fighting the forest manager, the regional bureaucracy, and an army of biologists."

He stood up to leave. "Daniel, don't turn this into a one-man show. Keep me posted."

Trokic waited patiently for the usual spiel about not taking things into his own hands, about his responsibility as a leader. Once in a while, Agersund threatened him with a transfer. He shrugged it off nowadays, sensing it was just for show; his boss had resigned himself to Trokic's way of doing things.

He fingered the two marbles he always carried in his pocket and glanced at Agersund. "I usually do."

Lisa Kornelius shook a cigarette out of the pack and lit it. Her colleagues respected her, even though her odd clothing, purple hair, and height led them to make silly comments sometimes. She'd spent three years in the Copenhagen Police IT division, and she'd been loaned out to the Århus Police twice: on a local hacker case two years ago, then later for a seminar on computer forensics. Agersund had been so impressed that he'd talked her into transferring to Århus. Now she assisted whenever computer technology was involved, no matter which department.

As far as Trokic knew, she lived alone in an apartment in the center of town, with no boyfriend and no kids. She was in her early thirties, though at times, the look in her eyes made her seem twenty years older. He had enormous respect for her work, and he had no problems with her, as long as she stayed behind her desk. He didn't understand why she'd been assigned to this homicide. In his opinion, everyone should keep to what they do best, and if that was working with computers, they shouldn't be out in the field, where trusting your partner to have your back in an emergency was essential. He simply couldn't see her taking part in a police operation or as an analytical interrogation leader. But for some reason, Agersund had decided to throw her a bone. And Trokic would have to make the best of it.

LISA SEEMED a bit distracted as she flipped the pages of her notebook back and forth, trying to familiarize herself with the details of the case. Clearly, she didn't want to show she was affected by the situation, but her eyes darted a few moments as she glanced at the photographs on the whiteboard. How many homicide victims had she seen in her career? Probably none. He wondered if she could handle watching the autopsy.

"You've been in Copenhagen? Was it a good trip?"

She nodded without saying a word, her eyes glued to her notes.

Trokic poured another cup of coffee and offered it to her. She spilled a few drops on her lime-green sweater on the hand-off.

"When will we hear from forensics and the techs?" Lisa said.

She wanted to show she knew what was going on, Trokic thought. "We'll get the reports from our people early tomorrow morning, the others hopefully sometime this week. Jasper will be coordinating the questionings."

Finally, she looked up at him. "What do you think happened here, why was she killed?"

He mirrored the cool look from her green eyes. Verdigris, like the copper roofs of old churches. "I think it's personal. Very personal." The telephone rang as he stood up. Bach.

"We're on our way," Trokic said.

"It's the plant," the pathologist said. "Your tech just arrived. He called a botanist in immediately." He paused a moment. "This is going to be interesting."

Chapter Seven

"IT'S one of the most poisonous plants in Denmark," Bach said, as he slipped the sheet off the corpse. "Hemlock. It can be lethal. It's not very common. Normally, it would be dead by now, if the summer hadn't lasted so long. But that's not the strangest part."

Trokic breathed through his mouth to avoid the smell. Instantly, he'd felt nauseous when they stepped into the autopsy room of the Department of Forensic Medicine. He would never get used to the place. Every time he came here, the smell brought forth images of things he wanted to forget.

There were seven of them in the room: the pathologist, Torben Bach, an assistant pathologist, an orderly, Lisa Kornelius, Trokic, Agersund, and the tech, Kurt Tønnies. It was Tønnies' job to photograph the procedure from start to finish and to take care of all the technical evidence, such as clothes, jewelry, etc.

"The bouquet scattered over her has been dried. When I first saw the plants, I thought they'd just wilted, but they're dry as a bone. Not one single drop of moisture left in them. In other words, they weren't picked recently."

"Dried?" the tech said. "What does that mean?"

Bach smiled. "When you find out, I hope you'll tell me." He measured the throat wound and made a note of it.

"If they weren't picked in the immediate area like we thought, that would indicate planning," Agersund mumbled. "Not a spur-of-the-moment rape that got out of hand."

The sight of the young woman was no less frightening, now that she'd been brought in from the forest. The gaping wound on her throat was black. Trokic noticed that Lisa held herself and shook a bit, and he kept an eye on her in case she got physically ill. She seemed to be holding up okay in that department, though.

"The murder weapon is probably a small, sharp knife with a narrow blade," Bach said. "You can see it from the cut, right there. Anyway, you're looking for a very fine instrument."

He slid his finger along the wound. "It's a very clean cut that severed nerves and veins…deep, very deep in fact. All the way to the spinal column. The person is right-handed. And a good deal of physical force was used. Or it could be rage."

THEY WATCHED FOR OVER AN HOUR, with Bach commenting along the way. At first, there was no new information, nothing they hadn't known from the postmortem done where they'd found her body. The time of death was Saturday evening, probably between seven and ten. The cause of death was the incision in her throat and the subsequent enormous loss of blood. There was no sign of sexual assault besides the semen. Anna Kiehl was twenty-seven years old, five feet seven, with medium-blonde hair cut in a page. Normal build. Trokic noticed that her navel had been pierced and that she had several birthmarks. Her skin was now an unnatural color, and her inner organs had been removed.

"So, she didn't put up a fight?" Trokic asked.

Bach stood quietly for a few moments, ignoring the question. Finally, he said, "She was pregnant."

"How far along?" Lisa asked, even more horrified now as she gazed down at the body.

"Hmmm…I need a measurement. My guess is ten weeks. Right now, I would say the fetus looks normal."

"Daniel!" Agersund thundered. "Boyfriends, ex-boyfriends, lovers, any men interested in her?"

Trokic shook his head. "We don't know of anyone yet. Obviously, it's our top priority now."

Bach's orderly took the fetus away. DNA tests would be performed to possibly determine the identity of the father. Trokic was relieved when it was gone.

"Hemlock," Bach said. "Bit of an odd statement from our killer."

"What do you mean?" Lisa asked.

"If I remember correctly, hemlock causes cramps, vomiting, abdominal pain, and a whole number of other very unpleasant symptoms. Even a small dose can cause respiratory paralysis and death. But it was used here only for decoration."

"They made Socrates drink hemlock tea after he was convicted of not believing in the state gods," Tønnies said. "They said he perverted young people. Could there be a connection?"

"Interesting," Agersund said. "It can't be a coincidence. I don't want a single bit of this leaked to the media, is that understood?"

"When can we expect a report?" Trokic said, sweating now. It was difficult for him to concentrate. And the dead woman already smelled, a sweet, heavy odor.

"When I get the results of all the tests," Bach said. "Would you mark these?" He handed Trokic two glass tubes and a permanent marker to give him something to do, distract him from his thoughts. A diplomatic move.

Bach took off his gloves, turned to the sink, and washed his hands thoroughly and systematically.

Several of the others looked at each other for some answer. The unspoken question hung in the air above the young woman's body.

"We're going to nail the bastard," Agersund said.

Chapter Eight

"HUMAN HAIR, YOU SAY," Agersund said skeptically. "Stuck in a necklace that's obviously been laying there a long time. It could be anybody's. We have three hundred thousand candidates from the city alone, not counting the surrounding area."

"You think so?" Trokic said. "I don't agree. The pond is quite a distance away from the trail; it's not the most logical place to be walking around. We've got to have it examined."

Lisa glanced at the whiteboard in the briefing room. Her boss had already sketched out what they knew at present. Several colleagues sat glued to their chairs, concentrating on what was going on.

"Yeah, yeah, okay, take care of it," Agersund said, ready to move on. "Until we have the techs' reports, we're going to focus on mapping out the movements of the victim. I want to know everything about this young lady. When we're done, I want to know who she saw, what she did, what she ate, all her habits, good and bad. I want to know her better than I know myself."

"That shouldn't be too hard," Jasper mumbled from somewhere back in the room.

As usual, Agersund ignored the insult and brought out a large map of the city and all the suburbs and forested areas. He hung it over the whiteboard. A stippled square in the southeast corner outlined where they'd found Anna Kiehl.

"We're looking for witnesses within this area." He drew an invisible circle in the air around the map and then pulled up his gray pants, which looked as if they might fall off any minute.

"We're going to question everyone who could have been in the forest in the time frame of the murder. Dog walkers, mountain bikers, runners, riders, tourists, residents of the area. I want all the reports on my desk, with a copy for Trokic."

Trokic spoke up. "We've got to assume we're dealing with an extremely disturbed person. We're checking all the lunatics not locked up, also everyone who could have had some problem with the victim."

"What about the MO?" one of the older officers asked.

"We haven't seen anything quite like this before, so it's probably not someone we know."

Agersund cleared his throat and sat down on the table. "We don't have a motive. It doesn't look like she put up a fight, which *could* mean she'd gone there voluntarily with the killer. Who then would be somebody she knew. But let's not eliminate anything. Nobody, I mean nobody talks to anyone who even looks like they might be media. If anyone leaks anything, this person will be fed into a shredder and squeezed into a ball smaller than my asshole."

"Is anyone from MCI coming?" Jasper said.

On difficult cases, they often were assisted by the Mobile Crime Investigation Unit, a division of the national police with special expertise and experience.

"We're not getting much help," Agersund said. "They're working on that case with the headless corpse that showed up in Copenhagen a month ago. But they thought they might be able to spare someone they just hired."

"Fantastic," Jasper said, acting as if he was about to clap. "We're so very grateful."

"It's better than nothing," Agersund mumbled.

Lisa looked at her boss and smiled. Despite his clumsy behavior and tacky appearance, she was sure he was an excellent leader. Once in a while, when he showed up in wrinkled, seedy shirts and trudged through the building, she nearly felt sorry for him. He'd been divorced for four years; his wife just couldn't take it anymore, was what she'd heard. The irregular work hours, all the talk about autopsies and other Department A activities during dinner. One day when he got home from a late shift, she'd tossed half of the house into a duvet cover and announced that their marriage was over. They had joint custody of their two teenage boys. So much for the gossip. Lisa appreciated him for several reasons: he'd made her feel welcome and treated her with the greatest respect, he'd made sure everyone working with child pornography had access to a psychologist, and he always had time for them. Even when he had way too much on his plate. He was popular on the force and with the public, and she was proud to call him her boss.

Agersund's phone rang, and he fished it out of his pocket and spoke shortly to someone. He hung up and looked at everyone. "The techs have just started going through Anna Kiehl's apartment. Trokic, Lisa—take care of that."

Chapter Nine

THE AIR WAS cold and crisp when they arrived and stepped out into the darkness. Their evening would be spent combing through Kiehl's apartment. Twenty-four hours earlier, Lisa had been on her way to another meeting. She smiled at the thought of her trip to Copenhagen. The man she'd met. Maybe she shouldn't have gotten involved with him so quickly, but she felt the chemistry had been right, and he had been incredibly attractive and gallant. And what else should she do with her fading youth? She'd met him on a dating site on the internet, and they'd written back and forth for two months, dozens of emails. She felt they'd become close. He was only a few years older, and he didn't reject the idea of having children or of moving to Jutland, two important things to her. Now she was in wait-for-a-call mode, and she was, in fact, grateful for something else to think about.

THE TECHS HAD FOUND a slip of paper under Kiehl's bathroom scale. The only small piece of the puzzle that for now piqued their curiosity. In her short career with the city's police department, Lisa had participated in searches for computers containing things you wouldn't show your worst enemy. Usually, though, those searches had taken place at the end of an investigation. This was something new for her. A beginning.

On one side of the paper stood a name: Procticon. A British pharmaceutical company, Jasper had said. On the other side: "C+I." It might have nothing to do with the case, but it couldn't be ignored. Writing the name of a pharmaceutical firm on a slip of paper and sticking it under a scale was odd. It must have been dropped on the floor and blown underneath by a gust of wind.

Lisa was responsible for the dead woman's computer, an older model that she disconnected and carried out to the techs' light blue van.

When she returned, she said, "Not a bad place to live for a student."

"According to her mother, all she lacked was her thesis," Trokic said. "Which is why she was only studying part-time. She freelanced, wrote for several magazines, and taught the younger anthropology students at the university. Over in that folder on the desk is a lecture on genetic anthropology; she was going to give it tomorrow."

Newspapers and magazines were piled up in a rack on the wall. *National Geographic, Norwegian Anthropology Magazine, Peoples of the World*. The techs had ordered Trokic and Lisa to keep their hands in their pockets until the apartment had been gone over for fingerprints. They'd already gathered up everything to be examined. Calendars, personal papers, contents of desk drawers.

Lisa walked around to get an impression of the person who had lived there. No murder had been committed in the neatly-kept apartment, but hopefully, it would produce details of Anna Kiehl's activities, her interests, her friends. Details that would form a picture, a type of truth about the anthropologist. Lisa could see the edge of the forest outside the window, the heavy fog hanging over it. She wondered if Trokic would have brought her along if Agersund hadn't said to.

"You live close by, don't you?" she asked.

"Half a kilometer closer to town."

Trokic waved in the direction. He had piercing dark-blue eyes, she noticed, not brown like she'd thought. And black hair, though in the sunlight she picked up hints of brown. He had a cowlick on one side that secretly amused her. Mornings, he almost had it tamed, but as the day wore on and he unconsciously kept running his hand through his hair, it got out of hand.

She tried to imagine his apartment. His private life. She couldn't. Maybe he didn't have a life outside of work. Or maybe there was some sort of unspoken agreement on the force to not talk about him. It wouldn't surprise her if he had a secret or two. But at least he didn't flirt around, which she respected. A few of the single office girls at the station seemed interested, but apparently, he hadn't noticed.

"Aren't there any photo albums?" he said. "And what about her mailbox?"

After the techs gave her the green light, she started looking through the drawers, on the shelves, on hooks, until finally, she found two small keys that had to be either for a mailbox or a bicycle lock. It was the mailbox. She emptied out the hordes of advertisements and a book, *The Chemical Zone*. A yellow post-it had been stuck on the cover. "Thanks for the loan, Irene." She walked into the kitchen and casually leafed through it.

Trokic poured himself a glass of water and handed her a piece of paper with a symbol written on it. "I found this."

The oval with a type of cross inside had been drawn by hand with a pen.

"What is it?" she wondered. "A religious symbol? Maybe she'd just been doodling while she talked on the phone?"

"It's from the inside of her calendar. Which is almost unused, by the way."

Lisa rubbed her eyes. The long train ride had been tiring. Also, the horrific murder was already wearing her down. She still saw Anna Kiehl's face when she closed her eyes, and that frightened her. Times like these gave her doubts about whether she'd chosen the right job. She wasn't able to look at people's actions like Jasper Taurup and many of her other close colleagues. For them, events were either legal or illegal, falling in under a paragraph in the law or a statistic, and evidence might or might not be sufficient to stand up in court. But to her, these events were nuances of good and evil, light and dark, and far too often they were mixed up in inscrutable patterns. And then, most of all, there were the emotions. If there wasn't enough positivity in her life, the darkness gained the upper hand. She felt it as an overwhelming exhaustion.

"You'll be in charge of the computer when we get back in," he said. That was an order, not a question. She'd hoped to be assigned other duties, and now she felt sidetracked.

She glanced up when she heard a scraping noise. A woman stood watching them from the doorway. Lisa couldn't tell how long she'd been there. Trokic had mentioned a woman in the apartment above, and this must be her. The tattered prima donna look seemed to fit.

"Have you talked to the neighbors?" she asked.

"Most of them. What do you mean?"

"I just remembered, there was some sort of commotion over there yesterday evening." The woman pointed over to the next row of apartment buildings. "It looked like some sort of party going on. I saw a man walk out, and a moment later he was lurking around out there along the field."

Lisa and Trokic stood up simultaneously. "Was it when Anna left?" she asked.

"I can't remember."

"Can you tell us exactly where the party was?"

Chapter Ten

HIS BLOND HAIR was pressed flat on one side of his head and his skin was puffy. As if he'd just woken up from a deep, sweaty sleep. Earlier that day, he'd escaped their first round of door-to-door questioning, and he clearly wished he could avoid their questions this time, too. His apartment was a mirror image of Anna Kiehl's, with his window facing hers —Lisa noticed the techs still rummaging around over there. Otherwise, the two apartments were total opposites. Beer and liquor bottles covered his living room coffee table. The place stunk of cigarettes and spilled beer, and judging from the odors and the tiny stubs in the ashtray, a few joints had also been part of the well-supplied festivities.

He was in his late thirties, and he claimed to work for a wireless carrier. She spotted a potentially attractive man hidden behind the Sunday hangover. Trokic explained why they were there. The man seemed surprised; he probably hadn't heard the radio or watched television that evening.

They sat down at a small, round table in the kitchen. Lisa smiled. "Was it a good party?"

"Sort of on the wild side."

"How many people were there?"

"Me, my brother Tony, and one of his pals, Martin."

"How well did you know Anna Kiehl?" Trokic said.

"Actually, I didn't know her. I didn't know her name before you said it. But I've seen her, yeah. I mean, her apartment is right over there, and I've seen her take out the trash and on the playground with her son. I've seen her running, too."

"Were you here all evening yesterday?"

"Yeah, all night. Tony and Martin didn't go home until five this morning. We were inside all the time."

His eyes darted a second, a very quick second. Lisa noticed the aquarium on the shelf a few meters away. Small turtles were paddling around eagerly. One of them watched her from a rock sticking up out of the water.

"Did you see her yesterday?"

He looked up at the ceiling, apparently trying to get his head working again. "Yeahhhh, I think I saw her yesterday afternoon, walking with her son. Could have been the day before yesterday. I'm not really sure, now that I think about it. But she was home yesterday evening, I know that. She was walking around over there."

"What time was that?"

"In the middle of the evening."

Trokic caught Lisa's eye. "Could you be more precise?" he said.

Obviously, this was asking a lot of the man's fried brain. "It was...wait a minute, no, it was when we started on the Irish coffee...I was doing the whipped cream. That was after the soccer match. I don't remember when it ended, but it was after the supermarket closed because we..."

"You what?"

"Nothing. I think the soccer match ended a quarter past eight or eight thirty."

His eyes darted again.

"Didn't you just say no one left the apartment?" Trokic said. "What's this about the supermarket?"

The man lowered his head a notch. "My brother went out to buy the cream."

"How long did that take?"

"I don't know. He might've gone to the gas station."

"So, it took enough time for him to drive down to the gas station and back?"

"I can't remember."

"Can you even remember if it was before the soccer match had ended, or maybe it was during halftime?"

"It must've been at the end of the first half," he mumbled. "He came back during halftime."

"So, how long was he gone, do you think?"

"Maybe a half hour. But I didn't whip the cream until the match was over."

"Are you sure?" Lisa said. "I mean…" She glanced over at the flooded coffee table. "You couldn't have noticed Anna Kiehl earlier, could you? When you were…how should I put it, less under the influence? You see, it doesn't fit with the information we already have. Apparently, she went out running at seven yesterday evening and never came back."

"But I saw her." The fog in his head seemed to be lifting. "I saw someone, anyway. It was dark when I came out here, and I caught a glimpse of her before I turned on the light. After that, I couldn't see anything through the window. It was only a moment…the light was pretty dim over there."

Trokic remembered what the woman who lived above Anna Kiehl had said. Either her memory was unusually bad, or else Anna had been out running twice. Which didn't sound likely to him. "Hashish can play games with your memory, especially if you're drinking too, and if–"

"I'm certain," the man said, not bothering to deny the

part about the hashish. It would have been useless anyway unless he tried to blame his guests.

"Okay, you're absolutely certain," Lisa said. "Do you know anyone who knew Anna?"

"No, I've only lived here two months. I've told you everything I know. Was she really murdered?" He rubbed his arms, which were covered with goosebumps.

"We don't know a lot yet," Lisa said, avoiding his question. "Anything you might happen to remember could help us. We'd like to speak to your guests, of course."

"My brother doesn't have anything to do with this. All he did was go out for the cream."

Lisa frowned. "We'll decide who to speak to. Let's have the names and addresses."

"HOPELESS," Trokic said, as they sat in the car five minutes later.

"The woman lives in an apartment building," Lisa said, "and half of the people living there are gone Saturday evening while the other half can't remember a thing because they were drunk."

"He lied about them being in the apartment. One of them could have been out, a neighbor could have seen them."

"His memory wasn't first class, no doubt about that."

"Let's check if his brother has a record." Trokic called the dispatcher. "And if it turns out he left during the first half, it could be within the time frame of her murder. He might have seen her leave the building and followed her."

"Let's talk to the other neighbors."

"Already done. No one saw anything unusual, and since her apartment is the one closest to the forest, she could get in and out on the trail by the field without most people seeing her."

Lisa glanced at her watch. A quarter past nine, and she was exhausted. What did he think they could clear up at this time of night? She noted the squashed insects on the windshield. Trokic put away his phone.

"The brother was convicted of rape three years ago."

"Oh, God."

"Let's pay him a visit," Trokic said.

"Now?"

"Why not? Maybe you have a life, but I don't."

For the first time, he smiled at her. He put the car in reverse.

Chapter Eleven

TONY HADN'T BEEN as successful as his brother, judging from the neighborhood. It was no mystery where last night's joints had come from; the old building's hallway stunk of hashish. After knocking on the door a third time, Tony's neighbor, a redheaded woman wearing smudged green makeup stuck her head out. Her eyes were swimming as if she'd had a fix a few minutes before. She spoke slowly. "Hell of a racket you're making. Don't you know what time it is? I mean, Jesus, people are trying to watch TV here."

"We need to talk to your neighbor."

"What's the idiot done now?"

She slammed her door shut the moment Tony Hansen opened his.

THAT THE MAN had gone out for cream was no doubt a crime in itself. Any chance of the beard stubble, red-rimmed eyes, and dirty T-shirt facing them ever being sober enough to drive a vehicle seemed minuscule to Lisa. And after an embarrassed Tony had reluctantly let them in his cramped, stinking apartment, she noticed Trokic frowning. Briefly, he explained why they were there. Without being invited, he sat down on a rickety chair. Tony was in his late twenties, but he had the face and movements of an old man.

"We'd like to hear where you were yesterday evening between six and midnight," Trokic began.

"What's this all about?"

"You know what. A young woman was found murdered not far from where you supposedly were."

Tony blinked. "I was with my brother."

"All evening?"

"Yeah. We watched a soccer match."

"I see. Did any of you leave the apartment at any time?"

"No."

"You're sure about that? I think you're lying. And I don't like that one bit, not this time of night."

Tony sat down on his stained sofa and rolled a cigarette with practiced hands. His nicotine-tainted fingers shook. Lisa was left standing with her notebook in hand.

"Yeah, I'm sure."

"You don't remember anything about driving your brother's car to buy cream?"

The silence was heavy. "Oh, yeah."

"What time was that?"

"I don't remember."

"You couldn't have been drinking, since you drove," Trokic said. "So, your memory should be okay. Was it before, during, or after the soccer match?"

"During. The first half."

"And what else did you do besides buy cream?"

"Nothing."

"So, if we assume you bought the cream at the gas

station, you should have been gone about ten minutes. Your brother says you were gone at least a half hour."

"They were sold out. I had to drive into the 7-Eleven in town."

Another pause. Trokic sighed and stared at a pair of worn sneakers a meter away from him. He picked one of them up, looked at the sole, and tossed it back down again. "You didn't follow a young girl into the forest?"

"No, I sure as hell didn't. I've never hurt nobody. Not even that person I did time for."

"We'll check that." Trokic looked around the shabby apartment. "What do you do for a living, Tony?"

"Nothing."

"You don't have a job?"

"I get disability benefits. My back is ruined. It happened when I was working for the railroad. I can't get around for very long at a time anymore."

"So, you hang around home all day and have a few drinks?"

"You could put it that way."

"Maybe it's not so easy getting out to meet girls in your situation?"

"What are you getting at? Hey, I do all right, I get what I need. Just ask the neighbor. She's more than willing."

Trokic stood up reluctantly. "We're going to check this out about the cream, and if your story doesn't hold water, we're bringing you in."

"HE'S LYING," Lisa said after they were out in the fresh air again.

"Yeah, that's my impression too. Even so—"

"No doubt about it. The question is, why? He had time

to follow Anna into the forest, make a move on her, and then kill her. Shouldn't we be taking him to the station?"

"Not now. I'm not so sure. We need to find out the timeline on all this."

Lisa persisted. "It didn't have to take very long."

Her boss bit his lip and fingered the marbles in his jeans. "Hmmm. It's at least ten minutes' run to where she was found. That would have taken too long. Then there's the dried flowers, where did he get them?"

"That doesn't eliminate him. Someone else could have laid the flowers on her, as some sort of gesture. People do the weirdest things."

"But then there's the blood. Could he have avoided getting blood on him? I doubt it. He would've had to change clothes."

Lisa chewed on that for a moment. "But we agree that he's lying?"

"Yeah."

"Why would he lie?"

"Good question. Let's check up on this. I'll send a few officers out to the gas station and 7-Eleven. If he wasn't in town, he's got a problem."

Chapter Twelve

THE CAT WELCOMED him home at a quarter past three in the morning. Its loud, devoted purring accompanied him as he slipped out of his coat in the back hall and kicked off his shoes, but it ended abruptly when he filled the cat's bowl up with Whiskas. Scruffy was used to the vet's best cat food, and currently, she was on a hunger strike, convinced that victory would soon be hers. From the time he found the kitten in his hedge, its fur matted and pus running out of its ears, not even old enough to be taken from its mother, it had been the boss when it came to food. Trokic always ended up paying out the nose at the nearest vet clinic to keep the peace.

He noticed wet paw prints on the kitchen counter, also leaves from outside that must have gotten caught in her thick tail. He didn't bother wiping up. At the other end of the counter lay a letter from a woman he'd dated for several weeks early that summer. He'd broken it off because it had gone way too fast for him. After skimming the letter yesterday, he wasn't sure whether she expected an answer.

He put on his latest luxury item purchase, a wireless

headphone set, and listened to Audioslave. The headphones had cost a fortune; he wanted absolutely no noise to disturb his journey into a spacious, isolated sound universe at a decibel level approaching the pain threshold. They also prevented complaints from the neighbors. It was as if the world disappeared, including the dark depths into which he occasionally fell. He tossed a stack of reports on the coffee table, sat down on the sofa, and poured red wine into a coffee cup. The music and alcohol were meant to dampen the thoughts swirling in his head so he could get at least some sleep.

He'd moved into this residential area eleven years ago after returning to Denmark from two years in Croatia. At first, he'd rented the house, thinking he would find something closer to the center of the city, but he bought it when it came up for sale a few years later. It had only one bedroom and not a lot of extra space, but after two years of sleeping on the sofa of a large Croatian family, it had felt like pure luxury. Now he couldn't imagine living any other way. The surrounding houses had all been modernized, but he'd contented himself with painting the walls. He was fine with the brown bathroom and peeling paint on the cabinets. He felt comfortable with the old dusty-green upholstered sofa, his cousin's rough, frameless abstract paintings, the wooden floor darkened with age, the bookshelf full of worn paperbacks. But it wasn't only a matter of feeling at home. Within these walls, he'd also gone through some of the most difficult times of his life. For hours, he'd sat staring at small lumps in the wallpaper with music enveloping him, easing the pain as his two years in Croatia gradually faded. In a strange way, he felt it would be wrong to move away.

He was the product of an impossible relationship, a passionate interlude between his Croatian father and Danish mother during a vacation. His mother had told him about her longing and the intense meetings, followed by frustration and misunderstandings. In the end, the relationship had foundered, and he was born in a cold Nordic country to a mother filled with bitterness and lost illusions. And yet, his mother had shown no qualms about giving him his father's last name. "So you remember there's a part of you somewhere else," she'd said.

He grew up in the slums, a gray labyrinth and colorless landscape that still existed inside him. He wondered when it had begun. While out on the balcony, a lonely child mostly on his own, watching the drunks sitting on benches and the addicts in hallways?

At ten years of age, he knew every detail of the concrete hell he lived in with his mother. He knew everyone's name, who bought what from whom, how the price of a gram of heroin fluctuated.

When he was fifteen, he decided to visit a small village in the cornfields at the foot of the Medvednica Mountains near Zagreb to meet the rest of his family—his father, a younger half-brother, and cousins. He was without exception met with open arms; it was as if he'd lived his entire life among them. When his mother died of cancer five years later, his Croatian family became more important to him, and he spent longer periods of time down there. Much later, his family's pain became his own when the country was torn apart and his father and little brother were killed in the war.

At times, he'd considered moving permanently to Croatia, to family dinners with spicy, heavy food, a sun that drew out strong unfamiliar odors, a less stressful everyday life. But his connection to his homeland was too strong.

Eventually, his childhood's extraordinary feel for and insight into the criminal world became one of the two reasons he applied for police school. The other was Milan.

He sighed and walked out into the kitchen, where the cat was sitting in the sink, drinking from the leaky faucet. He finished off his wine and tossed the woman's letter into the trash.

It took him a long time to fall asleep as the plants with the reddish splotches danced on the inside of his eyelids. They were trying to tell him something, but he couldn't make out what it was.

Chapter Thirteen

MONDAY, September 22

LISA WAS STILL YAWNING when she arrived at work at nine. She sat down and tried to concentrate on Anna Kiehl's computer.

No object in a home reveals more about someone's personality than their computer. During her career, she'd found incredible stuff on hard drives and discs. Occasionally, suspects tried to erase their tracks by deleting files or hiding them, but that was child's play for her to find. The more hard-core types knew that nothing vanished until the hard drive had been erased as many as seven times. Usually, she found something no matter what, thanks to methods she'd developed and existing data recovery software.

She'd also found out that psychopaths believed they were invincible, a character trait that had put many people behind bars throughout the years. She took a deep breath and reached for a cigarette, and a moment later her disappointment at having to go through the computer dissolved.

Her contribution was vital to a murder investigation; she held one of the keys to the victim, and therefore to the murderer. She was on a mission. An exploration. And Trokic hadn't cut her out of anything. Whatever lack of faith he had in her, he wasn't letting it show, she had to give him that much.

At first glance, Anna Kiehl's computer was a perfect example of meticulousness. After copying the hard drive, in case of any problems during her search, she began securing all significant data on the machine while taking notes on paper. The hard drive had only a few folders, including one with a spreadsheet dealing with her private finances and what looked like invoices from her freelance work, one with letters, and one containing her anthropology thesis and various related material. One separate folder held photos of her and her son, Peter. Every time she opened one of the photos, in her mind's eyes she saw Anna Kiehl on the autopsy table, followed by a mental sigh of relief at the sight of the woman on the screen, alive. Surely, there was something in her email. As she was about to open the program, Trokic walked in. He wore a thin, light blue sweater with creases that showed it was fresh from the store. Lisa felt sure he was the type who walked into Jack and Jones twice a year, grabbed a bunch of clothes off the shelves, and never worried about how they looked.

"Jasper went out to that gas station," he said.

"Yeah?"

"He found the girl working the Saturday evening shift and showed her a photo of Tony Hansen. She recognized him; he'd been drunk. She couldn't remember what he bought, but it's a hundred percent certain they weren't out of cream. So, we checked their surveillance camera, and there he was."

"I knew it," Lisa said.

"We'll put the screws to him, but we can't focus on him too much. I just can't see how he had time to kill her. We can't ignore the rest of the evidence. I sent a few men out to bring him in."

He took a deep breath. "Jasper and I are going out to make some inquiries about Anna's friends. The people she ran with, that woman with the book in the postbox. She and Anna were writing their thesis together. And another student said that for some reason they weren't getting along so well."

He left, and Lisa turned back to the computer. She opened Outlook and stared at the screen in bewilderment. This couldn't be right!

Chapter Fourteen

FOR THE PAST TWO YEARS, Jasper Taurup had been Trokic's favorite colleague. He had a dry, subtle sense of humor, and though Trokic didn't laugh a lot, he still appreciated it. Taurup was also rational and logical, with a startling ability to instantly analyze things. Rumor had it that as a child, his hobby was counting tomatoes in his parents' greenhouse with a pocket calculator. Trokic knew exactly when to tap into the man's intellect, such as during interrogations. He knew every single witness statement by heart, and he could connect them every which way.

Interrogations weren't Trokic's strong suit. A few months earlier, Agersund had casually commented that a robot would do better than him, unfortunately. Trokic had never developed a talent for extracting vital information from people brought in for questioning. Some of the others developed a rapport by talking about the weather, hobbies, family, work, etc., to get the person to relax before the tough questions came up. Trokic simply couldn't do that sort of small talk. He asked; they answered. Which was why it mattered to him that his colleagues knew what they were doing in the interrogation room. The day before, he'd noted with satisfaction that Tony had sought eye contact with Lisa and spoken to her, even though she had been blunt and persistent in her questioning.

FOUR OF THE five men in the running group were easily eliminated as suspects. One had moved to Gibraltar to work for a Danish company. Another had a broken leg and was in a district hospital. Another had been to a bachelor party in Lystrup with seven other people all evening. Another had been on a weekend trip with his family in Søhøjlandet. That left only one.

"ARE YOU MIK SØRENSEN?"

The man in the doorway had black hair and blue-green eyes. He was in his late twenties. They stood on the third floor of an older apartment building in the northern part of the city, and for once, the morning sun broke through the clouds and shot columns of light through the hallway's small windows. He was one of Anna Kiehl's former class-mates. His pink shirt needed ironing, and his light-colored jeans were torn. Normally, someone relevant to a case was taken to the station, but Trokic felt he needed context, needed to see people in their surroundings. To begin with, anyway. He wanted to see their reaction when he showed up unexpectedly, see what was on their kitchen tables, how their pets acted. Their social status. And he wanted to smell the places—were they clean? Did someone smoke? And if so, *what* did they smoke? Later, it could be more effective to bring them into a more formal setting. The station.

"Yes?"

"Police, Criminal Division. We have some questions about the killing of a young woman Saturday evening."

Sørensen looked back and forth between Trokic and Jasper before speaking. "Who? Not my sister, right?"

"No, not your sister. This is about one of the people you used to run with, a classmate of yours."

"Oh, no! Who is it?"

"Anna Kiehl."

He shuddered for a second, then he opened the door wide for them. "Come in."

He led them into a small green living room with a high ceiling and dark varnished wood floors. Nice place, Trokic thought. A bit messy though, with textbooks, coffee cups, a bag of candy, and the remains of a pizza on the table. The young man plopped down into the easy chair and buried his freckled face in his hands. A moment passed before Trokic realized he was crying. They stood quietly until finally he straightened up and dried his tears on his sleeve.

"How...?"

"She was found in the forest here yesterday morning," Trokic said, avoiding Sørensen's question. "Did you get along with her?"

Again, Sørensen trembled briefly before answering. "I was totally in love with her when we were in school. But she didn't feel that way about me, so that was that."

"When was the last time you saw her?" Jasper asked.

"I've only seen her once since the group stopped running together, except I still run with Martin, but he just broke his nose. Anyway, it was sometime this summer. Maybe three months ago. I ran into her while I was running. Met her, I mean."

He stood up and dried his eyes again on a napkin smeared with pizza sauce.

"And otherwise you haven't seen her? She ran three times a week."

"No. We must have run at different times."

"What else can you tell us about her?"

He looked uncomfortable as he sat down again. After a few moments, he sighed. "Anna was super. The most decent person I've ever known. She fascinated me, but I also liked her as a friend, as a person. I just can't understand this."

"We have to ask, what were you doing Saturday evening?" Jasper said.

Sørensen stared, wide-eyed. "Jesus, you don't think I—"

"No, not at all," Trokic said. "It's just routine. We have to ask, to eliminate all potential suspects."

"I was just hanging around home here, didn't do anything. I read some, ate dinner, watched some TV, then I went to bed early."

"Are there any friends or neighbors who can confirm you were home?"

"No...not really."

"Okay. Do you know if she had a boyfriend?"

He hesitated. "I think she was seeing someone this summer."

"How do you know that?" Trokic said.

"My sister talked to her a few months ago. She ran into her walking on a street in town. She told me Anna looked really happy, and she'd asked her if she had a boyfriend. And she said, yeah, she did. My sister wasn't sure how serious it was. And yeah, it hurt a little bit, but I was happy for her, too."

"She didn't happen to mention his name to your sister, did she?"

He shook his head and picked at a glob of red candle wax that had dripped down on the table.

"Do you know if she had any enemies?"

"Not really enemies. But some of our classmates didn't particularly like her. I think they were jealous. Anna looked really good, and even though she was sort of a quiet type, people listened to her when she spoke."

"Who were the ones who didn't like her?"

"Just some bitches. Then there was this Irene we ran with. They were writing their thesis together, but I think something happened. It was like one day they suddenly weren't friends anymore, is how I sensed it."

"You have any idea what the problem was?"

"No, I didn't ask."

Trokic stood up. They'd gotten all they were going to get from him for the time being.

Chapter Fifteen

THE REDHEADED GIRL in front of them hadn't cried when they'd begun questioning her. And though Trokic didn't think it was something she necessarily should do, it seemed cold to not show sorrow at a friend's death, despite whatever differences they'd had. Dark makeup circled her eyes, making them look small.

Her small apartment was filled with the type of African masks and figures popular several years earlier but quickly going out of style. Some of them had small bones in their hair, others stared emptily at him. They had found her through Anna Kiehl's mother. Irene had explained that she'd dropped a book, *The Chemical Zone*, into Anna's mailbox Saturday evening at eight when she saw Anna wasn't home.

"Did you know she was pregnant?" Trokic asked.

The girl hesitated, which he interpreted as surprise. Expressionless, she turned to him and answered, "No, I didn't know. Who was the father?"

"We were hoping you could tell us. She was ten weeks along."

"Anna didn't go out much, and I didn't know she was involved with anyone. She said she couldn't go out evenings. Peter's father lives in Helsingør, and he hasn't seen the boy since he was a few weeks old. So, if she needed a babysitter, she had to take him to her parents in Horsens. I offered to look after him several times, but she never took me up on it. Really, I think she preferred it that way."

"How well did you know Anna? Were you close?"

Irene's lips flinched slightly as if she were about to smile. She was thin, though she looked strong and wiry. "We studied together for five years. One year when we lived in a dorm, our rooms were next to each other. We knew each other very well."

"Don't you think it's odd that she didn't tell you she was pregnant?"

"I do. But ten weeks isn't all that long, is it? A lot of women don't say anything the first three months; things can go wrong, you know. And Anna kept things to herself anyway."

Jasper had been looking at a drawing of stick figures, small men behind bars smoking joints. He looked up. "Any man back then? I mean, when you lived in the dorm."

"I only know about one, other than Peter's father. His name is Tue. I can write his name down for you."

She stood up and found a paper and pen. "Do you have any suspects?"

"Not yet," Jasper said. "This Tue guy, was it serious, or maybe just more of a sexual relationship?"

"What do you mean by that?"

"Yeah, what *do* I mean by that?" Jasper said.

She stared at him. "I don't have the slightest idea."

"Why don't you tell us what your thesis is about?" Trokic asked, taking over now.

"It's extensive. An incredible amount of work. And now

I'm going to have to finish it by myself." She launched into a long discourse about genetic anthropology and a tribal society in Central Africa they had lived with for a short period. The young anthropology student appeared very wrapped up in her project; it was almost as if she'd forgotten why they were there. She broke off in the middle of a long explanation of mutations in genetic material and looked up at the ceiling as if she'd lost the thread. She continued in a quieter but steady voice.

"I'd like to ask her mother if I could have some of the information on Anna's computer when you're done in her apartment. She had very interesting angles whenever we met, and I know she's written several chapters."

"We're going through her computer," Jasper said. "It's part of the case, so don't count on having access to it anytime soon."

"What about enemies?" Trokic asked.

She paused before answering. "I don't know if she had what you'd call enemies. But she wasn't shy when she spoke up; she said what she meant. Sometimes that offended people. She wasn't scared of anybody, didn't matter who they were, and she had some pretty strong opinions. I heard her get worked up a few times."

"Did she strike you as being condescending?"

"No, not really, but of course it can get uncomfortable when people express their opinions bluntly."

"Maybe she angered you, too?" Jasper said. "We've heard you weren't on the best of terms lately."

"That's not true," she said. "Who told you that?"

"Never mind who. Did she have any special causes she was involved in?"

"She was left-wing, totally. And she hated cars. She always took the bus or the train. She should have lived with the Amish. She was against everything she felt was unnat-

63

ural. Pesticides, antidepressants, too much technology. The military in particular. She bought organic and washed her clothes in this horrible detergent that smells like coconuts."

"So, you're saying you two definitely got along well."

"Yes, absolutely."

Jasper glanced at his watch and pointed to his stomach. It was long past lunchtime. Trokic stood up. "If you think of anything else, we'd appreciate you contacting us. Anything you feel might be important."

Irene nodded. "Of course."

She stood to follow them out. "When can her parents be allowed into her apartment? They keep calling and asking me to pick up some of her things. They don't really understand that we're not allowed to take them. And they're not like Anna, they like things organized, taken care of as soon as possible."

Trokic ignored the girl's question and caught Jasper's eye. Slowly he said, "They like things organized, unlike Anna?"

He stroked the front of his throat. "What would you say if I told you her apartment is squeaky clean, everything picked up and in its place?"

She smiled wryly. "I would say you have the wrong apartment. Believe me, she was the messiest person I've ever seen."

Chapter Sixteen

LISA STARED at the computer screen in front of her. The deceased's email program was open. And it was empty. Both the inbox and outbox and the trash too. Nothing. She had contacted the university and now knew that Anna Kiehl had used a TDC account for emails, but there wasn't a single one on the computer. Her stubbornness perked up; this couldn't be right. Possibly the anthropologist had used an online email service—she would look into that. But then why did she have Outlook on her computer? Her emails were probably not far away. Emails weren't permanently deleted from Outlook like most people thought. Instead of generating individual files, they were contained in one large .pst file. And there they stayed, deleted or not until the folders were compressed. If she could find the .pst file, she could open it with a hex editor, corrupt it, and use a repair tool to create a copy. And when she opened this new file in Outlook, the emails would be back in the deleted folder, where they originally came from. Voila! It was like pulling a rabbit out of a hat.

Ten minutes later, she needed a cup of coffee. She was

worried; nothing had shown up from the .pst file. Either there were no emails, or else the folders had been compressed.

It was time for a plan B. She fished around in a drawer and brought out an old, badly fragmented hard drive. If she couldn't figure this out, they would need outside help, which would be expensive. They'd sent data too difficult for them to recover out of the country before, and usually, it took a week to get it back. She'd have to discuss that with her boss if necessary. Again, she stared at the screen; intuition told her something had been there. She installed the hard drive, started the recovery program to search for a range of data, and crossed her fingers.

SHE STOOD up to clear her head, then she walked over to Forensics to talk to Kurt Tønnies.

"Have you found anything?"

Normally, all evidence was sent to Forensics in Copenhagen, which was a part of the NIC, National Investigations Center. They had more than enough nerds there to find new creative ways of extracting information from evidence.

"Nothing important. The bastard must've used a nail brush on her. Maybe even a vacuum cleaner, that's how little we found. We did find a few fibers, but we can't know if they're from the clothes she was wearing. Her friend and the woman in the apartment above her said she usually ran in a T-shirt and bicycle shorts, nothing special. We also found two cigarette butts not far from her, two yellow Kings. They couldn't find any DNA on them though, so at the moment they're not much use to us. You'd hope they came from the killer, but it doesn't make sense. He does all that work setting up and practically sterilizing the crime scene, then he smokes a few cigarettes and leaves the butts behind?"

"He wouldn't be the first to do it," Lisa said. "People aren't even aware they're smoking a cigarette."

She thought about Tony Hansen. He rolled his own. Tønnies sighed and rubbed his eyes. Lisa guessed he hadn't slept last night. The techs were work addicts; they could run for days on black coffee. "What about the hair Trokic found on the necklace?"

"We put it under the microscope; it's definitely not Anna Kiehl's. So, we sent it out for a DNA analysis, which could easily be a waste of money. It could have come from anybody."

"And the apartment?"

"Nothing there either. Most of the fingerprints were from the boy."

Lisa thought about the three-year-old boy in the apartment, how he had woken up alone. Was he still in shock?

"And, of course, her fingerprints are there too," he said. "And a few others. My guess is they belong to the manager, the woman above, her friend, others who visited her sometimes."

Lisa shook her head. "Thanks. I'd better get back to the computer."

He squeezed her arm and gently nudged her out the door.

WHILE THE RECOVERY program worked in the background, she had a look at the websites that had been visited on the computer. Hundreds of sites in the program folders showed her internet habits: Google, Danish television stations, net radio, district government pages, library, daycare, weather, net doctor, a few bands, anthropology organizations both foreign and domestic, research results in English and French from foreign universities in a number of disciplines. Anthropology, ethnology, archaeology, microbiology, neurochemistry, cultural history, sociology.

Lisa sighed and grabbed a bag of Brazil nuts from out of a drawer. Flossy's favorite nuts. Hers too. They crunched when she bit into them, and they were filling.

Nothing on the computer looked helpful. Apart from the empty trash and an empty email program, Anna Kiehl appeared to be a very normal human being.

"Find anything?" Jasper pulled up a chair and sat beside her.

"No. That's the strange thing about it."

"Nothing in the trash?"

"No." She briefly explained the Outlook procedure. "Since I can't find the emails that way, I have to search for text fragments."

She pointed at the program on the screen, which had finished now. "Computers store data, which isn't used again until needed. That goes for emails and everything else written on them. So, it's only the shortcut to a file that gets deleted at first, you could say. But if it was deleted a long time ago, and with a tiny old hard drive like this one, it might have been overwritten and is gone forever. And it's like someone tossed a bomb in her hard drive, it's that fragmented."

She pulled her chair closer to the screen. "Okay, so the recovery program has gone through all the data on her hard drive. Let's see if we can find any emails. I'll search for her address, that would be part of any email."

She typed it in a search bar. "Now, it'll find everything deleted that has the address."

It took only a fraction of a second for the machine to find one hundred and two results.

"Aha!"

"That's a lot."

"Not really. The last time I searched my own computer, just out of curiosity, I found over eleven thousand fragments with my email address. But this shows she actually did use her address on this computer."

She clicked on the first result.

</BODY> </HTML> ....
"Anna Kiehl" <annakiehl@oncable.dk>
To: "Birgitte Aksen" <b.axen@get2net.dk>
Subject:
Date: Tue, 12 Apr 23:36:46 +0200
<p class=3DMsoNormal><font size=3D2
face=3DArial><span =
style=3D'font-size:10.0pt;
font-family:Arial'>Hi Birgitte – This can't be in an
sms.<o:p></o:p></span></font></p>
<p class=3DMsoNormal><font size=3D2
face=3DArial><span =
style=3D'font-size:10.0pt;
font-family:Arial'> about the party tomorrow.
I can't come, =
I have too much work
and I can't find anyone to take care of Peter on such
short notice.
<o:p></o:p></span></font></p>
<p class=3DMsoNormal><font size=3D2
face=3DArial><span =
style=3D'font-size:10.0pt;
font-family:Arial'> I have more hours
from the fall.
I'm looking forward to it. And if you think

********** End of Cluster **********

"WHAT A MESS," Jasper said.

"Yeah, most emails are written in HTML. This one is from last spring. It was deleted a long time ago, that's why it stops so abruptly. The computer has overwritten some of it."

"But does this mean she's only written a hundred and two emails?"

"No, her email address could have been overwritten on some, so I'll have to do a search with other words. I don't really know what I'm looking for, all I can say is that I can find something."

She clicked on the next result, which was even more chaotic. "This will probably take the rest of the day," she said.

"Mmm. But we have another problem."

"What?"

"We went out to pick up Tony Hansen, but there was nobody home. The neighbor says she saw him earlier today with a big backpack. He's gone."

Chapter Seventeen

LISA WAS DOZING off on the sofa at ten when her long ringtone startled her. The dancing silhouettes in the murky living room added to her sense of being only half awake as she reached for the phone.

"I know it's late, sorry for calling you."

Trokic. Why was he calling? "It's all right."

The thought popped up that the man from Copenhagen she'd met that weekend hadn't called, which didn't help her mood. She saw no end in sight to the single life. The past few years had been rough, especially because she was the only one in her circle of friends without a partner. And while everyone around her was having kids, buying houses, constantly on the go, she felt more alone every day. She lit a cigarette and resigned herself to talking to Trokic.

"Are you okay?" he asked.

"Yeah, I'm fine." Pause. "What about the semen we found on the victim? Do we have the results on the DNA?"

"We do, but we don't know who it is. Maybe we should ask the men who knew her to take a blood test."

He summarized the rest of the day's interviews. Generally, everyone agreed that Anna Kiehl was very messy, as her friend had claimed. Trokic couldn't understand why her apartment had been so immaculate.

"So, you don't think she picked up and cleaned her apartment, that someone came back and did it? That rules out Tony Hansen."

"This may sound a little bit crazy," he said, "but I think the killer took the key from her. Maybe he was looking for something?"

"Sounds risky. The boy was there; he could've woken up."

"According to the woman upstairs, he was a heavy sleeper. But, if he did wake up, there are ways to keep kids from talking. The boy was in shock, and no one can get a word out of him yet. Why?"

She pictured Anna's killer walking around in her apartment, the boy ignorant of what had happened to his mother.

Trokic sighed. "It sounds too far-fetched."

"Don't be too sure." She told him about the curious absence of emails in Outlook.

"That's another thing that fits. Something's going on here; it just isn't like Kiehl. The killer could've been looking for something, ransacked the apartment, put everything back in place. And then wiped off all the surfaces where he might have left fingerprints. That could be why it smells like it's been cleaned, and why the neighbors insist someone was in the apartment after Anna ran. Could the internet provider have any information about the emails?"

"I've already asked them," Lisa said. "Nothing there. But I ran the hard drive through a recovery program, and it found one hundred and two fragments that can be categorized as email."

"Really? I didn't know that was possible, great job, Lisa. Is there anything we can use?"

Lisa smiled. What she'd done was routine for her, a piece of cake. But there was no reason to tell him that. Let him think she'd done something extraordinary. "Mostly she emailed about practical things having to do with school and the people she worked for. There's nothing particularly interesting. Just a bunch of deleted data. I need something more concrete to search for. A name, for instance. Or someone's email address."

"I hope we can get something for you soon."

HER HEAD WAS BUZZING when she hung up. Trokic was going back to the office to look for a report from Forensics and finish his own report for Agersund.

She sat down at her computer and began playing Minesweeper on expert level to clear her head before going to bed. The past two months, she'd been battling her irritating little niece, who led with one hundred forty-six seconds to Lisa's one hundred seventy-two. Flossy Bent P. had finally fallen asleep on his perch after having used the word "fuck" a million ways, especially "fucking fine and dandy." Finally, she'd threatened to strangle the bird and opened a window, which she knew it hated.

She was exhausted; now she regretted opening the bottle of red wine and drinking half of it. And getting nixed by a Copenhagen antique dealer was even more tiring. She was going to let her hair grow and switch to a less aggressive style of clothing. And say nothing on the first four dates about her being a computer nerd, one that worked for the police to boot.

"I AM SO sick and tired of this," she said out loud as she crawled in under the comforter a half hour later. She wasn't sure just what she was sick and tired of. Finally, she squirmed around into her favorite sleeping position and was about to pull her comforter over her head, when her phone rang again from the living room. She swore loudly while letting it ring four times. Finally, she got up to answer it. "What is it now?"

"Hmm…" She could hear him smile. "That was quick. What, were you waiting for me to call?"

Why was he suddenly calling her so often to discuss the case? Surely there were other people he could call. They probably weren't answering.

"I was in the office a half hour ago." He sounded excited.

"And?"

"The results from Forensics were on my desk. Or some of them anyway. I found the hairs in the necklace by the pond, you know—"

"Yeah, I know, we've gone over that. Kurt said it wasn't her hair. What about it?"

"Right, it wasn't hers. But someone did a quick check on the DNA and sent the information over this evening. And I ran it through the database and found a match."

He sounded like someone who'd won a prize but didn't know what it was or what to do with it.

"What do you mean?"

"We're going out for a little drive early tomorrow morning. I know whose hair it is."

Chapter Eighteen

TUESDAY, September 23

An autumn solstice morning, nine-forty. The hairs had led them to this small farmhouse on the outskirts of a village a hundred kilometers south.

Trokic was glad to be away from the station and all the chaos. A forty-three-year-old man had shot his ex-wife in one of the western suburbs last night, and someone on the riot squad had received a tip about a cocaine deal in a nearby town; a raid was being coordinated with local police. As if anyone had time for that. Also last night, a few young kids had gone amok after taking a nasty new and popular designer drug, Kamikaze. The phone in Agersund's office had been under constant assault by families and others involved, and his swearing had rung through the halls and corridors as he, in turn, pulled his hair out, referred callers to the Superintendent, whined about the hundreds of thousands of citizens to keep an eye on, and generally tried to cover everything with the resources available to him.

But Trokic had found the most intriguing lead so far. A connection to Anna Kiehl. A man she knew, one who'd been close by to where she was killed.

A WOMAN in her mid-forties lived on the farm, apparently alone, surrounded by pine trees and fields with Iceland horses. The weather hadn't improved during the night; threatening grayish-black clouds lurked on the horizon. The place was lonely and remote.

Trokic thought it odd that a woman like Elise Holm isolated herself in this no-man's-land. She wore an angora sweater with oversized light-purple sleeves, and despite her unadorned appearance, he found her attractive. Her facial muscles twitched when she served instant coffee, mandarin oranges, and sweet chocolate biscuits while apologizing that it was all she had to offer. She began peeling an orange from the big bowl on the table, sending an out-of-season smell of Christmas into the small living room.

"Like I said on the phone," Trokic began, "during the investigation of a murder, we found some hairs that could be significant. We did a DNA analysis and cross-checked it with old cases in the area. It turns out that it's your brother's hair, which is why we're interested in knowing his whereabouts."

The house was remarkably quiet. "I haven't heard from Christoffer," she said, her voice nervous. "And what do you mean about this DNA? I haven't heard anything about that. Do you go around taking DNA from all sorts of people?"

Eight weeks ago, Elise Holm had reported her thirty-seven-year-old brother, Christoffer Holm, as missing. After attending a neurochemistry conference in Montréal, he hadn't taken calls or answered his door or kept his appointments. Trokic had checked his case the evening before and found that Anna Kiehl had been questioned about his disappearance, making him the first male they'd linked to her. She'd identified herself as his girlfriend, and she was sure something had happened to him, claiming it was highly unlikely he'd just run off. Christoffer Holm had to be the boyfriend that Mik Sørensen's sister had mentioned.

"At the moment, there's not a lot we're sure about. The police requested his DNA profile in connection with an unidentified burned corpse found at the time your brother was reported missing. We were convinced it was him, in fact. He matched the few remaining physical features."

Trokic had studied the report about the missing researcher. At first, his trail ended in a small Maersk airplane headed for Copenhagen airport, four days before he'd planned on celebrating his older sister's birthday with her. After trying to find him, she'd gained access to his apartment, but she'd found no clues there. A few passengers on the flight had been contacted; apparently, he hadn't spoken with anyone on the plane, and no one had noticed him in the airport.

The police discovered that two weeks earlier he'd given notice at his job at the hospital's research center, and with his reputation for being spontaneous and passionate, it was assumed that either he didn't want to be found, or something bad had happened to him; his credit card had been used several places in metropolitan Copenhagen. His case was shelved after a month, but there were many loose ends.

"Requested his DNA?" Elise Holm asked.

"Genetic material from his apartment was used to help with identification because my colleagues couldn't find any dental records. And it was determined that the corpse wasn't your brother. His neighbor let them in the apartment; he had a key."

He told her about Anna Kiehl, whose body had been

found two days earlier. And that Christoffer's phone had apparently been blocked because he hadn't paid his bill. Also, TDC had received no signal from it after his return to Denmark. Trokic guessed that its battery had run down during the flight.

"This can't be a coincidence, a murder takes place and we find hair from a missing person nearby, hair that belongs to someone who knew her. Do you recognize the name Anna Kiehl?"

She frowned. "I'm not sure. There were so many. But he did talk about a woman the last time he was here. Was she a student?"

Trokic nodded.

"Okay, then that's probably her. Usually, he doesn't talk about them, so...I have to admit, I don't remember much of what he said. Months can go by without us seeing each other."

"What's he like?"

"Christoffer? Very thoughtful. Very intelligent. Very ambitious. Sort of a rebel."

Her face softened as she spoke about her little brother.

Lisa took the color photo out of Trokic's hand and studied the missing researcher. There was something hippie-like about him. Someone you might see on a beach in the evening with a surfboard, standing around a campfire. Not a person she would have connected with laboratories and scientists. His hair was longish and medium-blond, his blue eyes smiled as he flirted with the camera. He wore an armband, the type used at festivals and outdoor concerts. There was something wild about him. A damn handsome man, she thought.

"I have to ask you," Trokic said, "do you think he's capable of a crime like this?"

Elise Holm stared at him in disbelief, as if he'd just placed a Martian on the table in front of her. "No way."

The two officers looked at each other. "Okay," Lisa said, "but do you have any idea why he didn't return after the conference?"

The woman shook her head. "His work took him there once in a while, of course, and some of his old schoolmates and colleagues live over there. But other than that, he had no ties."

"Do you know what the conference in Montréal was about?"

"Only that it was a big event, he was so much looking forward to it. He was going to present his book."

Lisa perked up, brushed a stray lock off her pale face. "The report didn't mention that. What's the book?"

"It's called *The Chemical Zone*."

"I thought I'd seen his name before. Anna Kiehl had the book." She turned to Trokic. "The book her friend brought back Saturday evening and stuck in her mailbox. It's about psychopharmaceuticals, right?"

Elise nodded again. "That was partly what he was going to talk about over there. He's very much conflicted with regards to the use of antidepressants in psychiatric treatment. On the one hand, he has the results of research, his own and that of others around the world—"

"Research at the hospital?"

"Yes, precisely. On the other hand, he's worried about it, the side effects, the long-term effects. His book deals with the two sides of the issue. He tried to present the results of his research and the latest knowledge, both pro and con, in layman's terms."

Lisa checked her watch and showed it to Trokic. "Meeting at one o'clock." They were supposed to go through the initial results from the forensic pathologist.

"I know. Just one last thing." He glanced at his notepad. "Since he does research in such things, have you ever heard him mention a pharmaceutical company called Procticon?"

The woman shook her head. "Not that I can recall."

Trokic downed the rest of his coffee, stuck a chocolate cookie in his pocket (Lisa noticed that and gave him a dirty look), and asked Elise Holm to contact them if she heard from her brother or if she thought of anything else. She followed them outside.

"Will you tell him to call me if you hear from him? It seems to me the police generally aren't good at keeping people informed. I had a break-in last weekend, and I've heard nothing about it. In fact, it was strange, nothing was taken. Maybe that's why they don't seem to care about it."

"They do care, definitely," Lisa said. "But right now, there's a lot going on. And, of course, we'll let you know if we hear from your brother."

"Tell him to call me."

"We will. This is a beautiful place you have here. Do you breed horses?"

"Yes. I have about twenty at the moment. It's not a good business, though. Christoffer likes to come out here once in a while. We ride for most of the day." She smiled to herself.

TROKIC SPED up as they entered the entrance ramp to the freeway. He was happy to be back behind the wheel. "We didn't get much out of her."

"Maybe we should focus more on finding Tony Hansen. There's something about him, I just know it."

Trokic stepped on it. He was frustrated; they were all working their asses off, and they had to set priorities. At the same time, a decree sent down from on high proclaimed that all their overtime had to be used in time off before the end of the year. An absolutely insane decision that made any planning impossible. "Can you search for Christoffer Holm's name in what's been deleted on her computer?"

"Of course. I'll do it the second I get back to her computer."

"There's not a whole lot more we can do right now."

His phone vibrated, danced around between the two front seats. "Grab that, would you?"

She listened for a moment then laid the phone back down. "Agersund. He wants to know where the hell we are and to remember about the meeting. We're ready to recon-struct her last day."

Chapter Nineteen

ONE MORE PERSON squeezed his way into the office, and Jasper had to sit on the floor to make room. Trokic caught sight of an officer in his mid-thirties and broke into a big smile—the first time Lisa had seen that happen. She guessed he was from MCI.

"Zdravo! Jacob!" He laid the autopsy report down on the table. "Haven't seen you for several months. When was it?"

The blond man, Detective Jacob Hvid, seemed reserved, perhaps even shy, as he came over and gave Trokic a friendly clap on the shoulder. He wore light jeans and a white hoodie. The number "12" was printed on the front. Streetwear.

"Agersund brought me in. It must be three or four months ago. You probably don't remember because you're repressing how I totally destroyed you in chess."

Hvid had spent the morning familiarizing himself with the case by going over all the documents, talking to Jasper and the techs, and visiting the crime scene. "I suppose you've already thought about the ritual angle? The forest, the hemlock, the way the body was arranged. A beautiful place. This country is filled with crazies, Satanists, God knows what other kinds of alternative lifeforms."

He leaned forward. "We were over in Sweden last spring, Gothenburg, they had a bizarre homicide too. They nabbed the killer in June. Absolute psychotic. He'd sacrificed a young woman to Ydun. You know, the Nordic goddess of youth. Besides cutting her open from head to toe, he stuffed an apple in her mouth to give her eternal youth. He thought he was doing her a favor, if you—"

"Not to disagree with you," Lisa said, smiling at him cautiously. "But all this symbolism could be a smokescreen for something much more ordinary. And we have a suspect who's been sentenced for—"

"Have we looked at this ritual angle?" Agersund said, eying Trokic. "And have you checked everything out, the psychiatric wards, paroles and so on?"

"Give us more bodies and we'll check Mars out too," Trokic said, defensive now. "We found a symbol written in her calendar; it could have some connection with a religion. So, yeah, a ritual might be involved, but it's hard to tell. The victim worked with tribal societies in Central Africa. What I mean is…it could mean anything. Christoffer Holm is much more interesting, in my opinion."

"Let me take a look at it," Jacob said. "Maybe I've seen it before; I know most of the new religions like the back of my hand."

"I'll make sure you get a copy," Trokic said. He clapped him on the shoulder. Lisa couldn't help but stare at him; for a moment, she'd seen an entirely different side of the man. A side capable of being truly happy.

"Great to see you," Trokic added.

Jacob smiled. "Same here."

Trokic wrote some things on the large whiteboard, and gradually, from the information supplied by the pathologist and techs, they began to get a grip on Anna's background and where she'd been the last day of her life.

She was twenty-seven and had grown up in the city with both of her parents. Her childhood had apparently been normal, and she'd been politically active as a teenager, left-wing. Had behaved like most teenagers. After high school, she enrolled in the Institute of Anthropology and Ethnology. There she met her first boyfriend, Poul, and they had a child, Peter. The relationship quickly fell apart, and Poul moved out. She'd adapted smoothly to her new status as a single mom and alternated between work and studies.

Her relationship with her parents became strained, and they seldom saw each other, especially after the parents moved farther away. Many of her friends and acquaintances lived across the country because of their education, and only a few were up to date on what she was doing.

People found her reserved at first, but usually, she opened up relatively quickly. No one had anything bad to say about her work ethic. She was a good mother who spent a lot of time with her son. And whenever possible, she took him to work with her. Even at the university. Several people mentioned her sunny disposition and that she loved practical jokes. No one had seen or heard much from her lately, and when they did, she was short with them and seemed a bit blue.

It had been difficult to track her exact movements on the last day of her life. Apparently, it had been quite normal. She and her son had been seen late that morning at a playground about half a kilometer from home; Anna had said hello to two people from her apartment building, a woman and her daughter. A receipt found in her kitchen drawer showed that she'd bought milk at a gas station kiosk at eleven thirty-four.

They were back home by one because Anna had called

her mother and apologized for a minor argument the evening before. After that, according to her mother, she presumably wrote an article for an anthropological publication. The pathologist reported that her last meal was lasagna and ice cream and that she had eaten around six. Peter had been put to bed immediately after.

At around seven, she left the apartment to run. It hadn't been possible to determine precisely which trails she took, but she was killed on the west side of Ørneredevej, relatively deep into the forest. She'd been defiled—the semen—and her throat had been cut from behind with one quick stroke. Or vice versa. They weren't sure about the sequence. She had died immediately.

The techs had determined that she'd been dragged through the forest immediately after, leaving a trail of blood to where she was found.

AGERSUND SLAMMED his pen down on the desk. "What about the kid?"

"What about him?" Trokic narrowed his eyes.

"Maybe we should let one of the girls have a go at him, see if we can get something. If someone's been in the apartment—"

"Listen, the psychologist and the doctor both say no to pressuring him to talk. He's nearly catatonic, and the doctor can't say what might happen. They both say we have to wait."

"Can't they be overruled?"

Trokic's stomach felt heavy as lead. "He's only three years old, he's just lost his mother, doesn't even know his father. His grandparents say he hasn't said a word since he walked inside their door."

"You can't be serious," Lisa added.

Agersund squirmed. "But what if—"

"If you want that child questioned, you'll have to fucking do it yourself and take the consequences," Trokic said.

The silence was awkward. "Okay, okay," their boss finally said.

I⊤ WAS dark by the time Trokic drove home through the city. It was like a journey through his past, when he was a cop on a beat, where split lips, vomit, vulgarity, and lousy explanations were all part of the drunken mosaic of his workday. The low moaning in public bathrooms, used needles lying around, broken mirrors, hashish dens. A forest of buildings, symmetry, and chaos that shielded the degradation he'd lived around most of his life.

The city seemed jittery now. The meeting that afternoon nagged at him. Something didn't jibe, and what had gone on in the apartment, who had the stoned neighbor seen so late that night? And how did the researcher, Christoffer Holm, fit into the picture?

Chapter Twenty

FINALLY, Lisa was back at Anna Kiehl's computer, after satisfying Agersund's appetite for reports and answering phone calls. Finally, she thought. She turned on the computer and started up the recovery program. Christoffer Holm's name hadn't been mentioned in any of the emails she'd already found, but they'd been a couple, and surely he was there somewhere. She typed his name in and waited. Four results. The first one:

FROM: "CHRISTOFFER" <christoffer-k-holm@get2net.dk>
    Subject:
    Date: Fri, 18 Jun 14:22:46
    <p   class=3DMsoNormal><font   size=3D2
face=3DTimes
    Roman><span =
    style=3D'font-size:10.0pt;
    font-family:Times Roman> Yes, you're right. But
    what the hell should I do. There's no time for
    this.<o:p></o:p></span></font></p>

```
    <p         class=3DMsoNormal><font        size=3D2
face=3DTimes
    Roman><span =
    style=3D'font-size:10.0pt;
    font-family:Times Roman'> Call you tomorrow,
    okay?
    <o:p></o:p></span></font></p>
```
*********** End of Cluster ***********

IT COULD BE ABOUT ANYTHING. For now, it wasn't important. She clicked on the next result, which only showed his
address surrounded by code. She had no idea where it came
from. On to the next one. Another email. No date. This had
more substance to it. What she got out of it was: *"Don't think
any more about it. I'll take care of it. I bitterly regret even considering
it. But now I have to get myself out of it. If this goes on, I'll have to
get a new phone number. Let's just forget about it for now. See you later.
Hugs, Christoffer"*

SHE STARED AT THE WORDS, trying to imagine what had
made him think about changing his phone number. It had
to be something significant. Was someone harassing him?

She clicked on the final result. No date there either.
*"Yeah, it's no problem. I'll take it over to Elise. It's not because I don't
want to leave it with you—I just think it's so stupid. I'll pick you up
later. Did I tell you that brochures have been printed for the book? They
look fantastic. I'm looking forward to taking them along to the
conference.*

AGAIN, no context. She needed more. It just didn't make
sense. She clicked her tongue in annoyance and turned on

the printer to print the results out. She racked her brain to find other ways of getting more out of the computer; there had to be fragments she couldn't locate because the To/From had been overwritten. If she had some keywords.

Jasper came in and plopped down on the chair beside her. "I've been thinking, how hard is it to do what you're doing here?"

"What do you mean?"

"Mmm, well, the thing is, a few weeks ago, I sold my old laptop to a student."

"Not very many people know you can even do this. But if you do know about it, it's not all that hard."

"It's an IT student."

She snorted. "Then I hope you don't have anything too indecent for anyone to see. And that the guy you sold it to isn't all that curious," she added, teasing him now.

The young officer blushed. "But I reformatted the hard drive. No one can find anything, can they?"

"That depends on *how* curious he is. Reformatting a drive isn't enough. The only thing you're really doing is telling the system that you're not using these data areas anymore, that it's okay to overwrite them. It's not actually deleting the data."

"So, what should I have done?"

"Well, unless you wanted to use a magnet or a big hammer on the hard drive, you should have gotten some of the serious programs that delete data."

"That's a little too much."

"Yeah. He probably won't look at it. Luckily, there aren't many people who want to bother with things like that. You have to know what you're looking for, too. Like in this situation. You don't have any ideas about words for a search, do you?"

"Try Montréal. Or *The Chemical Zone*. Or Procticon."

She typed all that into the search bar and clicked on it. "Nada. Damn."

"Not everyone is so into email."

"I suppose…"

"How about ducking out for a beer?"

Lisa closed the computer and sighed. "Yeah, what the heck. Maybe alcohol can get my brain cells functioning."

Chapter Twenty-One

A FEW DAYS AGO, he'd seen an advertisement hanging at the Central Station for a cell phone. Three-foot high red letters—Get a Life. He'd felt offended, strangely so. If a "life" meant some existence outside working hours, then he sure as hell didn't have one. Though he didn't regret it. And so what if it really was the pleasure of solving a criminal sudoku that got him out of bed every morning? It was enough for him. Now, he was home at eight-thirty, though, with enough time to digest the day's information while having a bite to eat. He opened the refrigerator door with high expectations. White shelves stared back at him. Empty shelves except for two cans of beer and a chunk of Turkish sausage. He'd been sure there was garlic lamb left over from Friday, but now he remembered eating the last of it for lunch yesterday. After a moment, he grabbed the sausage and a frying pan to sauté it in. Tomorrow, he'd ask Jacob if he wanted to come over for a decent goulash one of these days. Though he enjoyed being alone, he was pleased to have guests, too. There were two sides to the solitude he'd chosen for himself. He needed a place to sort things out, but he had yet to meet the woman who understood that. They quickly became jealous of where he chose to retreat, and they wanted either to be a part of that place—which he found intimidating—or to get him away from it. Neither of the two options had a happy ending. And yet, once in a while, the house felt empty. He pulled out a Joe Satriani CD; the power chords in a live version of "Time" rattled the walls. He imagined he could hear the space around the guitar. He smiled to himself. It felt like standing in the ocean and letting a wave ram into him.

Five minutes later, he was ready for a limited coffee-table meal of Turkish sausage with ketchup and a slice of bread, together with a stack of papers he'd brought home.

MILAN. He was the reason Trokic had transferred to the Criminal Investigations Department. He and his little brother, Mirko, had been friends with Milan, a carpenter who'd lived in an old house down the street. When Trokic began visiting Croatia as a teenager, the three of them had hung out together, with an eye for the same girls. None of them could have predicted what Milan was hiding, least of all Trokic. When Mirko had a car accident, it was Milan who spent the most time with him at the hospital, entertaining him, bringing him books. And Milan had made sure that Mirko's car was repaired and ready to go when he left the hospital. It was important to Trokic, who was in Denmark at the time, that Milan was there. He was a favorite with all of Trokic's family because of his generosity and willingness to help as a carpenter. But then came the war, and Milan wanted to serve his country, Croatia, even though he'd never shown any animosity to Serbs or interest in politics. They'd simply never talked about it when they were together.

For a long time, the family heard nothing from him. Trokic saw him only once, when Milan was home visiting his cousins. He'd brought along a bag filled with goodies—God only knew where he came up with them. Trokic had heard the soldiers did a lot of bartering, though. His friend had risen in the ranks and was an officer with many men under him. Complaints about conditions in the Army seemed to occupy much of his time.

Even then, Trokic hadn't noticed anything unusual about him. Trokic's childhood in Denmark among people with little respect for the law hadn't prepared him. The war had been over for a year, and Trokic had lost his father and brother; he'd needed someone to share his pain with, someone who'd known them. During his first visit after the war, Trokic asked his male cousin what had happened to Milan, but the answers he received were evasive. When he asked his female cousin, she spoke cryptically about were-wolves being human beings who acted normal most of the time. Finally, Trokic approached a long-time family friend who ran a popular bar, an old wooden barracks at the outskirts of town where he and Milan had often drank.

They called him the Werewolf of Medvednica. The evidence was clear. As an officer, Milan's position of power had brought out another side of him. Video evidence and witness statements from those close to him in the Army supposedly confirmed that Milan had single-handedly executed at least sixty people.

It was one of the few times in Trokic's life that he'd been emotionally numb. Not because of Milan, but because he'd lost faith in humanity.

SOMEONE KNOCKED ON THE DOOR. Thinking it was the neighbor, annoyed at him for not trimming his hedge, he grudgingly got to his feet. Lisa stood in the doorway wearing a thin, flowered chiffon blouse, her arms folded around her in the cool evening air.

"Hi...?" Unsure of herself, she smiled wryly and handed him a sheath of papers. "Hope I'm not disturbing you? I know it's late."

"No problem. Come in."

She stepped into the hallway and took her shoes off. "Isn't she sweet!"

He followed her eyes; the cat was playing with a bite of sausage on the floor. So much for the rest of his meal. It wasn't the first time it had happened.

"That's Pjuske."

"Just thought I'd drop these papers off on the way home. We've been so busy...I didn't have time until now."

"Okay. Would you like a cup of coffee or a beer?"

"No, thanks, I had a beer with Jasper, and I've got to get home. But I just wanted to say..." She took a deep breath and squeezed her wrist. "At first, I felt out of the loop, working on the computer, with no partner."

He pulled his hair while choosing his words. "It's my job to make sure everyone's being utilized the best way possible. Especially because we're under so much pressure. We can't—"

"I know, I know. I just wanted to tell you, I appreciate the opportunity to get out, do something more interesting, with more substance. The interviews, for example."

He thought for a few moments. "I could put you with Jacob; he's been working alone up to now...MCI couldn't spare any more officers...and it's my job to get the most out of him. And you can also learn from him."

"That sounds good. Thanks."

She seemed satisfied. She glanced around a few moments, then she pointed at a photo of a street that took up most of the side of a kitchen cupboard. "Is that where you're from?"

"I come from here, Århus." Trokic ran a hand through his hair. "But that's the town where my father lived."

Lisa tilted her head and took a closer look. "Nice-looking place. Beautiful flowers…I love oleanders."

She looked away. "Better get home. That's a report, the attachment specifies what I got out of the computer today. Thanks for the chat."

HE SANK down on the sofa, pleased with his decision to pair up the two detectives. Jacob was going to get along fine with Lisa. Same age. Same sense of humor. He was happy to have Jacob on the team.

AT FIRST, he wasn't sure where he was. Light surrounded him. Way too much light. Sunlight streamed through the filter of the forest's branches and leaves, down onto the snow-covered ground. He could just make out the pond to the left, covered with ice and surrounded by frosty cattails.

Someone was behind him, he heard a quiet rustling, and the faint odor of excrement was in the air. Scraping sounds. He hunched over. His clothes clung to his skin. Then the snow, the first of the year, began moving, twisting around in clumps in every direction. But it wasn't snow; long rows of gray rabbits ran down to the pond, thousands of them. He gasped for breath, and the small furry animals turned to him, showing their small, sharp teeth. Not rodent teeth, not at all—they were ice picks behind the peeled-back lips. He stumbled over the first rabbit and felt the back of another one break as his foot came down. Their eyes glowed from inside caves, and they began hissing loudly.

Pink and gray clouds dotted the sky, and he tried running through the rabbits, fell down into their cold ashen fur in the white forest, and their screams rose as the darkness fell. Chimes weaved around him in the air.

HE WOKE UP WITH A START. Papers lay over the blanket covering him, case reports were scattered everywhere. Instinctively, he looked at his watch; it was just past eleven, he'd slept forty-five minutes. A stack of papers fell as he sat up, and he grabbed them midair just above the floor. A half-empty bottle of red wine stood on the coffee table. His temples were hammering, a cold sweat covered his back. Something had woken him. A sound. Trokic shook his head. He could still see the gray animals on the floor, in the corners, under the table. He rubbed his eyes and reached for his cigarettes. Slowly, the images of the rabbits vanished, and the floor became the floor again. His phone rang.

Agersund. "There's something strange about that pond," he said. "We got the analysis on the hemlock. You're right. It's almost certain that little dry bouquet on Anna Kiehl's chest is from the plants close to the water."

"You think our murder weapon might be in there?"

"It's possible. The killer's familiar with the area; those plants were picked earlier this year. This summer, maybe even spring. We're sending divers in, I want to know what's in there."

Chapter Twenty-Two

WEDNESDAY, September 24

THE WEATHERMAN HAD PROMISED a last gasp of summer, a final desperate attempt to hold off autumn. Wrong again, he thought, as he looked out the office window at the thick, low-lying fog.

"The forest manager isn't all that wild about us," Agersund said, as he and Trokic drank their morning coffee. It was nine-thirty.

"He's not happy with the mess we're making in his pond," he continued. "You wouldn't believe the names he came up with, all the absolutely vital creepy little insects and breeding grounds for all these mysterious birds. So, I had to apologize. But I just talked to Falck, their divers are out there now. Let's keep our fingers crossed they find our murder weapon and hopefully a few other interesting things, so at least we get something out of all our destruction."

"How long will it take?"

"Good question. They're not sure they can finish today."

He stared at Trokic's small CD player spouting out Rammstein. "That music's from hell, you need to see a shrink. Which reminds me, how are we doing on the nutcase angle?"

"We found a few," Trokic said. "But they could account for their whereabouts, so right now it looks like their alibis check out."

"And Tony Hansen has flown the coop and we can't find him. So, we're not getting anywhere, is that it?"

"We have a connection between Anna Kiehl and the missing researcher, Christoffer Holm. We're looking into that."

He'd called Christoffer Holm's phone again, in hopes that it suddenly had been turned on. Unrealistic hopes, as it turned out. He was convinced the hair he'd found was significant. That the neurochemist had been near the crime scene recently. And he wanted to know why.

Agersund tousled his gray hair. "Jacob says the symbol drawn in the victim's calendar is used by a local sect. The Golden Order, they call themselves."

"Really," Trokic said.

"We'll have to check them out. Anything else?"

He slurped his coffee; some of it spilled onto the table. Trokic frowned at him. "A few wives have called in and ratted on their husbands because they weren't home Saturday night."

Agersund shook his head. Whenever someone was killed, women accused husbands and fathers, while psychotics, convinced of their guilt, gave full confessions. Many man-hours were wasted on these dead ends. "Check them out," he sighed. "I got a joke, by the way."

Trokic wrote a note to himself on the day's newspaper in front of him. "Out with it."

"Nah, you don't want to hear it," his boss said. He sounded wounded.

"I have no sense of humor."

"That's the truth," Jasper said, as he passed by outside the door.

"But everyone has *some* sense of humor," Agersund said.

"Not Daniel."

"I'll check that sect out," Trokic said. He spent more and more of his time on desk work, and it felt like a strait-jacket. He needed to be alone.

"Watch your back out there," Agersund said. "Those types can make a loony bin look like the sanity hall of fame."

Chapter Twenty-Three

THE HOUSE WAS on one of the side streets bordering the edge of the forest. A two-story house, built in the seventies. It stuck out in the midst of all the Danish orderliness with its shameful lawn of long, dead grass and tangled, overgrown bushes. The gable was painted a dour light-brown, touched up in places with a different color. The windows were almost too dirty to see through. The place had no charm whatsoever. He shivered.

A bald man in his late forties opened the door. He wore dark flared jeans, an orange knitted sweater, and wooden shoes. His fingernails needed clipping, and around his neck, he wore a metal chain with the symbol they'd found in Anna Kiehl's apartment.

"Hi," the man said, as he looked Trokic up and down.

"Detective Trokic." He flashed his ID. Through the hallway, he glimpsed the living room, where women and men with shaved heads moved silently around, lost in their own worlds.

"Hanishka," the man said. He stared at the ID. "Daniel? That's a good name."

"I have a few questions in connection with a homicide last weekend."

"What does that have to do with us?"

"I need some information."

Hanishka opened the door and Trokic followed him into the tiny square entryway with chessboard linoleum.

"Please, remove your shoes." That sounded like an order to Trokic.

Trokic took off his black shoes and walked gingerly on the cold floor into the kitchen, which many people obviously used. Hordes of teacups stood around the sink, and the odd smell in the room reminded him of rabbit food. He thought of the nightmares last night and he shivered again. A dark-skinned, barefooted woman chopped carrots at the kitchen counter. She didn't even look up when they walked in. Trokic wondered what the neighbors thought about this blot on their tidy residential landscape; was the sect's mailbox skipped when invitations were delivered for the annual street party, with its meatballs and songfest?

The sect was based on an interpretation of the Bible, and Hanishka was the local leader. Jacob had explained that many of the larger sects started this way, with a charismatic person who studied the Bible and gradually attracted students. Did Anna Kiehl have something to do with these people? An independent-minded woman, strong political convictions, anthropologist? That was hard for him to believe. She must have been studying them or crossed paths with them some way.

"We're only a small part of a larger flock that's growing day by day, all over the world," Hanishka said, as he offered Trokic a glass of some foul-smelling herbal tea. "We study the Bible and try to remain pure. We believe that God's word should be understood in its proper context."

"Something like Jehovah's Witnesses?" Trokic sipped at

the drink and wondered if he had offended him. But the middle-aged self-proclaimed apostle simply shook his head.

"Jehovah's Witnesses are a part of this depraved society. We keep out of it."

Trokic thought about what the district authorities would say to that; did these holy people exist on sacred air, or did they perhaps accept alms from society?

"*The reward for humility and fearing the Lord is riches and honor and life,*" he said, answering the unspoken question. "But how can I help you, Daniel?"

"The Golden Order's symbol was found in the calendar of a young woman who was murdered. We'd like to know if you have any connection to her."

"As I explained, we don't take part in society, and therefore there is no connection between us and the beings who still do. Revelation says that only—"

"As long as you people reside in this society, you will cooperate with the police and provide information." Trokic had neither the time nor the inclination for any long explanation.

"But we don't, the borderline between us and society lies just outside the door," Hanishka patiently explained. "In here, you are outside of society. And—"

"Would you please answer my questions? I don't have much time."

"Because your name is Daniel, I will answer what must be troubling your heart. We know of no woman by the name of Anna Kiehl."

"How do you know her name? I didn't mention it."

He stared cunningly at Trokic. "We happen upon a newspaper now and then. The fish we buy at the harbor is wrapped up in them."

"I see." Trokic raised his eyebrows. He reached for his cigarettes but left the pack in his pocket when the man across from him shot him a look of disapproval. He wasn't impressed with their professed righteousness. Many killings had been committed by people brandishing a Bible; a few short years ago a female member of a sect had died during a sadomasochistic exorcism of impurities. No sect looked kindly upon defectors. And to top it all off, the room was cold and impersonal.

"What about your disciples?"

"The members of the Golden Order keep no secrets from each other, and we are always around here."

"Would you please ask them at your next service, or meeting, prayers, whatever you call it—if anyone knows or has heard of her?"

"Of course. But their answers will be the same as mine."

TROKIC WALKED outside and down the small, weedy trail from the house. He stopped to light a cigarette; the hairs on his neck rose and his skin felt cold. When he wheeled around, a pair of eyes was looking down at him from a second-floor window. The figure's head was shaved, his face gray, his eyes empty. The eye contact lasted only a few seconds. Trokic took a hard drag on his cigarette. He could return to the house, but there was an entire army of hairless men inside. He wouldn't be able to tell them apart. The man vanished from the window.

Chapter Twenty-Four

IRENE OPENED the door almost before he rang the door-bell. Had she seen him park his car? Or maybe she'd heard him on the stairs.

"Detective?"

"I have a few questions. Very brief."

"Yes?"

Anna Kiehl's thesis partner leaned against the doorway without inviting him in. He looked her over; she almost seemed embarrassed, and her hair was tangled as if she'd just gotten out of bed. Instinctively, he touched his head, reminding himself that he needed a trim. The longer his hair, the wilder his whorl became.

"I worked late yesterday," she explained, a bit apologetically. "The thesis."

Trokic tried to hide his intense dislike of her. Experience had taught him that showing animosity made it difficult to ferret out information from people. He explained shortly about the Golden Order. "I'd like to hear what you know about it."

"I've never heard of that sect. It's not the type of thing Anna and I have been working with."

"Could she have been researching it on her own?"

"I doubt that very much. She would have talked about it, definitely. When she was seriously interested in something, she wouldn't shut up. Maybe she knew someone involved with the sect. Or maybe it's just a coincidence that what she drew looks like their symbol?"

"Maybe." He thought about it for a moment. "Do you know any connection between Anna and a man by the name of Christoffer Holm?"

"No, no, I don't."

"Even if I told you he was her boyfriend?"

"I didn't know she had a boyfriend."

"You didn't? I don't understand, I thought you two were close? Or maybe you really did have some sort of falling out with her?"

Irene shrugged.

"Do you know anything about him?"

"Never heard of him."

"He wrote the book you returned to Anna Saturday evening."

"Oh, that guy." She looked as if she could care less, which disappointed him.

"Hmmm. I guess that's it, sorry to bother you."

"No problem."

He stood his ground until she closed the door. He was sorry he couldn't think of more questions to put to her, to dig deeper underneath her façade. He decided to pay a visit to someone else who knew Anna Kiehl.

HE RANG THE DOORBELL. Isa Nielsen, the woman he'd met

in the forest near the crime scene, looked surprised when she opened the door, but she smiled. "Trokic—isn't that right? Please, come in."

She wore dark jeans and a knitted beige cardigan, a contrast to the sweatsuit he'd seen her in a few days before. Her hair hung free and she was wearing light makeup. He noticed her attractive collarbone, a scoop of revealed skin; he forced himself not to stare. "Thank you. Sorry to barge in on you like this, hope I'm not interrupting anything. I just have a few routine questions."

She opened the door wide. "You're not interrupting a thing."

He glanced around. The second-floor apartment was in an older building on the south side of town; it had been newly renovated and painted an antique blue. The old furniture, crowded floor-to-ceiling bookshelves, and Persian rugs were a bit too much for Trokic's taste. The place smelled of perfume and something else he couldn't put his finger on, a bit sweet; he didn't like that, either. Europa lifted her head up in a corner of the room and wagged her tail.

"I don't have a lecture until after lunch, so we have lots of time." Isa Nielsen gestured toward the sofa. "Have a seat."

She placed coffee and cups on the coffee table. While she poured, she talked about her work at the Department of Political Science. Primarily, she taught sociology and worked on various interdisciplinary research projects.

"Including anthropology?"

"Yes, sometimes the two institutes have common interests. But mostly I work with theoretical sociological models in connection with political science projects."

Trokic imagined the male students stuck around when she lectured. Even though you couldn't call her beautiful, her eyes and smile were lively, her movements graceful and feminine. "So, maybe you knew Anna Kiehl outside of the running group, from the university?"

"It's a big university, thousands of students and researchers and lecturers in every discipline. I didn't know her there."

"What about personally?"

Isa Nielsen turned her hands over in her lap. "Only superficially. There were eight of us in the group, and we only ran once a week." She sounded apologetic.

She looked him in the eye, straight into him. He felt it all the way down to his toes. "Does the name Christoffer Holm ring any bells for you?"

The sociologist thought for a few moments. "I think I've heard that name. Should I know him?"

"Maybe. He wrote a book called *The Chemical Zone*."

She smiled. "Oh, yes. Tall, blond, handsome? Works at the university?"

"Holm was a researcher at the psychiatric hospital, but he seems to have disappeared."

"He was the one with the other anthropology student in our running group. Irene. I remember because he drove her out a few times to where we met in the forest. He didn't run with us, though. Her last name escapes me right now. A redheaded girl…"

Trokic frowned and straightened up. "Are you sure about that?"

"I think so. Wasn't she Anna's friend? It seemed so, anyway. But that was a long time ago."

"It was. Tell me about her, what you know about her."

"Nothing other than what I've already said. She seemed a little…no, she's actually nice, very nice. But really, I never spoke with them much at all."

Trokic wrote down what she said. Irene had *lied* about

what she knew about Christoffer Holm. That was obvious. Why? The missing researcher was involved in some way, he was sure of it. And now there was a new angle. "Would you please excuse me? I have to make a call."

He walked into the next room, a small library. Europa padded after him good-naturedly and laid down at his feet. He called Jasper and immediately said, "Bring Irene in, she lied to my face an hour ago. Something's not right here. I'll be in as soon as I can."

So. Christoffer Holm had a connection to Irene. The tall bookshelf in front of him was filled with textbooks and folders. He wondered if Isa Nielsen could help with a few observations; she was a sociologist, she must know a few things about human beings. And her familiarity with the forest. He wouldn't mind coming back here.

He hung up and stuck his phone back in his jacket pocket, wrote down a few words in his notepad, and distractedly scratched the dog before turning. The sociologist watched him from the doorway, her arms crossed.

"Nice dog you have here," he said.

She nodded, then her eyes suddenly changed expression. "She's also the only one I have."

Trokic didn't know what to say. "I guess I better get going."

"Have you done a psychological profile of the killer?"

"We don't use that type of thing so often."

She smiled and shrugged. What he'd said wasn't completely true. Agersund had met that very morning with the psychologist they normally used. But it was more a dialogue—contentious, in his opinion—than an actual profile. Jacob had mentioned a few short takes from the meeting on his way out the door. He was convinced they were wasting their own and the psychologist's time.

"I have to go. Thanks for talking to me."

His phone vibrated in his pocket. It was Jasper again. "We have the DNA analysis. It's certain that Christoffer Holm was the father of Anna Kiehl's unborn child."

Chapter Twenty-Five

TROKIC PACED in his office with a pencil between his teeth. Two sandwiches lay on the desk. He was moving the pieces of the puzzle around in his head while absorbing all the new information. So. Holm had gotten Anna Kiehl pregnant. His DNA was in a hair found at the pond and also in the unborn child of the victim, but the semen on her stomach belonged to someone else. Who? Jasper leaned back against the door and stretched his legs.

"I sent someone out for Anna's friend."

"Where the hell are they?" Trokic asked.

"Things can only go so fast, Daniel."

Trokic grabbed the phone and dialed Lisa's number. "You have Christoffer Holm's sister's number. Call her and see if she'll talk to us again. We need to know more about Anna Kiehl's boyfriend, maybe we've overlooked something."

He did another lap of his office as he thought about what to do. "No, wait. Go down and talk to her, Lisa. To speed things up. We'll take care of the friend—"

"I just promised Poulsen I'd take a quick look at a

computer from a fraud case. It won't take long, but apparently, the speed of light isn't fast enough for him."

"What! They must be crazy, he'll have to find someone else to help. Find someone to bring Elise Holm in then, it's important. Have you heard anything about the pond?"

"They say it's going slow. The bottom is muddy and it's almost impossible to see anything. They have to feel their way around in it."

"I'll run out there this afternoon." Trokic hung up.

IT FELT as if his brain was working even when thinking of other things. While he slept, fragments of the case drifted around in circles, creating new structures, curves, energies. This time it was the details in Anna Kiehl's apartment that kept dancing around. Her friend Irene was sitting near his office, waiting, ready to be questioned. He needed to get started, asap.

Chapter Twenty-Six

"WOULD you like to go out for a bite to eat?"

Lisa looked up from the computer into Jacob's calm expression. She hesitated a moment. They were busy, and she'd decided to skip lunch. On the other hand, she couldn't be expected to run on Mars bars all afternoon just because everyone thought they could just boss her around. Then she remembered what Trokic had told her yesterday evening: Jacob was her new partner.

"Okay. A quick lunch."

She lifted the lavender jacket off the chair behind her, wishing she'd worn something more neutral. She would draw attention beside the tall, pale officer, but there was nothing to do about it.

He smiled. "We're partners, after all. Let's grab something light down on Åen."

THEY ORDERED PASTA AT SIDEWALK. "We got the search warrant," he said after the food came. It smelled delicious.

"Reasonable grounds for suspicion and significant importance to the investigation. We'll go out there this afternoon."

"What?"

"A search warrant for Tony Hansen's apartment." His eyes were focused on her. He was a few years her senior, with boyish features, a straightforwardness, a lack of cynicism. His arms were splayed out on the table between them, his off-white hooded sweatshirt slightly open at the neck. Her skin prickled.

"Yeah, okay, but how'd you manage it? I mean, it's not easy to prove he had time to do it."

"We have to be able to cross him off the list. So, we emphasized his record, that he'd been in the vicinity, that he lied. We drove out there, but he's still not home. The techs are going through the apartment, they haven't found anything of interest yet. The guy is just a dedicated alcoholic. It's a waste of time if you ask me."

"I'd like to know what he's hiding. There's *something*."

They ate for a moment in silence. The crowd on Åboulevarden streamed by, the baby buggies, high heels, piercings. The longer she lived in the city, the better she liked it. Much of her family also had moved here. She liked the Latin quarter, in particular, all the small, winding streets, brunch on Sundays. A young woman at the table beside them was obviously trying to make eye contact with Jacob. She kept playing with her hair on the back of her neck.

"How do you know Trokic?" she said.

He wiped his mouth with a napkin. "I met him in Croatia several years ago. I was a UN soldier stationed in Sisak for a while, and he worked for a humanitarian organization in Zagreb."

"Humanitarian work?"

"Yeah, it was an Irish-Catholic aid organization, St.

Patrick's. Its headquarters was a former school on the outskirts of the old city of Zagreb. He helped relocate families who'd lost their homes some way or other. Often, they'd burned down. Most of them came from Krajina. That was where they refused to recognize Croatia as an independent country."

So, Lisa thought, she'd have to give up the idea that her somber colleague was a Croatian fascist. It annoyed her a bit. "Okay. But how exactly did you meet?"

"He was going around the hardest hit areas, making contact with the homeless. It was bad when he started, really bad. The Serbs burned entire villages and drove out the Croatians. But to make a long story short, I actually met him in the middle of the war zone. I thought it might be interesting to meet someone with a Danish *and* Croatian background, so when I had some time one day, I looked him up in Zagreb. I met one of his younger cousins…and well…Trokic lived with her big sister and husband during the time I was seeing her. Sinka. That was her name."

The corners of his mouth sank; something bad had happened, she sensed it, but she didn't press him.

"He's had a rough life, all in all. A tough childhood here, and his father and younger brother were killed by the Serbs down there. He took it hard."

She drooped inside. She hadn't known, but of course, it was something he wouldn't tell just anyone. She wanted to know more, but she didn't want to pry, either.

"We've seen a lot of the same things," Jacob said. "Not that we sit around and dwell on it when we're together, but anyway…"

He ran his hand through the tufts of his blond hair, and she lowered her eyes.

"But what about his disciplinary case several years ago?"

she said, bringing up one of her other reservations about him. "Unnecessary use of violence, wasn't that it? Against a woman. That's the kind of thing I can't handle very well."

"You probably also know he was acquitted in city court. He was on a beat back then. She was a heroin addict, sort of crazy."

Lisa looked at him skeptically and lowered her voice; she'd noticed that the couple to the right seemed to be eavesdropping. "Violence is violence."

"He's okay. And a damn good cop. He punched her a few times, she attacked him while he was confiscating four grams of heroin. I know, because he talked a lot about it. She tried to scratch out his eyes. Sometimes, you just react."

"Okay, I didn't know that. I just thought—"

"Yeah, I know. But I trust him three hundred percent, and you can too."

AFTER HE FINISHED HIS PASTA, he leaned back and looked at her carefully. "I was thinking, maybe you'd like to see a movie with me some evening? It gets lonely sitting by yourself in the hotel room, watching TV."

"Sure," she said, surprised that he'd asked. And relieved at the thought of not being alone for an evening.

"Jasper said you were a sort of female film freak, underneath all your computer expertise. He said I should ask you who said…what was it, let's see if I can remember…'*This is a .44 Magnum, probably the most powerful handgun in the world.*'"

She laughed. "That crazy bastard won't leave me alone. He challenges me all the time."

"So, do you know?"

"Of course I know. Tell him hi from Dirty Harry. Surely, he can find something harder than that."

Jacob laughed. "He said that's what you'd say."

His phone rang. He looked at her across the table as he spoke. The wind swirled his short hair and made him shiver a bit. He hung up, focused again.

"We have to pay a visit to the sect. One of them claims he knows who our killer is."

Chapter Twenty-Seven

"WHAT IS IT NOW?" Hanishka frowned sternly at the two officers. "Don't you have anything better to do? I told that Daniel detective guy this morning, we had nothing to do with what happened."

"One of your...supporters called us, said he had some information," Jacob said.

"I doubt that very much."

"Don't waste our time. It's the truth, the call came from your phone."

The leader of the sect looked at them for a moment before sighing. "All right. Wait here and I'll ask around."

Two minutes later, he returned. "No one here knows anything about the case."

"Is everyone here?"

"Yes."

"Then we're going to have to ask you to let us in. This is important, it concerns a serious crime."

"All right," the leader repeated in annoyance. He opened the door.

They stepped into the living room, their usual meeting

place, it looked like. An old yellow rug lay on the floor, potted plants stood on a large windowsill. No furniture. Lisa held her arms at her sides and peered around. Groups of people sat on the floor, about twenty of them in all, their heads shaved. Even though their clothes weren't identical, she wasn't sure she could tell them apart.

Hanishka clapped his hands, and abruptly their murmuring ceased. "Someone here has information for the police. I don't know who, but I want that person to come along so we can get this settled!"

You could hear a pin drop. Some of them looked at the floor, others stared frankly at the two detectives. One person coughed, a few others looked terrified. Lisa studied them carefully and noted every move. Nothing. Absolutely nothing.

"WHAT DO YOU THINK?" she said when they reached the car.

"We could bring them all in, one by one, maybe?"

"That would take time. But we may have to. Let Trokic decide if it's worth it."

Lisa sat in the passenger seat, leaning slightly toward him so she could watch as he drove. "Strange place. You think they're happy?"

"Probably. According to Sartre, we're all doomed to be free, so if you put yourself in a situation where there are rules for everything, maybe you feel all your choices have been made."

"What do you mean?"

"I mean that freedom gives you responsibility, but responsibility can create a lot of anxiety. And like somebody said, we feel trapped, even though our lives are made up of free choices.

The members of that sect in there aren't doomed the same way because it's written out what they're supposed to do. And that eliminates a lot of dilemmas and makes life less of a problem."

"Opium of the people, is what you're saying?"

"I think they're at peace with themselves. Maybe that's a type of happiness. They're not the ones adding to the depression statistics, that's all the rest of us."

BACK IN THE OFFICE, Lisa was happy she'd gone to lunch with him. She felt better, now that her blood sugar had stabilized. The short stint with Jacob had been good for her, and she looked forward to spending an entire evening with him. She smiled at the thought.

The officer sent to pick up Elise Holm was grouchy when he returned. "She's all yours. Maybe next time you can do your own pickup; your cases aren't necessarily more important than ours."

"Sorry about that. The orders came from higher up."

Lisa had heard about a pile-up on the freeway in the northbound lanes at a turnoff, and the police were short-handed.

She'd just sat down when her niece called. "Can I come over this evening, Aunt Lisa?" She was blubbering.

"What is it?"

"I can't stand her, she's a complete nul, a basic bitch. She promised to give me money to go to the movies with Line and Oliver tonight. So, I'm getting ready and she says I can't go after all."

Nanna was sobbing dramatically. She'd begun using Lisa as an escape hatch a little too often, and even though she enjoyed Nanna's company, she wasn't sure it was helping the mother/daughter relationship. Besides, this could be a stunt to improve Nanna's chances of getting her way.

Lately, Lisa was worried about her niece becoming a bit unstable. She was dropping all her interests, and her appearance and behavior were more provocative nowadays. Or was Nanna just being a teenager? Hadn't she herself run around with a rainbow of colors in her hair, wanting to rebel against her parents? She couldn't remember exactly where the lines had been drawn.

"I don't know, Nanna. I'm working late this evening."

Another agitated voice came on the line. "You can have her; I'd love to get rid of her. She insults me over and over and then expects me to finance her little escapades, and the crowd she hangs with? You don't want to know. Honestly, I can't knock any sense into her head. But I'm cutting her off, she just has to learn."

"I'm working late this evening," she repeated to her sister. "But I can bring it home with me, and if she's there first, she knows where the key is."

"I'm moving in with Aunt Lisa!" her niece screamed in the background.

Someone knocked on the door of her office. "Just a sec," she told her sister.

Elise Holm opened the door, walked over, and sat down across from Lisa. Her face was pale, bloodless. "Something's horribly wrong," she said, shaking her head.

"It's okay with me," Lisa said into the phone. She turned to the woman.

Chapter Twenty-Eight

IRENE WAS CORNERED. Her pupils were slightly dilated, every muscle in her body tense. It was easy to stand in a doorway and let drop a little white lie or two, but sitting in a police station with two officers staring her down, ready to give her a verbal beating, was an entirely different animal. And there might be consequences. Trokic sat in the chair across the desk from her, while Jasper leaned against the wall.

Trokic began slowly. "You told me earlier today you didn't know Christoffer Holm personally or know about any connection between him and Anna. Now we know that's not the case."

"I just didn't think—"

"You didn't think what? That it was relevant? Or that it looked so good? Because it doesn't. Once, you were Christoffer Holm's girlfriend, and now it turns out your friend who was murdered was carrying his child."

"I didn't know she was pregnant; I told you that."

"No, but when you did find out, you must've known he was the father. Yet you kept it to yourself."

"And he wasn't my boyfriend."

"No? What would you call it?"

"We went out a few times. It never got to that point."

"To what point?"

"We only went to bed together once, if you absolutely have to know."

"But you were in love with him?"

"I suppose so. Yes."

She looked like she'd eaten a piece of absolutely forbidden cake. She stared to the side.

"So, what happened? Did she steal him from you?"

"I suppose you could put it that way. Even though I hate that expression."

"How long were they together?"

"Since my birthday early this summer. That's where they met each other." She sighed. "I threw a party for a bunch of my friends, and they started talking. And kept on talking. They went out into the kitchen, and they were so wrapped up in each other that they forgot where they were. Not that they started kissing or anything. They were just talking, but intense, nonstop. So into what they were talking about that it was like everyone else was just so fucking uninteresting."

Trokic remembered the note they found in Anna Kiehl's apartment. He grabbed his notebook and wrote: Christoffer and Irene. Then he held it up to Jasper.

Irene swallowed nervously and looked directly at him. He should feel sorry for her, but he didn't. He couldn't. He sensed a selfishness in her way of being in love. It sounded as if she were talking about other people, but in fact, she was talking about herself.

"She knew very well how I felt about him, and that's why she never talked about him to me after they started seeing each other. But, suddenly, one day he was gone.

Anna was totally crushed, I could see that. Now I can better understand why. Of course, she knew she was pregnant."

She bit her lip. "Maybe she told him about it, and he just took off." She didn't look unhappy at the thought.

"Now you're guessing. Let's stick to the facts here. You weren't angry with Anna because she was pregnant with a man you loved?"

"But I didn't know it, did I?" she snarled.

"You have no knowledge about anyone involved with Anna's murder?"

"No," she spat. "And now I want to go home."

"Take it easy. We're only talking."

Trokic tipped his chair back and tried to digest what the woman had said.

She took a sip of the water in front of her.

Trokic's phone rang. He almost ignored it, but he decided to check who was calling. Agersund. "Yes?"

"What the hell have you been doing all afternoon?"

"We're right in the middle of an interrogation—"

An interrogation that was over, he realized, from the tone of Agersund's voice. "They're busy out at the pond. You'd better get out there, the sooner the better."

Trokic raised his eyebrows. "Murder weapon?"

"Still looking. But we found Christoffer Holm, and he doesn't look one damn bit good."

Chapter Twenty-Nine

ON A LATE AUTUMN day a few years earlier, Trokic had seen a body washed up on a beach. He'd been dead three weeks. Two kids from a free school had found him. Trokic had never been able to rid himself of the image.

But this was worse than that, worse than anything he'd ever seen. The forest loomed over them, darkness was about to fall. Trokic studied the gruesome sight.

The body of the blond man had been handled very carefully to avoid damage. His brown skin had loosened over most of his body; only the once-white shirt and jeans seemed to hold it in place. Most of his hair, nose, and eyelids were gone, also the lower part of his face from his lips to his chin, revealing his white, wide jawbones. His marble-like row of teeth was bared at Trokic. A leg was covered with sludge and duckweed, and the pond's small insects had burrowed in a few places.

The area around the pond was a scene, like an operation room set up in the fading day, lit by intense spotlights. The sweet odor spread and Trokic instinctively held his breath while stepping around to keep out of the techs' way.

The absolute worst stench in the world came from rotting human beings. For example, a body quickly transferred its odor to the upholstery of a car seat, after which the car was worth a match and a few cans of gas.

Forensic Pathologist Torben Bach had been called in once again to investigate. He spoke quietly into his dictaphone.

"Are you sure it's Christoffer Holm?" Trokic asked one of the techs.

"His driver's license was in an inside pocket. It's the only ID we've found so far. Maybe something more will show up. I'm guessing he wasn't anywhere else since he got back from Montréal. Doesn't look like he's been in there less than eight weeks. He was hidden over in the southwest corner. It's really not so deep, only about three or four meters. Jesus, he stinks! Incredible."

"Why didn't we spot him earlier? Don't bodies rise up to the surface?"

"Yeah, he probably drifted up to the surface after a week or so, when the decomposition process was at its peak. It's the gases that cause bodies to rise in water. But this guy sank to the bottom again when the air leaked out of the balloon, so to speak."

Trokic shivered at the thought of the diver who found the body. The thought of touching it, perhaps even his face brushing against something so nauseating in the muddy water.

"A little like one of the old bog people," the tech said.

"Maybe."

The historic area and the symbolism didn't interest him; he was convinced this was a more ordinary murder. Christoffer Holm had most likely been killed on the way home after several days in Montréal. And almost eight weeks later, the mother of his unborn child met the same fate. He wanted to bring in everyone who had worked with the researcher. Plus neighbors, friends, former lovers. He wanted to know the man's financial transactions, business connections, legal situation. There could be other people rejected in his past. People would kill for a gram of heroin or because of an offensive remark, but this was different, this was something evil, a crime committed by someone seriously screwed up.

He called Lisa. She already knew and was about to try to comfort the victim's sister, who was in deep shock.

"I want you and Jacob to investigate his professional life. His projects, the reviews of *The Chemical Zone*, his standing in neurochemistry, everything you can find about him, nationally and internationally."

"We'll get right on it," Lisa said.

Trokic was sweating, even though it was cool in that isolated part of the forest. He could stand a glass of fine red wine. His facial muscles were starting to twitch, a sign of overexertion. After a final glance at the decomposed remains of Christoffer Holm, he turned and left.

JASPER WALKED in to deliver the latest witness statements. "Can we do this while we drink a cup of coffee?" Trokic sighed and rubbed his eyes. "I'd like your opinion on something."

"Here or somewhere else?"

"How about my place? I'll drive you home later, or you can sleep on the sofa. I just need to run some reports over to Lisa…let's say in an hour, okay?"

"No problem." Jasper had no family responsibilities. In fact, Trokic doubted he'd ever had a girlfriend. And really, it was less complicated that way.

Chapter Thirty

LISA WRESTLED her apartment building's front door open with one arm while practically dragging a much too heavy grocery sack from Netto. She wanted to cook a decent meal, Mexican, and have a serious talk with her niece before getting back to her work. Her bag was filled to the brim with papers, and the strap bit into her shoulder muscles as she lumbered up the stairs. The events of that afternoon had tied her stomach into knots. She hadn't seen Christoffer Holm's body, but the description had been vivid enough to etch the sight in her mind.

A few steps past the second floor, the handle of the plastic sack ripped off. The small cardboard tray of cherry tomatoes placed strategically on top fell out and trickled down the stairs like miniature red balls. A bottle of balsamic vinegar followed them.

"Freaking sack!"

She set the sack and her bag down and gathered all the small runaways while breathing in the fumes of red wine vinegar. The front door below slammed shut. Nanna! She could use an extra hand with the meal; otherwise, they'd be eating awfully late.

It wasn't her niece. The startled face of her new partner appeared, and he hooted when he saw her in the middle of all the chaos. "On a scale of one to ten, how popular will I be if I help pick all this up?"

"You'll earn a few points, no doubt about that. Especially if you carry the bags up, too. And lose the grin on your face."

She smiled at him and handed him a sack.

"I stopped by to invite you out to eat."

"I can't this evening. My niece is coming in a bit, and I promised Trokic I'd do some reading on Christoffer Holm's professional life."

She gave him a disappointed look, then she said, "But you could stay and eat, and help with the reading if you like?"

"I won't be butting in?"

"Absolutely not."

"What's on the menu?"

"Mexican."

"I'm in. I'll make the gravy."

"Gravy? There's no gravy in Mexican!"

"Yeah, I know."

They laughed as they climbed the last few steps.

"It's a bit of a mess in here," she said.

That was the understatement of the year. Bombay during tourist season would have been a better way to put it. She glanced around in embarrassment at the ravaged landscape of case files, overflowing ashtrays and orange peels on the coffee table, the stacks of glasses and plates and a half-empty bottle of wine in the kitchen. Topped off by Flossy screaming: "Fuuuuck—good you're home!"

"Whoa!" Jacob said. "The bird talks."

He looked around at the room. "You have been one busy cop, haven't you?"

"You could say that," Lisa mumbled.

They set the sacks down. She glanced at him to see how he was taking all this, but he was already focused on the contents of the sacks.

"This looks great. Give me a few minutes, I'll run down for a few bottles of wine."

"You don't need to do that."

"Of course I do."

She watched him every step of the way until he was out the door, then she turned to her apartmental anarchy. How quickly could she pick up?

Chapter Thirty-One

"DID ANYONE TAKE care of Elise Holm?" Trokic asked. An hour had passed; they'd made Nescafe and scrounged up a bag of peanuts and a Swiss roll out in the cupboard. TV2 late news droned in the background. Tomorrow, they'd be doing a segment on the researcher and his girlfriend, but apparently, they hadn't heard about Holm's body in time for this broadcast. Which pleased him.

"Lisa found a friend," Jasper said. "Elise's parents are dead. Am I seeing things, or is that a plant over there? A real living plant, Daniel! So how long has it survived the drought in this hostile environment?"

"My neighbor gave it to me a few weeks ago; I took care of her guinea pig while she was on vacation."

Jasper always had a comment ready about his house. In his opinion, the dark gray walls were "sinister," even though Trokic had pointed out it was a greenish-gray. His eternally empty refrigerator was also "sinister," also the fact that Pjuske would never talk to him.

Trokic thumbed through the witness statements to find

Irene's. "What do you think about Anna's friend's reaction to all this?"

"I think it shocked her."

"I'm not so sure."

"Doesn't seem like an act to me," Jasper said. "So, you don't have anything with a higher alcohol content than coffee?"

"Wine?"

"That would qualify."

Trokic went out to the kitchen for two glasses and a bottle off the wine rack.

"She seemed more on edge when we saw her a few days ago," Jasper said.

Trokic poured two glasses of wine and drank most of his in one gulp. His favorite wine. A Chilean Cabernet Sauvignon. Inexpensive, but as smooth on the palate as a marshmallow.

"It doesn't look good that she had such close relationships to both of them. She could be involved."

Trokic leafed through the papers. He would go through all of it again more carefully tomorrow.

WHEN HE FINALLY GLANCED UP, the young assistant detective had fallen asleep on the sofa. Trokic sighed and emptied the rest of the bottle. No reason to waste Chilean grapes. He was about to doze off when his phone rang a meter away from him.

"Yeah?"

"Bach."

"What's up?"

"We're starting early tomorrow. At seven."

"Okay. I can't say I'm looking forward to it."

He scraped a wad of chewing gum off the coffee table. Jasper was snoring now. He could stand some sleep himself.

"I think it's going to be interesting," the pathologist said. "It looks like he wasn't killed at the pond."

"What do you mean?"

"Something else happened to Christoffer Holm before he landed in the water. That much I can tell you."

"Why do you think that?"

"You'll have to see for yourself. See you tomorrow, Daniel."

Chapter Thirty-Two

LISA'S NIECE slept curled up in her bed. They had kept her from going to the movies, though she'd tried to talk them into it when she arrived. As they expected she would. But, before long, she was giggling at Jacob's comments and tales from work. Line and Oliver had been forgotten. The evening, including the Mexican food, had been a success. Work awaited them, though, and they each grabbed a stack of papers and sat down on separate sofas. She started reading *The Chemical Zone*, and Jacob leafed through several articles. A soft female voice sang in the background.

"I don't understand much of this," he said, after an hour of reading. He reached for his wine glass. "This stuff isn't for amateurs."

"This is okay," she said, holding the book up. She'd made a good start on the three-hundred-twenty-page book version of the thesis, a discussion of the pros and cons of antidepressants in layman's terms. At first, she'd battled with the slightly convoluted writing, sorting out the differences in neurotransmitters such as serotonin, noradrenaline, dopamine, glutamate, and a new one, nitric oxide, but now she was making progress. Her respect for the young researcher was growing; he seemed to have been very concerned for the mentally ill, but he also recognized the long-term risks for society, the opportunity for abuse. The book had personality, and many cases from the laboratory as well as psychiatric and neurological hospital wards were described. It also contained a statistical section to help give an understanding of the issue.

"Actually, it's strange to think we have these types of people here, in this small of a city. People helping solve one of the greatest mysteries of the human mind. And the nature of happiness."

"But what's the book about?"

"It's a sort of reckoning with the media's distorted picture of biological psychiatry and psychopharmacology, and it tries to put the knowledge we have into a modern perspective. He does a pretty good job. You feel like he wants to discuss what it means to be happy."

Jacob stretched his legs under the coffee table. He looked comfortable. "Happiness is freeing yourself from the world's eyes and giving up the hunt for material goods."

He let that hang in the air for a moment. "What's that music we're listening to? I'm glad you don't share our mutual colleague's sick musical taste."

"It's an EP by Aztrid, a band I heard in town one night. A demo. Nanna found it for me. I like it a lot."

"Me too. Unusual voices."

She put the book down. "It would be nice to know if any of this is relevant to the case, or if we're just stuffing our brains with all this knowledge."

"What do you think?" he asked.

"He was at the top of his field, looks like. There's always someone wanting to take people like that down. It brings out the worst in us."

"You might have something there. I'd better get home. If you can call that lousy hotel room a home."

She followed him to the door and turned on the hallway light.

"Okay, get a good night's sleep," he said.

She nodded. "You too."

He waved goodbye and closed the door behind him. She permitted herself a sly smile.

It was one-thirty in the morning when she finally settled in on the sofa. She could sleep five and a half hours before getting up and sending her niece off to school.

Chapter Thirty-Three

THURSDAY, September 25

As ALWAYS, Bach sounded neutral and sober when he began describing his observations at the autopsy. They were all there again, several of them holding up handkerchiefs to avoid the sickeningly sweet odor of the corpse on the table. Lisa stood at one end, frowning, pensive, but apparently not even this could throw her off. And it was bad.

"The dental records are arriving this afternoon. The medical authorities found his dentist, and the forensic odontologist will have a look at it later. The body fits the description of Christoffer Holm. Late thirties, one hundred eighty-five centimeters tall, medium-blond hair. There are no special identifying marks or objects, no rings, tattoos, old broken bones, nothing except an older scar in the groin area. The condition of the corpse corresponds to what could be expected after being submerged underwater for eight weeks, in a state of advanced decomposition and partially skeletonized."

He adjusted his glasses and caught Trokic's eye. "From here on it gets more interesting. There are fractures of his right leg and three ribs. Also his right jawbone, and I found shards of glass in some of the remaining tissue around one ear. I'll send it to the lab in Copenhagen later."

"What caused the fractures?"

Bach hesitated. "Hard to say, but I think he was in a car accident. The glass is splintered in a special way, it could be from a side window."

"Are you sure?" Agersund said.

"It looks like the type of injuries inflicted by a vehicle ramming into the side of someone. But it's probably not the cause of death, at least not entirely."

He pointed to an open section of the skull. "Here, there's a sizable oblong, jagged fracture. It extends five centimeters into the brain. Unlike the other traumas, it's on the left side, and I've also found traces of red coloring."

"But why—"

"Let me finish." He smiled and leaned in closer to the corpse. Carefully, he touched the area with his gloved hand. Several of those watching looked as if they were about to throw up.

"I've also found some particles of lacquer. Of course, I can't be one hundred percent sure, but if somebody took a small ax and hit somebody else over the head, hard as they could, this is how it would look."

TROKIC RETURNED to his office where he continued the painstaking work of going through the latest reports.

It was unusually hectic at the station for a Thursday morning. More episodes involving the newest designer drug had taken place. A fourteen-year-old was still in a coma after taking the drug last weekend, and a seventeen-year-old had tried to strangle his mother two days after being stoned on Kamikaze. A team of officers had arrested four "new Danes" in connection with a knifing. Trokic had met one of them on the way in, a tall, skinny kid fifteen-years-old or so, wearing a red sweatband and an Outlandish down coat. He held a bloody rag to his arm. His right eye was swollen, his face streaked with blood from a cut on his eyebrow. Even though he must have been in considerable pain, his face was expressionless. Occasionally, one of them tried to break loose, and they yelled obscenities both in Danish and Arabic at the police, as well as the others who had been arrested. Further away, a filthy drunk they'd just brought out of detention sat on a chair, grinning as he watched the scene in front of him.

Trokic concentrated on the witness statements concerning Christoffer Holm trickling in from officers querying practically the whole city about the researcher. Was it possible the neurochemist was the primary target, that Anna Kiehl possibly found out about something and had to be eliminated? Or did it have to do with jealousy? Regardless, they had to concentrate on everyone connected to the researcher. Motive was of vital importance. And Christoffer Holm had been much in demand in many ways.

He grabbed his phone and called Bach. He had to know the killer's physique. Most of the officers at the morning briefing had agreed that the killer was very strong.

"The biggest giant can be taken down by anyone clever enough, you know that," Bach said. "But it requires a certain element of surprise."

"Anna was in good shape and probably fast too; she was no sacrificial lamb."

"That may be, but someone was faster than her. And anger is also a major factor."

"But the researcher couldn't have been easy to take down."

"I don't think you're looking for a ninety-pound weakling. Just don't rule anything out; there may be angles you're not seeing yet."

Trokic sighed and hung up. That's why Bach was so good, though; he refused to eliminate any possible line of inquiry, no matter how much Trokic pressed him.

He grabbed his jacket from a chair. It was time to pay a visit to Christoffer Holm's workplace.

Chapter Thirty-Four

"THIS USED to be one of the four psychiatric hospitals in Denmark," Lisa said. "Some of the buildings are gorgeous, but a lot has happened here, too. Over the years, these walls have seen the history of psychiatry. Since back when they used instruments of physical restraint. Several people in there did groundbreaking work, internationally recognized. I read about it in a book at the doctor's office once. It's actually pretty cool."

Trokic opened the door for her. "Maybe we ought to just hang around. Seems nice and calm in here."

"Yeah, it does now. There are also rumors that when psychopharmaceuticals were first used, in the middle of the twentieth century, property values in the area shot up. There weren't nearly as many crazies running around in the streets."

"Incredible what women remember."

She stared at him. His rooster tail was sticking up in the air again. "What do you mean by that?"

"Just what I said. Let's find that head doctor, okay?"

CHRISTOFFER HOLM'S FORMER BOSS, Jan Albrecht, was a white-haired, bearded man in his late fifties. He had a friendly smile, and his oval eyes were relatively big and wide-set, which for some reason made him look easy-going, Lisa thought. His gray-green V-neck sweater was a bit too large as if he'd recently lost weight, and behind his friendly façade, she sensed sadness.

"I'm not sure I can be of much help to your investigation," he said, after showing them into his long, narrow office and offering them a cup of coffee.

"We're interested in any information that could be important," Trokic said. "Why did he resign? Who did he work with? Things like that."

"It might be more useful to talk with our Ph.D. candidate, Søren Mikkelsen. He's probably the one person who can explain Christoffer's research in detail. Their work overlaps each other's in certain ways. Christoffer left us a few months ago. He didn't give us a reason as such, but we thought he needed a break."

"Why?" Lisa said.

"Christoffer was an exceptionally talented human being. Too talented, it seemed at times. He spent most of his life within the walls of academia. And he'd been pushed by teachers who recognized his potential. I was worried. I felt he'd lost his spirit this past year, his faith in what he was doing. His research results were excellent, even on an international level, but he was also an energetic man who needed to see some of the outside world."

He smiled to himself. "He wasn't what you would call suave. Some of the older ones here—no, not me—didn't approve of his worn jeans, loose shirts, and long messy hair. But he was extremely likable once you got to know him. And then when, all of a sudden, no warning, he resigned, somehow it didn't seem all that surprising. Even though many of us were sad to see him go."

Lisa nodded. That fit in with the positive impression Holm's book had made on her. "So, he was very well-liked?"

"Definitely. He was a very decent man. And he made time for other people. That's not a given in our profession."

The doctor looked away. His voice broke as he said, "I can't believe he's gone. Who could want him to suffer such a horrible death? It's a great loss."

"What exactly did he focus on in his research? Was it only antidepressants?"

The psychiatrist corrected her automatically. "SSRI's. Actually, even narrower than that. Lately, he did research on nitric oxide. Søren Mikkelsen can explain that to you more precisely."

He smiled. "Mostly, I attend to patients out here, by choice. So, I don't really follow along with the research like I used to. I'm more interested in the human contact—"

"The results of his research…is it possible to get a copy?" Trokic said. "We have his book and several articles we found on the net, but we'd like to have everything."

Albrecht handed him a large stack of papers. "I thought you might ask that. Here's everything he had published, several copies of articles and so on. It includes all the published research he participated in. It should give you some insight into his work."

"Thanks," Lisa said. "What about his computer, any stored data?"

"I'm afraid I have to disappoint you on that. He deleted everything on his computer before he left. And the computer wasn't modern enough to save, according to one of our IT people. It's been destroyed."

"What about laptops, other workstations he might have

used, anywhere there might be some information? Professional or personal."

He shook his head. "No, there's nothing along those lines either. Most people prefer to keep everything in one single place, and Christoffer was that way, too."

He shrugged in apology. "We had no idea that the computer might be important in some way."

"No, of course not."

Lisa sipped at her coffee. It tasted horrible, like reused coffee filters. Institutional coffee. But sometimes caffeine desperation set in. "We'd appreciate a list of everyone you know who had a close working relationship with him. And a short note about how he knew them."

She handed him her email on a slip of paper. "Is that possible?"

"I'll send you a list later today."

"Could we speak with Søren Mikkelsen?" Trokic asked.

"He's in the basement. I'll take you to him."

He led them down a long hallway and several stairways. "There's been a lot of water under the bridge since people believed insanity was an imbalance in body fluids."

"Who believed that?" Trokic asked.

"The ancient Greeks did. People were treated with warm baths, herbs, that sort of thing. Which was much more reasonable than in the Middle Ages, the exorcisms and witch burnings, locking people up in madhouses."

"A lot has been done in the name of Christianity," Trokic said.

"That might be a bit harshly put," Albrecht said. "But a long time went by before we returned to a more humane treatment of the mentally ill. We'd like to think we played a role in that."

THE SMALL ROOM was filled with rat cages, each one occupied by a small white rodent whose beady red eyes watched them suspiciously. Lisa could smell them, as well as the wood shavings that filled the cages. The animals along the right wall were disfigured by five-centimeter-long stitches on their backs; it looked as if some long object had been implanted. She felt nauseous, sympathetic toward the small, despised animals.

Søren Mikkelsen couldn't have been much over thirty—younger than what she had expected. His eyes were slightly bloodshot, his skin sallow, as if he lacked sunlight. He wore a buttoned-up white coat, horn-rimmed glasses, and black wooden shoes. He smiled amiably.

"I ran the Swim test," he said to the psychiatrist. "It looks promising."

"Is this where Christoffer worked?" Trokic asked.

"He had his own animals further down the hall." Mikkelsen nodded his head in that direction. "Sorry, I didn't get any sleep last night. Too much work to do. And I'm still shaken up; I didn't know about Christoffer until several hours ago. You have any suspects?"

"We're keeping an eye on a few people."

Mikkelsen led them out into the hall and closed and locked the door behind him. He looked back and forth between them. "Okay then, how can I help?"

Trokic again explained what information they were interested in, as well as what they'd been told. "Are you doing research in the same area as Christoffer Holm?"

"No, my thesis deals with tissue damage in the brain related to mental disorders. Christoffer was interested in eliminating the side effects of the new antidepressants."

He explained in detail about serotonin receptors, animal trials, and nitric oxide.

"Okay, okay," Trokic said. He hadn't understood a word, and he glanced at Lisa to see if she'd followed him.

"How far along was he? Had he published any results?"

"No, not since last summer, when he wrote an article for the *Journal of Psychopharmacology*." He pointed at the stack of papers Trokic was holding. "You can find them there. There's a lot of competition in his field nowadays."

"Does Procticon ring a bell?" Lisa was thinking about the note found in Anna Kiehl's apartment.

"It's a British pharmaceutical. A newbie in the industry, with a lot of money behind them."

He paused for a moment. "They're bragging about becoming the first to produce Pink Viagra. And they're also one of the new competitors to the heavy hitters like Lundbeck in antidepressants."

"Do you have any idea if Christoffer was in any way working with Procticon?"

The researcher laughed. "They wouldn't be the first to try to hire him. He made jokes about the price on his head among the pharmaceuticals."

"Could that be why he quit?" Trokic asked. "Maybe he got an offer he couldn't refuse."

Mikkelsen shook his head. "I really don't think so. Christoffer liked being where he could do whatever research he wanted. He didn't care about money. At all. And he liked this town, the down-to-earth atmosphere. But, of course, I can't rule it out completely. He could've had his reasons."

Lisa wasn't convinced; a slip of paper that shows up with the name of a pharmaceutical company in his dead girlfriend's apartment was no coincidence, when the two murders were added to the equation. Someone had a connection to the industry. She caught Trokic's inquisitive eye.

"We might have more questions for you after we look through all this material," she said.

"What was your personal relationship to Christoffer?" Trokic asked.

"We got along fine."

"Friends?"

"Colleagues who enjoyed each other's company."

"You didn't get together after work?"

"Once in a while. But it was mostly to discuss work or an article."

"Were you two in competition?"

"Not at all. On the contrary, I looked up to him. Why? Am I a suspect?" He sounded a bit guarded.

"Right now, everybody is a potential suspect," Trokic said. "Do you know anything about his private life? Who his friends were? Girlfriends?"

"Yeah, but it wasn't something we talked about a lot. He didn't keep things a secret. Actually, it wasn't easy to keep up on all his women."

Lisa thought she heard a hint of disapproval in his voice. "Was Anna Kiehl one of them?"

"Yeah, I remember her. She stopped by once in a while early in the summer."

"You have any impression of what the relationship was like?"

"I have no idea. I didn't pry into his private life."

"Any others you remember?" Trokic asked.

"There were a lot of them, but I don't remember the details." He looked thoughtful for a few moments. "I think they had problems understanding his dedication to his work, also all the traveling. It was sort of a revolving door with his women. But usually they were blondes, that much I can tell you. And there was one right before Anna. I never saw her, but she called all the time. Never introduced herself, just said, 'Can I talk to Christoffer?' Rude. The way I understood it, they were together a lot. He got more and more annoyed with her, and then finally it ended. I remember one day him saying, 'You are *so* sick, really sick,' like, he couldn't understand something, or she disgusted him. And then he hung up."

It could be Irene, Lisa thought. They still hadn't ruled out her having something to do with it all. "Could you tell us what you were doing Saturday evening?"

"I was watching TV with my brother."

"Do you remember what you watched?"

"No, I can't. I watch TV every evening. Give me a TV Guide and I'll tell you what I watched. Have you talked to the sister?"

"We've spoken with Elise Holm," Lisa said. "Any special reason why we should?"

"I was just thinking…she must be a rich woman. Parents killed in a car accident, the inheritance. The insurance must have been a lot of money. Now she probably gets his half, too. Plus all the other stuff."

Søren Mikkelsen stared at them. "A rich woman."

Chapter Thirty-Five

BACK AT THE POLICE STATION, they headed directly to the third floor for lunch. The new cafeteria manager there had become very popular in a short time. Good food made everyone happy.

"The coffee out there was horrible," Lisa mumbled. "Let's have a decent cup."

Trokic nodded. "Not so strange that people want out of there as fast as possible. That coffee could cure even the worst psychosis. Speaking of which, those damn antidepressants are quite an industry nowadays." He poured for them both. "We're running around in a country full of doped-up zombies if you believe the statistics."

"There must be a need for it. Something about the times. Our way of living."

She felt offended on her sister's account. Anita had been taking antidepressants the past year after a breakdown. Whatever else Lisa thought about them, Anita was definitely a hundred percent better, which in turn was a great help to the family.

Trokic shrugged and stuck his hand in the back pocket

of his pre-washed jeans. "It's living in an artificial condition. Like fighting a fever with aspirin. It doesn't solve anything. It's incredible that—"

"So, cure society," Lisa snapped.

"That's taking the easy way out," he said, a bit annoyed with her now. "We all have to take responsibility for our lives. It's stupid to lay all the blame on environment. Or say it's just the times. People have always lived under pressure. If there wasn't a war going on, there was a plague or an economic crisis. More likely, the problem is that people don't have much else to do than chase their own tails. Or money, I should say."

Lisa narrowed her eyes. "But the fact is, many people aren't okay. You can call it whatever you damn well please. People wouldn't be killing themselves if they were having a great life."

"I'm not saying they are." Trokic ran a hand through his black hair. "I just think that people have the wrong attitude. And then we're back to this business about taking responsibility for your own life. Everyone's free to sell their house and car and take a less stressful job, or move to India, for that matter."

"So, basically, you're saying that people have only themselves to blame?"

"Do you have to put it so black-and-white?"

"Yes, I do."

She slammed down her coffee mug. Who the hell did this idiot think he was, judging other people's emotional state? "What kind of attitude is that? Maybe you should read the deceased Mr. Holm's book, Daniel. Maybe you'll learn to keep your mouth shut about something you obviously don't know shit about."

To her surprise, he laughed. She wasn't sure she'd ever

heard him do that before, but in this context, it sounded like a definite insult.

"You surprise me, Miss Kornelius. You've got some fight in you."

That only made her angrier. "Just shut up, okay?"

He stared in amazement as she shoved her coffee away. She realized she was going too far, but his intolerance was too much. Before her boss could answer, she stood up and left.

SHE RAN into Jacob in the hallway. She was still in a rage, but he probably wasn't the right person to talk to about it.

She took a deep breath. "Would you like to go out for a glass of wine later?" She surprised herself, daring to ask him out. She could hear her own voice, more gentle. More Lisa, less detective.

"I promised Trokic I'd have a beer with him this evening."

"Okay," she said, lamely trying to hide her disappointment. That morning, after sending her niece off to school, she'd looked at a dusty bottle of '95 St. Emilion in the wine rack, a gift from her thirtieth birthday, two years ago. And she realized she wanted to share it with him, alone. She wondered if there was something wrong with her. She resisted the temptation to run to the bathroom to check her hair. Maybe it was time for a change.

"Well, I guess..." She fumbled with a button on her jacket.

"Another day, Lisa," he said, staring into her eyes. "I'll let you know. And it'll be soon, you can count on that."

He squeezed her arm. She stood there, feeling the warmth spread throughout her body, watching him disappear around the corner.

Chapter Thirty-Six

LIEUTENANT DETECTIVE DANIEL TROKIC drove too fast. A traffic cop would probably consider clipping his driver's license, but it was Jasper sitting beside him. And he made no comment. Showing consideration for his colleague, Trokic had given Rammstein a breather. The German band wasn't popular among the people he spent his time with. A musical personality disorder is how Jasper put it. Instead, Spleen United was out on the field, kicking ass with its dark electronic rock. Long runs of heavy synthesizer and shadowy minor chords. He smiled to himself. *Live the dream, stay in bed, with heroin unlimited.*

It was all about stimulants nowadays. A young girl had called in connection with the case and had made a serious accusation. About drugs.

He'd seen enough powder and pills during his childhood as well as his time on patrol. Drugs, like small pearls of nothingness on a long chain. He often wondered: how much different was he from the dregs of society? The ghetto's bleakness clung to him, and he couldn't muster up any sense of reproach when he saw people lying around stoned. He could feel the holes inside them.

"Take a right here," Jasper said, pointing to a shortcut.

THE GIRL in front of them lived in a mess that seemed to be a goal in itself. The neon-green walls stood in contrast to the piles of dirty clothes, bags of advertisements, makeup, gossip magazines, and CD covers on the floor. Three cacti were drying up in the windowsill, together with a few apple cores and a lemon.

She was only one of the countless many who had called, but for some reason, Jasper had insisted they talk to her, even though Trokic thought they were wasting their time. He'd never seen anyone with so many piercings. Chains of them in her ears, her eyebrows, her tongue, and lips. A black Mohawk dyed red at the bottom stood like a crown over her pale skin. He'd thought that had gone out of style fifteen years ago. Her name was Randi.

"I don't quite understand..." Trokic tried to not look at the black vinyl dildo on the floor. "Why do you think your drug use has anything to do with our case? As far as I know—"

"The paper this morning said the dead guy did research in antidepressants...and, well, I tested some pills for a guy like that. This spring. I met him at a private party. They hang out with all of us now. Maybe it was him, the dead guy."

Trokic raised an eyebrow. Jasper sat beside him, absent-mindedly picking at two snuffed-out tea candles.

"Are you saying Christoffer Holm had something to do with the sale of illegal drugs? He was a respected scientist; that's a serious charge."

Randi stared at a poster of Ozzy on the wall. "I didn't buy anything. The guy gave it to me. But he didn't tell me his name."

She lit a cigarette she'd rolled herself; a sharp odor spread throughout the small room. Jasper brought out a photo from his pocket. "Is this him?"

She glanced at the photo. "Nope."

Trokic and Jasper both sighed.

"He gave me enough for a few weeks. Test the quality, he said. I was feeling like shit, so I did it."

Jasper looked up and nodded to the side, checking to see if Trokic thought it was time to go.

"Test the quality?" Trokic said.

"Oh, yeah. One every morning, he said."

"And you did what he said?"

"Of course. Listen. I felt like shit. I took them, goddamn right I did."

"And how did they work?" Trokic was curious.

She puckered her pierced lips and thought that over. "First, I didn't feel a thing. After a few days, though, I felt so great."

"How, exactly?"

"Well, you see how it's…sort of a mess in here?"

They nodded.

"I cleaned everything up. I ran every evening. Had sex like you wouldn't believe and slept three hours a day."

"Some type of ecstasy?"

"Yeah, but some new kind, like I never had before. It lasted a lot longer, and it builds up kind of slow. It's scary shit. I read that monkeys get brain damage from taking ecstasy just once. The brain can't make the stuff that makes you happy anymore." She stared at her fingernails, bitten to the quick. "He said it was pure Kamikaze."

Her voice was emotionless, and Jasper and Trokic stared at each other. Narcotics was going to be interested in this.

"Believe me, I've tried it all," she said. "But…"

"But what?" Trokic said.

"Then I ran out of it."

"And that's when everything turned messy again?"

"Even worse. I got really strange. It wasn't me anymore; someone else was living inside me. Someone I really didn't like."

"What do you mean? You felt sick? Depressed?"

"You see that cage over there?"

She pointed at what looked like a small birdcage. It was empty. Trokic nodded.

"I strangled my gerbil." She had tears in her eyes.

"Did you see him again?"

She shook her head and looked thoughtfully at Trokic. "Did you ever see the seven suns?"

"Seven suns?"

She looked away. "They're all black. Now I'm on normal antidepressants. But they don't make me feel like picking up."

TEN MINUTES LATER, Trokic drove Jasper home. "What do you think?" Jasper said.

"With what we know about Christoffer Holm? I don't think he had anything to do with this, and she said herself the photo wasn't of him. And besides, there's lots of kids experimenting with their own little formulas. Maybe she needed some attention, too. She's a sad case."

"But there *are* new drugs out there," Jasper said.

"Yeah, we'll pass this information on tomorrow."

Trokic jumped the curb in front of Jasper's red apartment building and stopped. The day was over for many people, including the young detective. But Trokic decided to have another look at Anna Kiehl's apartment. There must be *something* he'd missed.

Chapter Thirty-Seven

HE PARKED the car and locked it. The feeling hit him when he opened Kiehl's apartment building's front door, and he jogged to her door. Chills streamed through his body when he saw the seal on her door had been broken. Had one of his colleagues stopped by? Hardly. No one he knew would leave the apartment open like that. Instinctively, he touched his gun and carefully pushed the door handle down. The unlocked door opened soundlessly. He pulled the gun out of its holster and entered with his back to the wall, peering around the apartment. Nothing looked suspicious. He glanced into the kitchen; it was just as dim and empty as the last time he'd seen it. The apartment, though, suddenly felt cold, different. It *was* colder, by several degrees. And that odor...

Something metallic rattled loudly behind him, and he crouched and whirled around, but it was only the metal buttons on his coat scraping against a radiator. He breathed out and squeezed his gun. Alert now, he walked further inside. Someone else was in the apartment, he could sense it, smell it, the odor of a human being and some sort of weak, neutral perfume he didn't immediately recognize. He wasn't sure if it came from the bathroom with its long row of perfumes on a shelf. It seemed familiar; where had he smelled it before?

The bathroom door creaked loudly when he pushed it open. Adrenaline shot through him and he gripped his gun even harder. The bathroom was empty, with no sign of it having been disturbed. He turned, and now, several feet away, he noticed a faint light in the living room. A bluish glow on a small, round table.

"Hello," he yelled. "Police."

No answer. He walked over, pushed the living room door open, and cautiously stuck his head inside and glanced around the room. He blinked. Something was wrong here, all wrong.

All at once, the back of Trokic's head seemed to explode. He fell forward and took a lamp down with him. The lampshade crackled under his weight. Something was dribbling down through his hair as he began fading out. His neck hurt, the pain from the heavy blow was blinding as he turned on his side and fumbled around in panic for his gun. His sight cleared up for one short second, enough to notice the silhouette in the doorway—a figure with a hood over his head, looking down at him and waving Trokic's gun around in his right hand. A cold, enraged movement. Then, the figure threw the gun down and ran out of the apartment. Trokic collapsed and lost consciousness.

THE PAIN WOKE HIM UP. Judging from the light outside, he sensed he'd only been out a few minutes. He looked around the room in panic, fully aware of his vulnerability, but the apartment was silent again. He crawled over and reached underneath the coffee table for his gun. He felt around on the back of his head; it was wet and sticky with blood, but there didn't seem to be an open wound. He fumbled around in his pocket for his phone, and a few seconds later he called Jasper and told him to come over with a tech from Forensics.

Slowly, he sat up and looked around. The bulb in the lamp was broken; small shards of glass lay all around. The flattened lampshade was close by. He noticed a small, smeared pool of blood. Not enough to be concerned about. As he got to his feet, he saw what had hit him—an African figure a foot and a half tall, made of ebony. A Masai warrior with a spear in his hand. One of Anna Kiehl's knickknacks. He felt dizzy, and he walked into the bathroom. There had to be a medicine cabinet or a first aid kit somewhere. He found a bandage in the third drawer by the sink, and he wrapped it around his head to stop the bleeding.

The second he stepped back into the living room, he noticed it lying in the glare of the lamp hanging over the small table in the corner. A startling sight. He tried to make sense of it as he carefully stepped around the glass and approached the table. It looked almost like a museum piece. An exhibition. Trokic glanced around one more time to make sure he was alone.

It was a hand. A dried hand, gnarled and twisted with its palm turned upward. He nudged it. Though he had absolutely no knowledge of anatomy, it wasn't necessary. Anyone would say it was a chopped-off human hand.

Chapter Thirty-Eight

JASPER STARED at the absurd object. "This is crazy, I've never seen anything like it. Who the hell put it there? You didn't see him?"

"No."

He checked out Trokic's wound. "You're going in to get this sewn up. What do I have to do to get a few hours to myself? I just get my bathtub filled up and you call."

"I'll go by the doctor on call later."

Behind them, a tech dropped the dried hand in a small plastic sack. The tech and Jasper had discussed its origin, but in truth, there was no doubt about the species.

"Emergency room," Jasper said, his voice firm. He clapped Trokic on the shoulder and took a good look around the room.

Trokic was about to leave when the tech grunted. "There's something on the other side, scratched into the skin." He spelled the word out loud.

"Eudaimonia," Trokic said. Silently, he let that sink in. This wasn't just a game here; this was deadly serious. He turned to Jasper. "It's the Greek word for happiness. Or actually, a type of happiness."

It was almost dark when Trokic parked at a small rest area and grabbed a heavy-duty flashlight from the trunk. In a half hour, he wouldn't be able to see his hand in front of his face. Jasper had insisted he stop by the emergency room. Maybe he would. Or maybe not.

Slowly, he walked along the trail to the pond. Could there be more bodies buried around here? He needed to check for any digging close to where Anna Kiehl had been found. A jolt of pain followed every step. The officer posted to keep an eye on the area the past few days had been reassigned. Scattered patches of cold fog filled the forest. A young guy whizzed by on a mountain bike, swerved dangerously around a curve, and disappeared on the trail leading east.

The barrier tape at the crime scene hung loose between the trees; it flapped in the wind a few places where it had broken. He searched the ground painstakingly with the help of the flashlight, but it looked no different from before.

Finally, he sat on a nearby tree stump and lit a cigarette. Did the killer have a special connection to this place? He knew how that felt. When the sea air filled your lungs, and the wind tugging at you became a background, a mood that defined you. Places could change your perception of reality.

He glanced around. Two people had been found dead here. Could there be a third? Tomorrow, he was going to assign a small team of officers to go over every inch of the area again.

Eudaimonia. Another cryptic message referring back to classical Greece. But how? Eudaimonia wasn't a private, individual happiness. It referred to respect and recognition and strength. It was a status. For some, he thought, it may be the only happiness. Something told him the killer had never had it, had never been happy. In any form. There was something melancholic and weighty about it, though he couldn't say exactly why. Among many other things, he and Jacob had discussed it during the many evenings they'd spent at cafés in Zagreb. The perception of happiness, what drove people to war. The various types of happiness people were willing to kill for.

A limb cracked deeper in the forest. It was nearly dark now, and he stood up to get his bearings. He glanced over his shoulder frequently as he made his way along the trail to his car. Maybe the emergency room wasn't such a bad idea after all.

THE CAR PULLED hard to the right as he started to drive away. Oh, no, he thought. He got out with his flashlight; both right tires were flat. His thoughts raced as he peered around in the dark. He crouched when he heard a rattling, metallic sound behind the trash can to his right, then he grabbed his phone in his pocket. It beeped every five seconds—just enough battery left to call.

"Yes?"

The voice on the other end sounded surprised. He whispered as softly as he could into the phone, then he hung up. Though Jacob was on his way, he felt only a hint of relief. Should he stay by the car or take off down the asphalt road through the forest? He heard the rattling noise again, twenty yards away. If someone wanted to get rid of him, why didn't they make their move? Had they been following him since he left Anna Kiehl's apartment? A rock landed at his feet—now he was convinced, someone was watching him. He drew his gun.

Chapter Thirty-Nine

THE MINUTES PASSED. One, two, five... The darkness surrounded him now. He leaned back against the car, his 9 mm Heckler and Kock pointed outward. Where the hell was Jacob? It felt like ages since he'd heard any movement. His breathing was rapid, shallow—was he alone, or still being watched, about to be attacked?

When Jacob's white Ford turned into the rest area, Trokic collapsed in front of his car from sheer exhaustion; the pain and stress had drained him.

"What the hell's going on?" Jacob said after they were in the safety of his car.

Trokic briefly explained what had happened.

"Falck's coming to pick your car up. Something's all wrong here." Jacob thought for a few moments. "This is about control. Power. It's about breaking you. It's a common military tactic, so you can't analyze the situation. So you lose focus. Someone's working on you."

Another pause. "It's your attitude," Jacob added.

"What do you mean by that?"

"You never take anyone at face value. And that pushes

people's buttons, people who are used to being in control."

Trokic leaned his head against the window and studied Jacob. They had both loved the same woman. Not in the biblical sense, but she had been a part of their lives. Small and thin, with green eyes and a compassionate character remarkable for such a young woman. She was Trokic's cousin, Sinka, a younger sister of the cousin he'd lived with for two years during the war in Croatia. Trokic and Jacob had forged a trust in each other during that time, despite the war. Jacob wanted Sinka to return with him to Denmark, and everyone had been happy for them. But it wasn't to be. One day, Sinka went swimming on an island, Krk, and she never returned. She disappeared like so many other women during the war, and though they had searched for her, she was never found. It was a horrible loss for both men. The thought about what happened to her, into whose hands she'd fallen, enraged him. And it was too painful to talk about. But the two men had remained close and in touch.

They turned onto the southern beltway.

"Where are you taking me?" Trokic said.

"The emergency room."

"Why don't we drink that beer instead?" Trokic hated the thought of white coats. And needles. "I was going to make goulash for us. With ajvar. I've been working on the recipe."

"For ajvar?"

"Ajvar, yes. It has more taste. And it's hotter. Red bell peppers, eggplant, garlic, chili peppers, wine vinegar, olive oil, cane sugar, salt, and pepper. It was all ready for the gullasch. But it's a little late for that now."

Jacob looked disappointed. "Okay, but let's stop at the emergency room first then grab a pizza on the way home. We'll put some ajvar on it."

Chapter Forty

LISA GLANCED into every single mirror or reflective surface she passed by that morning. She still couldn't get used to it. Her longish, messy look had been replaced by a page, and her hair color was toned down with light golden highlights. It changed her appearance quite a bit; the nuances in her face were less striking in her new frame of hair. She and Anita had also bought new clothes for her in Magasin. She'd never let her too-mainstream sister influence her style before, but the losses on the romance front kept piling up, and it was time for new tactics. You don't want to scare the bird off before it lands, either, her sister had warned her. And maybe Anita knew what she was doing after all, judging from the compliments she raked in at the station on the way to the office.

She met Trokic on the stairs. The pale detective looked like he'd been in a car accident. His swollen left cheek was yellowish green, and a bandage was wrapped around his head.

"What in the world happened to you?"

He gave her the short version. "I'll tell you the rest in my office. I need to be briefed about the interviews yesterday."

"God, you look terrible."

Trokic instinctively touched the sore spot on the back of his head. "Twelve stitches. They had to shave quite a bit of hair to get to the wound and avoid infection. It'll grow back, they said." He sighed heavily. "I was so close, we could have him, right now."

His office phone rang. He answered and handed the receiver to Lisa. "It's for you."

"Kaare Storm. I'm one of Christoffer Holm's friends. I read in the paper that he'd been murdered."

He paused before going on, his voice unsteady from emotion. "I don't know what…we corresponded quite a bit."

"Yes?"

"I was going through our emails last night. From the past year. I was hoping there might be something that could help you. I don't know if this is important, but we emailed back and forth this past spring about his research."

Lisa perked up. "What about?"

She caught Trokic's eye across the desk and put the phone on speaker.

"I think you'd better have a look yourself. I can forward them to you. I can count on your discretion concerning the private parts of our correspondence, right?"

"Of course."

A light bulb came on in her head. When they had spoken with Søren Mikkelsen at the psychiatric hospital the day before, she'd wondered if Christoffer's work played some part in the case. She'd spent the evening trying to gain an understanding of it, but her lack of knowledge in the area was a major handicap. And if Christoffer did have professional secrets, they were most likely not buried in the stack of papers she'd been given.

"I'm also interested in any correspondence about girlfriends and lovers he might have had."

"I'll send you what I have, right now," Storm said.

Lisa hung up. "This could turn into something."

"Follow it up. And talk to someone from Procticon. Take Jacob with you. And for the time being, let's not say anything about the investigation to the hospital."

"I'd like to see his apartment, as soon as I read what Storm sends."

"I'll make sure you get the key."

Yesterday, Jasper and Kurt, the tech, had ransacked the small apartment on the edge of the city center. In contrast to Anna Kiehl's place, it had been a mess, as if someone had left in a hurry. They'd found hair they presumed came from women, along with several fingerprints. Everything was being analyzed. But if some research material had been overlooked, it wouldn't necessarily take up much space.

Chapter Forty-One

HE HADN'T SAID anything about her hair or clothes, and the mood was oddly strained. As if there were a distance between them, a space filled with possibilities.

They unlocked the fifth-floor apartment and walked in. The view extended over most of the city. "What exactly are we looking for?" Jacob said.

"I'm not sure. A CD they missed, research material, reports. Something along those lines."

Jacob made a face and looked around. "He didn't have a computer here at home?"

"No, we didn't find one. He probably just used the computer at the psychiatric hospital when he worked there for whatever he needed. We'll have to go through everything."

She opened her laptop and turned it on. The mail correspondence between the two friends had been sporadic and, at times, intense.

THIS MORNING, I ran the Swim test again. Stunning. These rats are breaking every barrier. I must have overlooked something. Working day and night and have sent a sample of altromin for analysis.

MAYBE SHE WAS WRONG, maybe they were wasting their time. On the other hand, they didn't have a whole lot to go on, and they couldn't leave a single stone unturned.

They planned to drive over to Copenhagen to talk to a Procticon employee around noon. It would be a lot of driving, but they could switch off and each get some work in on the way, too. They'd return late in the afternoon after the meeting. A long day.

Silently, they worked their way through the apartment. Christoffer Holm didn't seem to have much of an interest in electronic media, but at last, they found a small stack of CDs hidden in a bookshelf.

"Check these out." Jacob handed them to her. She felt a spark when their hands brushed.

She sat down and stuck the first CD into her laptop.

"Nothing here," she finally said, disappointed after going through all the CDs.

"The fish are dead." He opened the doors of the mahogany cabinet on which the aquarium sat. "Or whatever those pitiful things are on the bottom. I had some black guppies when I was a kid. Sometimes more, sometimes less. Fish eat each other."

He pulled out a drawer and looked inside. "Nothing, not a single thing."

"Let's think about this a moment," Lisa said. "Let's assume he stumbled onto something incredibly important. Who would be interested in it?"

"The pharmaceutical industry, for sure."

"Definitely. And how many people could he have told?"

"The people closest to him. Family, girlfriend, maybe a few friends."

"Colleagues?"

"Maybe, but potentially they're competitors," he said.

"And where would he put the research results?"

"A bank box?"

She squinted in concentration. "I don't think he was the type who'd use a bank box. He'd keep it with someone he trusted completely. Some place he knew it would be in good hands."

"Anna Kiehl?"

They looked at each other, then chills ran down her spine. "His sister," she whispered.

He checked his watch. "Do we have time?"

"We can catch her on the way back."

"Okay, let's get our ass in gear, and then we'll see what she's got."

Chapter Forty-Two

TROKIC HAD JUST FINISHED a depressing phone conversation with the pathologist, and now, on a sudden whim, he was at Isa Nielsen's apartment. She might know something about the hand. Over time, he'd learned to use all available resources.

"What exactly can I help you with?" she said, after they'd sat down, he in an armchair and she on the sofa.

"I want to get your professional opinion about something involving our case."

"What in the world did you do to your head?" For a split second, her arm twitched, as if she wanted to reach out and touch his wound.

"I got in someone's way."

"Well, it must have hurt. By the way, would you care for a glass of wine? I have an extraordinary Chardonnay cooled down. You look like you could use it."

"No, thank you. On duty, you know."

"Cappuccino, perhaps?"

"I'd appreciate that."

She disappeared into the kitchen. He listened to her

rattling around as he leaned back in the comfortable chair. The apartment smelled almost sweet. He peered at a few painted marionettes hanging in one corner of the room. His mother had owned a few similar to them. From Romania. He'd never liked them.

"What makes you think I can help?" She smiled oddly as she handed him a steaming cup. She wore a loose, cream-colored blouse with silk sleeves and a pair of light jeans. Casual. Yet elegant. To him, the woman's appearance simply didn't fit the somberness of the apartment.

"You study human behavior."

"That doesn't necessarily make me an expert. As I told you before, I mostly work with politological models. Everything else is simply a side interest."

"What does interest you?"

"Is there something specific you need help with?" she said, avoiding his question.

He nodded and straightened up in his chair to get a bit closer to her. "Yesterday, I was out at Anna Kiehl's apartment. We found a mummified hand on a small table. Our pathologist inspected it this morning, it's a human hand. Male."

Isa Nielsen showed no signs at all of being shocked. She folded her hands underneath her chin. "Interesting, no doubt about that. Could the killer be telling you something? That he's being led by the hand of another, perhaps?"

"But whose hand?"

She shrugged. "I have no idea. The thought just struck me. It seems very…cunning."

She fiddled with her watch. The calm, professional look on her face melted away, and now she looked gracious yet vulnerable.

"I guess it's possible…"

"You asked my opinion, and that's what immediately came to mind."

He glanced around the apartment, then, after staring at each other a few moments, he said, "Do you live here alone?"

"I do have Europa."

He remembered her saying that the dog was all she had. Europa lifted her head at the sound of her name.

"What about your family? Where do they live?"

"I have no family."

"No one special in your life?"

"Not at present. That's not my strong side." She smiled apologetically. "I'm somewhat of a loner, and relationships never seem to work out. But I'm helping you, aren't I?"

"You are, yes."

"Tell me more, I might be able to help you zero in on the killer."

Trokic hesitated a second too long as he tried to gather his thoughts. She was leaning back in her chair, her cup resting on her right thigh, relaxed as she looked at him in curiosity. He fumbled around for his cigarettes until she shoved a yellow pack over the table to him.

"I guess you don't mind me smoking?" He looked around for an ashtray.

"Not at all. Smoke all you want, I'll join you."

She stood up and found an ashtray, then he lit a cigarette and began to tell her in general terms about the two related cases.

Isa Nielsen pointed demonstratively at her watch. "It's one o'clock, lunch time. Would you like something to eat?"

"No, thank you. It's nice of you to offer, but I can't stay that long."

It was Friday, his day for making Croatian food. Hot and spicy, the way he liked it. Usually, he didn't eat all day so as not to spoil his appetite. She smiled at him and pulled her feet back under her chair.

"Are you married?" she said.

"No."

He waited for the obligatory "why not," but it never came. The sociologist knocked the ash off her cigarette. Her hands were long and slender.

"What do you make of what was carved into the hand?" he said.

She narrowed her eyes a bit. "Do you ever dream?"

That took him by surprise. He wondered if his interrupted, fitful night's sleep was so obvious. "We all do, I guess."

"Do you have nightmares, I mean."

"Yes."

"What about?"

"Rabbits."

"Rabbits?"

A hint of a smile appeared on her lips. Not a contemptuous smile, though; she seemed curious. Anyway, he felt she was digging into him, exploring. "Where do the rabbits come from?"

"Croatia."

"What's their meaning?"

"They have no meaning," he said, hoping that would satisfy her.

"Everything has a meaning. I dream about the forest. The forest at night. Maybe it's because of all the newspaper headlines. What about this sect you mentioned? You said you found a symbol. Surely, that has some significance?"

"We can't seem to connect it with anything." He drank the last of his cappuccino. "I have to be going."

"Going." Isa Nielsen stared blankly at the wall. Suddenly a coldness entered the room. As if he had brought up a painful subject.

"Thank you for the coffee and for talking to me."

"You're welcome."

AGERSUND'S OFFICE WAS EMPTY. Which was a bit odd; these days the boss hadn't been straying far away. Trokic walked back to his own office. The phone was blinking red, which reminded him; he'd turned off his cell phone at Isa Nielsen's apartment so he wouldn't be disturbed. The message on the answering machine was fifteen minutes old. Agersund.

"Where the hell are you?"

Trokic sighed. How many times had he heard that?

"We've been called in; someone from the sect is dead."

Chapter Forty-Three

THE YOUNG MEMBER of the sect lay in a crooked, unnatural angle on the bed in the sparsely furnished bedroom. The pale, naked body was in an advanced stage of rigor mortis, and the bulging eyes seemed about to leave their sockets. The sheets underneath him were soaked with urine. Torben Bach ran his hand through his gray hair and exhaled loudly.

"What's the cause of death?" Trokic said. "Some sort of narcotic, or sleeping pills?"

The pathologist shook his head. "I don't know. Something's wrong here. It looks like he's been strangled, but there aren't any marks on his throat."

Trokic breathed in deeply. Was this the sect member who had called and said he knew the killer's identity? Why didn't he tell them if he'd known? And why hadn't they rounded up the whole lot of them and brought them in for questioning yet? Why hadn't they taken it seriously? He felt powerless. Things were going too slowly; there were too many people to question. Too many calls from people who thought they knew something, but didn't.

"Armageddon is approaching," the sect leader whispered. "But this, he didn't deserve."

"You're the one who found him?" Agersund said.

Hanishka spread his arms. "He didn't make it down to our morning meeting. One of the others came up and knocked on the door and called him several times. She assumed he was deep asleep. We never imagined anything like this. So, after a half hour, I came up to get him. It was a shock—he was already cold."

"Who was the last person to speak to him?" Agersund said.

The leader thought that over. "Probably me. About ten o'clock yesterday evening."

Agersund turned to Trokic. "It must've been after you were attacked in the apartment."

Trokic nodded.

"We're bringing your entire holy flock in, Hanishka," Agersund said.

"None of us are guilty of this."

"All right, listen up. There's a dead man in this house, and we want to know if Palle knew…"

Trokic jumped when music dominated by a light harpsichord suddenly streamed out of a speaker in the ceiling. It sounded strangely innocent in his ears.

"What the goddamn hell is that?" Agersund said.

"It's the call to prayers."

"Can't you stop it? My God, man, people are working here; we can't have that racket bothering them."

The sect leader looked grim. "It will stop in a moment. It was about nine o'clock this morning."

"What was?"

"The answer to your next question. When he was found."

"Nine o'clock, you say?" Agersund looked pointedly at

his watch, then he tapped on it. "It's two thirty now. What's been going on in the meantime? You been having a little party with this man?"

"We've been praying with Palle."

Like many of the others there, Palle had led a hard life before joining the sect. He'd been mentally unbalanced. Then he met one of the disciples at the beach. "That's why loving God is the most important thing in life," Hanishka had told Trokic earlier in the kitchen. "Palle had been lovesick over an earthly woman, a thorn, and only God's love could save him."

When Trokic opened the curtain to get more light in the room, a sheet of white paper fell out. He grabbed it before it reached the floor, and immediately he thought: a farewell note. Trokic skimmed Palle's brief apology to his parents for what he was about to do, then he handed it to Agersund.

"There's not a whole lot more to do here," Agersund said. "No matter what he took, it looks like an open and shut case. Speak to the others living here, maybe he talked to someone. And we'll take a DNA sample. Theoretically, he could be our man, even though I don't see any connection, plus it seems he was very religious. And that's about it."

Bach took a glass down from the shelf to the left of the bed and inspected it with a frown. He looked startled after sticking his nose in it and sniffing.

"What?" Trokic said.

Bach looked back and forth between them. "This odor, it's the same as the flowers on Anna Kiehl's body. If I'm not very mistaken, our friend here has taken his own life with hemlock."

Chapter Forty-Four

"I KNEW him from several conferences, national and international. Nice guy," Abrahamsen said after Lisa and Jacob sat down in the spacious living room. The comfy apartment was close to Trianglen in Copenhagen.

"How long have you worked for Procticon?" Jacob said.

"A year. I've worked for two Danish pharmaceuticals, but Procticon is British."

"And what exactly do you do?"

"I'm part of a team, several researchers with various backgrounds. We're based out of Birmingham, that's where I'm usually at, so you're lucky you caught me here. I'm only home because my sister just had her first child, and of course, I had to come home to see it."

He lit a cigar and blew large, well-defined smoke rings into the air. "I'm leaving again this evening. I'm afraid I can't tell you precisely what I do, but in short, it involves a product that stimulates the female libido. Our goal is to be the first ones to market a good product."

"Do you know anything about Christoffer Holm's research?" Jacob said.

"Yes. We've known each other for years. He was a good friend, we got together when we had time. Last I talked to him was at the conference in Montréal, we stayed at the same hotel. We went out on the town one evening."

His voice was shaky. "I'm really sorry he's gone."

"So, you knew he'd resigned from the psychiatric department?"

"Yes, he told me. He said he needed some space, talked about maybe traveling six months with a girl he'd met. As I understood it, the situation was complicated, there was a child involved."

Lisa frowned. They'd heard nothing before about travel plans. But, of course, the police hadn't learned about it, since Peter Abrahamsen had been sitting in his lab in England, messing around with female sexuality. "He didn't mention it to anyone else."

Abrahamsen shrugged. "It's what he told me in that Canadian pub, anyway."

"Did he mention where they were going?"

"Not anywhere specific, it sounded like it was still in the planning stages. But as I understood it she was working on her thesis, and he was going along with her to a few places in Africa she wanted to visit, maybe even work on a new book while he was gone."

Lisa mulled that over. "I've heard he was very talented?"

"Christoffer was extremely talented. That's why I was surprised he threw in the towel. Almost everyone working in our branch knows his name. We talked a lot about our culture, the stress and rat race, about how it influences our view on happiness. And how our way of life in the Western world affects the imbalances in our brain. He called it the serotonin craze. He used a metaphor, stress factors were leeches living off serotonin in the brain, making us crave experience and stimulants to feed the little monsters. And when the imbalances set in, we can reestablish balance by taking antidepressants. He was against that."

"Odd. I was under the impression that he supported SSRI's," Lisa said.

"Don't misunderstand me. Christoffer did research at one of the country's leading psychiatric centers. He wrote his thesis there. He was convinced the interplay between neurotransmitters in the brain is in some cases inherited and biologically determined. And he was very focused on helping these people, to relieve them of as much pain as possible."

To Lisa's great relief, he put down his nauseating cigar and stretched his legs before continuing. "But he felt these leeches were influential, and it was important to eliminate as many of them as possible, to lessen the need for medication. It's more commonly called the stress-vulnerability model. Christoffer was very interested in the scientific and political perspective, in relation to the everyday life of individuals."

Lisa finally asked the question that had been on their minds the past few days. "Is it possible he discovered something new?"

Silence. The researcher fidgeted in his chair for a few moments.

"Is there something you'd like to tell us?" Jacob said.

"This is top secret stuff, you understand."

"We're aware of that."

"If my company finds out, I will be in serious trouble."

"The only thing we're interested in knowing is if his work is in some way connected to a motive for his murder."

"Yes, I understand." He sighed. "Christoffer and I compared notes. We weren't supposed to, of course, but our research took two different directions, and there's no way we could exploit what we told each other."

"So, this was a mutual thing? You two trusted each other?"

"Absolutely." He paused few moments. "Christoffer thought he'd discovered something that might form the basis for the new generation of antidepressants. His research involved one of the recently discovered neurotransmitters, nitric oxide. The hypothesis has been around a long time, that inhibiting it could act as an antidepressant because it influences the circulation of serotonin."

"That's a bit above our heads," Jacob said.

"Of course. When you take antidepressants, you're trying to raise the level of serotonin in the brain. This influences a number of things, like mood, sleep, sexuality, control of impulses, memory, learning, and so on."

He brought out a notepad and pen and drew a circle. Then he drew a cross off to the side. "This is very much simplified, but basically it works like this: a neuron sends serotonin to a receptor. There's a space between the neuron and receptor, a synapse, where serotonin is absorbed by enzymes. Antidepressants work in different ways to ensure that as much serotonin as possible reaches the receptors. One way is to break down the enzymes that break down the serotonin."

He rapped on the drawing with his knuckles and looked to see if they were following him. "The big problem is the side effects of antidepressants. A lot of people think it's related to these receptors. There are several different types of them and they all have different functions. This was one of the things Christoffer was doing research on. But the past year, he was concentrating on the nitric oxide system, which indirectly affects this system."

"But how much did he tell you?"

"A lot, and yet nothing. Are you absolutely sure you're not going to reveal this conversation to anyone?"

They nodded.

"He said he could develop new medications completely different from what we have now. New antidepressants that kick in faster and without all the side effects."

"But I thought people worked together to develop anti-depressants?"

Their host smiled. "Normally, that's true. But this was a coincidence. He told me that several of his rats demonstrated incredibly favorable behavior, and it puzzled him. Their rat food came from Germany, and one time last winter, Christoffer received a shipment of food with the wrong composition of proteins. He was testing a drug he'd developed, and up to then there had been no effect on the rats' behavior, but suddenly that changed, drastically. It was a combination of the amino acids in the food and his drug."

"And you didn't steal his secret?"

"It's of no use to me without knowing precisely which product and which amino acids were being used. But that information must be in his records; he stored them somewhere, right?"

Lisa and Jacob looked at each other. "We don't know where they are," Lisa said. "But we're looking."

"They've disappeared? That can't be true, can it? It would be a tremendous loss."

"But if the drug was really that good, why didn't he announce it?"

"I don't know. Maybe he needed some time to think it over. I remember him saying once that the day we develop an antidepressant with no side effects, we'd be in a dilemma. What I'm saying is…well, the drugs on the market have side effects that stop people from taking them casually. You have to be suffering before you'll keep taking antide-pressants. But what if a drug made you feel cheerful and energetic without any short-term side effects? A miracle drug. A discovery like that, you can't let it fall into the wrong hands."

Lisa stared straight into Abrahamsen's brown eyes. "Do you have any idea why Procticon keeps showing up in connection with Holm?"

"No." He sounded genuinely surprised. "He would've told me if he was thinking about coming to work for us. I'm one hundred percent sure. And he knew I was working in Birmingham."

"Did his research have anything to do with Procticon?" Jacob said. "I mean, could it have been important to the company?"

"Definitely. Maybe you already know that Procticon is a leader in this branch of pharmaceuticals and they're constantly trying to improve their products. Picking up a researcher of Christoffer's stature and reputation would be a serious feather in their cap. I told him that, but he just laughed at me. Which is what I expected he'd do."

"You knew him really well. What do you think he would've done with a discovery this valuable?"

"He would have done the morally responsible thing. He would never have profited personally by it. He was a bit of a hippie. Peace and love, flower child." He laughed.

"And what if somebody else got hold of his research results?" Lisa said.

"Think about how much the pharmaceutical industry invests in research. What it costs to have a large team of highly-paid researchers employed for years. Getting the jump on any drug can be worth a fortune."

He narrowed his eyes. "So, if anybody did get hold of Christoffer's records, they have something very, very valuable."

Chapter Forty-Five

EVERYTHING around the house lookedgloomier and more deserted than she remembered. The birch trees along the road were hanging from the heavy showers, and the yard was muddy; even the cats had to patter around in weird, twisted routes to avoid all the puddles. The air reeked from the acrid smell of the manure pile behind the stalls.

Elise Holm was wearing riding boots and pants and a tattered blue work jacket. She met them at the barn door and led them inside.

"You don't know exactly what it was he gave you?"

Lisa peered around the small, damp, dusty, chilly room. The floor was covered with straw and small pellets of something that looked like rat shit, though possibly it was some sort of animal food. It stunk in there, too, and the dust tickled her nose. Outside the small window, she noticed a field with grazing Iceland horses.

Christoffer Holm's sister shook her head. She looked frightened and older than the last time Lisa had seen her. She would be inheriting somewhere around a million kroner, too. Probably enough to save this small stud farm, Lisa thought.

"I knew immediately when you called what you were talking about. It's true, he gave me an envelope. He called one day and asked if he could bring it out to me, said it was important, that it involved confidential documents. So, we put it in my filing cabinet."

"Is your office normally locked up?"

"No, you have to go through the house to get to it, so I never felt it was necessary."

"When did he bring it?"

"I'd say about two and a half months ago. A few weeks before he left for Montréal. But let's go in and find it."

They walked through the house and into a small addition with an office. It was cramped but homey, and it smelled of horses. Elise Holm walked over to the far wall, pulled out a bluish-green cabinet drawer, and thumbed through the contents. Her face was white when she turned to them. "It's not here."

"Maybe it's in one of the other drawers," Jacob said.

"No, I'm absolutely sure this is where I put it."

"Take a look anyway."

She pulled the other four drawers out and searched meticulously through each one. "It's gone."

"Is it possible he stopped by and got it?" Jacob said.

"No. He hasn't been here since he brought the envelope. And he would've told me. It's an hour's drive, after all."

A horrified expression spread over her face. "Oh, no, no. The break-in."

"What do you mean?" Lisa said.

"Last weekend, didn't I tell you? The window was broken, and I knew someone had been inside the house, there was mud on the floor. I wondered why nothing had been stolen. I reported it, but I haven't heard anything back from the police. What's going on?"

"It's strange, anyway, if you're absolutely sure it was here and that he didn't come get it himself."

"I'm five hundred percent sure."

"Did you ever look inside the envelope?" Lisa said.

She blushed. "Yes, I admit it, I did. It looked like some sort of scientific paper. A lot of numbers and graphs on separate sheets. I didn't really understand it. He always wrote in English."

"We'll come back later; we have to leave," Lisa said.

"So, you don't think the thief will return? It's been keeping me awake at night. I do live a bit far from everything."

"We don't think so, no," Jacob said. "I don't think you have anything to worry about now."

JACOB LOOKED TIRED as they drove away. "I'm convinced that someone who knew about his research killed them both. I think we have the motive. Christoffer Holm is the key."

"Søren Mikkelsen would be a likely candidate, except he has an alibi for the evening Anna Kiehl was murdered. Remember, he was with his brother."

"Did we check that out?"

"We did."

"It's not the world's best alibi. But even if we assumed it was no good, why kill Anna Kiehl? Why wouldn't it be enough to kill Holm?"

"She could have suspected something. Which explains the note about Procticon in the bathroom."

Jacob nodded. "There could be others involved. How

about going out to eat tonight? Forget all this? Then we'll check him out tomorrow."

Lisa smiled. "That sounds nice."

She watched the fields of stubble glide by outside. She couldn't think of anybody she'd rather be with right now.

Chapter Forty-Six

THE SMALL RESTAURANT WAS PACKED, and they'd barely managed to get a tiny round table. Through the window, she watched the busy populace rushing by, dressed up for the evening, on the way to see a movie, to the theater, to the train station, to the many restaurants in the city. The street was wet, the various colors and patterns of umbrellas danced in the air.

Lisa thought about the emails between Kaare Storm and Christoffer Holm; from the way they wrote, the sense that so much didn't need to be said or explained, they obviously had been friends for years. And yet, Christoffer's emails at times seemed vague, ambiguous, and several times she'd had to backtrack to figure out what he meant. As if he'd been afraid that someone was looking over his shoulder as he wrote.

And then there was the woman he'd referred to repeatedly. Was she the one who, according to his colleague, had kept calling but then suddenly was out of the picture?

I'M SEEING A GIRL. Another dead end. A kamikaze woman, like Woody Allen says. She flies high and crashes, and takes me along with her. This can only end badly.

HE WROTE in glowing terms about a number of women during the year-long correspondence, and it was hard to pick out who was who and what actually had happened. She'd called Kaare Storm again and read aloud several passages, hoping to shed some light on them, but he was also unsure about how influential the various women were in Holm's life.

THEY ORDERED OCTOPUS AS A STARTER, also French wine, and Jacob stared out at a long-haired man in dark clothing, holding an old blue coffeepot as he begged for change.

"I'm exhausted, how about you?"

"I'm not going back to Copenhagen anytime soon; it wears you out. I'd rather knock on doors."

He gestured out the window at the poor guy on the sidewalk. "It's easy to get rid of a cell phone and a credit card. I'll bet a lot of people could use them, to get by on a few days. Hand them over to some homeless person in Copenhagen, and suddenly loverboy Christoffer is doing some shopping over there, in places that don't require a PIN code. It's not like he was around to report it stolen."

"Do you think that's what happened?"

"I'm guessing it's something like that. I doubt that whoever got rid of him kept the phone and wallet very long. And giving it all to someone who'd use it would make it look like he was still alive. Which, in turn, would sidetrack us and delay any investigation."

"Yeah, we'll probably never find the phone and credit

card," she said. "We checked the phone provider — no signal after arriving back in Denmark; it hasn't been used."

He nodded in agreement. She couldn't help looking at him. Noticing his arms on the table. The shape, the hollows, the masculine form of muscles under the healthy skin. She wondered if he had any tattoos under his shirt. It wouldn't hurt. If there were scars, stories her fingers could track. Their eyes met, his like magnets drawing her in, and she had to look down.

"How long did you work in IT in Copenhagen?" he said.

"Three years."

"That must have been interesting."

"It was, yeah. But actually, I was close to quitting when Agersund offered me a job here."

"Why?"

She shrugged as she watched an older couple give a few coins to the homeless man outside. "It started to wear on me. Crazy hours. It's like hackers never sleep. Anyway, not when you're working all over the globe. But that wasn't the worst."

"What was?"

Jacob looked at her a bit shyly, though with a genuine interest; her stomach felt like it was melting.

"The pedophiles and child porn," she said, her voice faltering. She wasn't sure she wanted to talk about this over dinner. "There was too much of it. At first, I hung in, even though it was gruesome, sickening, and I had trouble sleeping at night. But it was almost worth it when we nailed some of them. So many cases kept popping up, though, and we watched them get off with these ridiculous sentences. Sometimes they didn't even stop. You can't underestimate their technical know-how. They're slime, but technically advanced slime, and we had to bust ass to keep up. They're very aware that nothing gets deleted from hard drives by emptying the trash. They use programs to make sure everything disappears completely, forever."

"But so many people say you and your team do a fantastic job," Jacob said. "We're one of the leaders internationally, aren't we?"

Lisa nodded and picked at the octopus in front of her. She felt a flash of the nausea she'd had to live with back then. "We spent an enormous amount of time tracking down networks, and sometimes the sentences handed out were shorter than the time it took to round them up. The worst case I ever had was right before I came over here."

"Selandia, is that the one?"

"No, it was another. A small case, actually. But for me, it was the last straw."

He sipped at his wine without taking his eyes off her. "But don't you still work on these cases?"

She smiled sarcastically. "Yeah, I'm a big expert with a lot of experience—because I did it for so long. We all went through a lot of long, expensive courses and training. Computer forensic courses in the States a few times. I had to threaten to quit to get this job. Agersund knows I'm sick of those cases, and he's smart enough not to push me too far. I only spend about ten percent of my time on them."

"Enough of that. I've got something else for you to think about, a line from a film…"

"What is it?"

"*Nine million terrorists in the world and I gotta kill one with feet smaller than my sister.*"

"Not you, too!"

"Of course, it's entirely possible you don't know the film."

"I know it, I just need a little time to jog my memory."

WHILE THEY ATE lamb chops and a great chocolate mousse, he told stories about his two teenage nephews and their escapades. She couldn't stop laughing. He also talked about his first year as a police officer, then about his stint on the Emergency Response Unit and the lasting friendship with a colleague there.

"Have you been back to Croatia after the war?" she said.

"Yeah, I was down there last year, matter of fact. I drove around several weeks. Saw all the places I didn't manage to see before."

"How was it?"

"Strange. I remembered it as almost a black-and-white urban landscape, with the last signs of communism hanging in the clouds of smog. Now the streets are full of new expensive cars, the streetcars are full of ads for cell phones. Lots of places they rebuilt incredibly fast after all the destruction from the war. Like they wanted to erase all the memories."

"That sounds natural, don't you think?"

"Definitely," Jacob said. "But it feels weird when you talk to them about it. It's like there's a hole, or a short-circuit or something in their memories when it comes to their role in what happened. They were absolutely ruthless when they retook their territories during Operation Storm in 1995. I saw Croatian soldiers mow down Serbian civilians running away, saw them burn their houses down. That's why they won't hand over anyone to Haag. In their eyes, there are no war criminals. Only heroes. They were only taking something back they believed was theirs."

"But that was the military's doing; surely other Croatians can't be judged for it."

"No, but anyway they allowed it to happen. First, you stop talking to the local flower shop owner like you always used to because he has a different background. Because hostility has gained a foothold through the media over the years. And then war psychology takes over, suddenly one day the flower shop owner is the bad guy, according to propaganda. You snitch on your neighbor. Too many people have too much on their consciences to want to talk about back then."

"It sounds like you don't particularly like them."

Jacob pushed his plate aside and rested his elbows on the table. "On the contrary. It's a beautiful country. I don't believe they were any different from others back then, or that they're worse than other Europeans."

"How does Trokic feel about it?" Lisa said.

"That's not something people talk to him about. It's too touchy because of what happened to his family."

"I won't, definitely not."

They sat in silence for a few moments. "It was Bruce Willis," she finally said.

"What?"

"Die Hard I. The film dialogue."

Jacob smiled. "Aha. So, you win the prize—a decent beer. Let's head over to Waxies."

They left money on the table and stepped out into the cool evening. "I've never been there," she said.

"You're kidding! I've been here less than a week, and I'm the one who has to show *you* all the good places?"

"Well, take me then," Lisa said.

He laughed. "Take you to Waxies, or just take you?"

She felt herself blushing for the first time in years, and she swung at him, but she couldn't stop the smile from spreading across her face. Quickly, he grabbed her hand, then her arm, then her neck and her mouth. He touched her hair and played with it lovingly.

"I don't think we're going to Waxies."

SHE WOKE up late that night. Confused. Her throat was dry, and she instinctively reached for the glass of water on the table beside her bed. Jacob lay spread out, only halfway under the comforter. She felt a stab in her groin at the sight of his naked body, at the thought of him. So absolutely perfect, his angular body against the sheet. He had taken her, all right. Kissed her everywhere. A long time. Woke her up with his tongue, touched her like no one had in years. And she had given herself up until her intense longing faded. She felt at peace.

She drank half the water and laid back down beside the sleeping man. The faint odor of his aftershave was wonderful. She slipped her hand down his hips and gently pressed the right places until he made small sounds of pleasure in his sleep. He reached for her.

Chapter Forty-Seven

SATURDAY, September 27

THE HEAD DOCTOR was watering flowers when Lisa entered his office.

"Passion flowers," he said.

"They're very beautiful."

"They were my wife's favorite plant. She always had a few of them around. Have a seat."

Lisa smiled politely, and she and Jacob pulled chairs over to the desk. "We're sorry to bother you on a Saturday, but we received certain information yesterday, and we have a few more questions."

"Nothing to apologize about. I'm here anyway."

Lisa hesitated. As usual, she wasn't sure how much she should reveal about their investigation.

"We have reason to believe that some of Christoffer's final research was very valuable," Jacob said. "Also, a report was apparently stolen from his sister's home. We need to know who has detailed knowledge of his research area."

Albrecht gasped. "If that's true, it's disastrous. If you had any idea of how much money we've spent on this research. The rats alone…see, we import them from the States. Rats that have already been stressed out sufficiently, to save us time. But these types of research results are difficult to understand. And someone would have to repeat the experiments described."

He rubbed his forehead. "But that would probably just be a formality. Christoffer was extremely thorough."

"Does all this somehow have anything to do with Søren Mikkelsen's research? We know he's taken a different direction, but is it possible that— "

Albrecht shrank back. "Is Søren a suspect? Because I simply can't believe— "

"No, not really, but we have to eliminate everyone who knew Anna Kiehl and Christoffer Holm." Jacob was being diplomatic, if not strictly truthful.

"Well, their fields of research are very closely related, of course he is very knowledgeable in the area."

"But no one here has talked about his research results?"

"No, not to my knowledge. I have to admit, I'm very surprised if it's true Christoffer made a significant discovery without sharing it with us. Results like that aren't something you're supposed to keep to yourself. But he must have had his reasons."

Lisa thought about Anna Kiehl as she looked at the pale violet passionflower. Could loving a woman make a man change this way? Yet the researcher had earlier expressed reservations about how biological psychiatry was advancing. At most, the female anthropologist had supported his growing conviction.

Bo Mikkelsen wasn't just Søren's brother; they were

twins. Lisa and Jacob spotted him walking out to a garbage can in front of his house on Stadion Allé, and apart from their haircuts, they were indistinguishable. Lisa got straight to the point.

"Can you tell us where you were last Saturday?"

"I already told the police. With my brother."

"And what were you doing?"

"Not much. We ate dinner and watched a movie."

"What time did you arrive?"

"About six."

"And no one left the house that evening?"

"No."

"Do you remember the film you saw?"

Bo looked as if he was trying to remember, then he smiled. "I don't remember the name of the movie. But it was on TV3."

"Who was in it?"

He blinked. "It was something with Andy Garcia and Richard Gere."

"*Internal Affairs*?"

"Maybe."

Jacob squinted and pointed as he said to Lisa, "Back in a sec, I'm going to run over to my car." He sprinted across the street.

"Do you live here alone?" Lisa continued.

"No, my girlfriend lives with me."

"What do you do?"

"I'm a lawyer. I work for Dahl and Laugesen."

Jacob returned, panting now. He was carrying a magazine. "I bought this last week. You have to have something to do alone in a hotel room every night." He found the TV listings. "There's no film here with those two actors."

"Maybe it was another channel," Bo said.

"None of these channels showed that film. Or any other with those actors."

"Maybe they changed their program."

Jacob looked at the previous page. "But they showed *Internal Affairs* Friday."

The twin suddenly looked uncomfortable.

"So, are you still sure it was Saturday you watched TV together?"

"Yes, definitely. Maybe I watched the film on Friday and got the days mixed up, thought I watched it Saturday."

Lisa lowered her voice. "This is a homicide case. It's serious. So maybe you should sharpen up that memory of yours and get it right this time."

He squirmed. "Maybe we saw it on Friday. Now that you tell me what was on."

Lisa smiled at him triumphantly. "Thank you. That was all we wanted to hear."

BACK IN THE CAR, Jacob said, "Let's pick him up. Right now, I can only see one reason for him to lie. He doesn't want us to know what he did that Saturday."

Chapter Forty-Eight

THE YELLOW BRICK house with the black roof wasn't particularly attractive, but Lisa knew this neighborhood was high dollar. The forest and water were attractions. Specifically, the place wasn't all that far from the part of the forest where Anna Kiehl had been found.

It struck her how devious it would be to disguise the murder as a rape that got out of hand. Placing his semen on the woman was taking a big risk, but it would imply the wrong motive and lead the police astray. The killer probably hadn't counted on them searching the pond.

The pale creature in the half-open doorway was losing it. His mouth had an aggressive set to it, his muscles underneath the tight, striped shirt were taut, and his hair looked like it had been mashed by a cap.

"What is this? It can't be legal to bust right into people's homes."

"Just open the door," Jacob said, a bit annoyed now. "We're investigating two homicides; it wouldn't take much to get a search warrant. We would appreciate your cooperation. We need Christoffer Holm's research reports. Either you can find them for us, or we can look for them ourselves."

Jacob stepped halfway between Lisa and the young researcher. Finally, Mikkelsen opened the door and stepped aside, looking resigned now.

"I didn't know someone working in the public sector could live this well," Lisa said, as they walked into the large living room. "How much is this house worth?"

"Find out yourself."

"Don't worry, we will," Jacob said.

"I don't have anything that belonged to Christoffer."

They entered a room with large windows. Had he just moved in? The heavy black leather furniture looked brand new, and unlike hers, the wooden coffee table had no scratches or stains from wine or coffee. It seemed more like a display room, unlived in. The walls were bare, except for one narrow side wall, where a single piece of needlework stuck out as the only personal touch in sight. They searched systematically, looking into cupboards, shelves, and rooms, while two officers kept their eye on Mikkelsen out in the kitchen. He'd grabbed a cola from the refrigerator, and he took several quick drinks as he watched them.

Lisa was halfway done in the office when Jacob yelled out from the other end of the house. A trapdoor in the back hallway stood open.

His voice sounded hollow. "Come on down...Jesus, you're not gonna believe this."

Lisa climbed down the ladder and joined him. Even without much knowledge of medicine, it wasn't difficult to figure out what the various bottles and distillation equipment could be used for. It turned out to be simple.

"No wonder he didn't want to let us in."

The small basement lab smelled of something acrid.

Jacob picked up one of the several small bags on the table. "Gotcha," he mumbled.

"What?"

He handed her a small, lilac-colored pill. A small "K" was imprinted on one side. She turned it in her fingers. "K for Kamikaze. I think we've just put a stop to all the bad trips in town. At least until the next new shipment comes in from Holland."

THEY MET Agersund on the way in.

"We arrested Søren Mikkelsen for illegal manufacture of narcotics. And we also have reason to believe he's the killer. We didn't find Christoffer Holm's research records, but he's hidden them somewhere, and we'll get it out of him."

Agersund's expression was inscrutable. "It's *not* him. I just got an email that points elsewhere."

Chapter Forty-Nine

SO MUCH FOR THAT WEEKEND, Trokic thought, as he arrived at the station. Agersund had called him in earlier that morning. No less than fifty-two officers had been questioning people from near and far with some sort of connection to the murdered couple, and now the case might be coming to a close.

The whiteboard had been a central focus for the small team leading the investigation. It was completely covered with photos, scribblings, and notes. And now an enormous circle had been drawn around Palle, the sect member.

"We requested a DNA analysis of Palle on the basis of finding hemlock in his room. It was strange when we found it on her body. Made no sense. But sometimes these analyses are money well spent. They're absolutely certain, the semen found on Anna Kiehl is his."

Several of those in the room looked relieved.

"On the surface, it looks cut and dried, a rape that got out of hand. But several things point to him knowing her. First and foremost, the symbol of the Golden Order we found in her calendar. The sect also says he was an emotional wreck when he arrived, because of a woman. It's easy to imagine him being in love with Anna Kiehl. Secondly, someone from the sect called—probably him—claiming to know the killer's identity. And finally, he takes his own life by drinking hemlock."

"But Anna Kiehl wasn't his first murder," Jasper said.

"No. I think we can assume that jealousy was a motive for Christoffer Holm's murder. Holm was in Montréal, and he runs into Palle before he gets home. There could be lots of reasons why Christoffer picked him up in his car. On the way home, he or they had an accident. Maybe someone smashed his windshield, or maybe he lost control of the car. Whatever happened, Palle killed him and dumped his body in the pond. A short time later, someone from the sect finds him walking around on the beach, almost in a state of psychosis."

"Am I the only one who thinks this business with the semen is a little suspicious?" Jasper said.

Agersund turned to him. "What do you mean?"

"We found almost no other evidence. Everything was cleaned up, everything around both bodies was almost sterile. Except for the semen we found on Anna. Which is practically the same as using your DNA as a signature."

"Okay, but where are you going with this?" Trokic said.

"I don't know, really. I just think it sticks out."

"Yeah, okay, there are a few loose ends in this case," Agersund said. "But the man was totally deranged. We'll follow up on the—"

"What about the hand we found, where does that fit in?" Trokic said.

Lately, he'd felt the male hand was the most intriguing part of the case. He'd searched cases from the past few years, though he couldn't say precisely what he was looking for. No one had reported any grave robberies or desecrations, and no one knew where it came from. A sample had been sent for a DNA analysis, but the results weren't in yet.

"We simply can't spend any more time or resources on this, Daniel. Palle must have had a weird sense of humor, he placed the hand in the apartment that evening before killing himself. He was mentally ill to some extent, and we may never find out where he dug the hand up or why. These types of people have their own agendas."

EVERYONE HAD LEFT the room except Jasper and Trokic, and they felt they could breathe again. The young detective picked out small blocks of licorice from a bag of candy. "I don't buy it, do you?"

"It's really strange, anyway. I'm going to look for the owner of that hand. To hell with that resource business; I've got to know where it fits in all this. Go home for the weekend, at least what's left of it."

Agersund stepped in the doorway. "A Tony Hansen wants to talk to us."

"What?" Trokic said. Hadn't they eliminated him?

"Okay, okay, I'll see if Lisa has time."

Chapter Fifty

THE APARTMENT WAS AS CLUTTERED as the last time they'd talked to Hansen. It was late morning, and Lisa and Jacob sat very close to each other on the stained black sofa. Almost illegally close.

"So, what is it you want to tell us?"

They waited as he struggled to roll a cigarette, spreading the tobacco unevenly. He lit it, but there was too much paper on the tip, they could all smell it. He was nervous.

"We know you lied to us," Lisa said. "And wasted our time."

She was sick and tired of the lies, and the reasons for them. Such as Søren Mikkelsen wanting to hide the fact he'd been dealing drugs the evening Anna Kiehl was killed.

"I didn't hurt her."

"No, we know that. But you lied to us about something. The clerk at the gas station remembered you, and so did their surveillance camera. You did your shopping close to where you watched the soccer match. What did you do the other twenty minutes?"

After several seconds of silence, he breathed out cigarette smoke and said, "I followed her."

Lisa nodded. "I thought so. But did you follow her into the forest?"

"She walked by in her running clothes just as I came out of my brother's apartment. I wasn't going to do anything to her. Just wanted to look. I admit it, I'd been drinking, I was a little…my brother kept saying I had to tell you. That's why I called." His eyes were swimming. "She looked really good."

"How far did you follow her?"

"She went down behind the apartments, down along the fence by the field."

"Was she running?" Jacob said.

"No, just walking. I followed her."

"Did she spot you?"

"No, she didn't even look back, it was like she was walking somewhere. So confident." He paused again, a look of fascination on his face. "I like that kind of woman."

"Okay, and then?"

"Then we reached the forest. It was getting dark, but you could still see. She turned off on a trail."

"Did she start running then?" Jacob said.

"No, she just kept walking. A running partner was standing by a small bridge a little further down the path, waiting for her."

"Running partner? What do you mean, did she meet someone?"

"I don't know for sure. That's how it looked to me. The person was waiting there, they raised a hand and said hi to her. That's when I turned around. Probably fifteen minutes passed by the time I got back. Then I went and got the cream."

He raised his head and looked Lisa right between the eyes. "I just wanted to look at her. Not do anything to her. Maybe talk to her."

"Right, uh-huh," Jacob said. "Would you recognize the man she met?"

"It wasn't a man."

Jacob leaned forward and frowned. "You're absolutely sure? It couldn't have been a small man?"

"No, it was a woman. Absolutely sure. She was really thin. Had a ponytail, down to here." He held his hand at his shoulder.

"What color?"

"Her hair? I couldn't see good enough, but it was light."

"Not red?"

"No, no way. Are you going to charge me for DUI?"

Lisa shook her head slowly, deep in thought now. The group of runners. There were three women; one of them was dead and another had red hair.

"TROKIC WAS the one who questioned the sociologist," Lisa said. "The third woman in the group."

Jacob grabbed his phone and punched his number. He let it ring eight times. "That idiotic answering service again."

"We both read the report," Lisa said. They were back inside the car now. "It could be her, the one Tony saw. She didn't mention anything about meeting Anna, and why not? It's suspicious. Maybe she's involved in some way with Palle. We're going to have to check this, just have to keep our heads down. Should we look her up and talk to her?"

Jacob fastened his seat belt and backed the car out. "No, let's wait to hear what Trokic has to say. I'm a little bit worried, not being able to get hold of him, I'm thinking about that blow to his head."

"Maybe he just needs a little time to himself. Meanwhile, we can take a look at the sociologist's past."

Chapter Fifty-One

"A SINGLE MOTHER lives there now, Benedikta's her name. She rents it from an old lady," the man said. He stuck his nose in the air as if he were sniffing for something. "She has a cat, long-haired. I give it shrimp and caviar."

The man was short, around five-three, and slightly hunchbacked. There were crumbs on his knitted sweater, and his large ears were filthy.

"But you remember the family who lived there twenty years ago?" Lisa said, pointing to the house on the other side of the hedge. Isa Nielsen was an uncommon name, and it had been easy to track down the address on Siriusvej.

The man spoke slowly. "It's because I dreamed that cats are going to take over the world. Yeah, I remember them all right. He was in the military. I never did like them. Those career military people. There's something perverted about that."

He focused on a point behind Lisa's neck and sighed as if there were something they didn't understand. "He acted like a big shot, the way he marched up the sidewalk every day. She was nice, very nice. We had a chat over the hedge once in a while. That's before I got sick."

"What did she do?"

"She was a housewife. I guess she polished the buttons on his uniforms. And drank. I could hear her carrying the bottles out to the garage. Makes your skin ugly. Unnatural. But what's natural anymore in this semi-artificial reality we live in? The PVC-fortified prettified landscape. My God, Coca-Cola almost has less acid than the rain, and the "

"What about the daughter?" Lisa said.

The man shrugged. "A quiet girl. I never saw her play with the other kids on the street. I used to watch her toddle around the yard. As you can see, I've got a good view. There was a time…"

Suddenly, he looked sad, and for a moment Lisa imagined he felt sorry for the girl. But then he said, "One day a blackbird flew into their front window. It just laid there on the porch, dying. The little girl watched it, like…like it fascinated her. Then she buried it in her sandbox."

"And?"

"A week later she dug it up. Plucked the feathers off, carried it around all day. Finally, I saw her throw it into the living room. I mean, I think she did anyway, her mother screamed bloody murder in there. It must've been full of maggots."

Lisa stared uncomfortably at him and cringed inside her coat. "You don't happen to know where they moved?"

"No. I think the girl might have been put in a foster home when the father disappeared. He drowned, they said. She must've been about thirteen. The mother moved out a few years ago."

"Where to, do you know?"

The man shook his head.

Lisa peered over at the yellow house. It looked quiet.

Almost as if no one lived there, or at least hadn't been home for quite a while. Advertisements hung out of the mailbox on the wall, the Venetian blinds in the kitchen window were halfway up. Time had stood still here; it could just as well have been a wet October day in the mid-1980s.

"I might have the address on a piece of paper somewhere," he said. "I don't know why she gave it to me. It's probably in the bureau, but I don't go in that room. I'm afraid of snakes."

"I'm not," Jacob said. "Show me where it is, I'll find it."

"Someday the world is going to end. Then there won't be any more snakes."

Chapter Fifty-Two

WHEN THEY PULLED out on the freeway late that afternoon, Lisa sensed they didn't have much time. That wasn't unusual; they were always working against the clock while following leads that turned cold and faded out. But now she felt it physically, a vacuum in her stomach and chest as they drove south.

IT STUNK of cabbage and urine out in the hall, and she unconsciously held her breath while Jacob rang the doorbell of the first-floor apartment. A few moments passed; thinking she might not have heard it, he knocked on the door. They heard steps, and a few seconds later a small woman opened the door a crack.

"Police, my name is Jacob Hvid. I'm the one who called earlier." Lisa kept her feet moving on the cold floor.

The woman eyed them. "Where's your uniforms?"

"We're detectives; we don't wear uniforms." He brought out his badge and showed it to her.

"Let me get my glasses, just a second."

Lisa stifled a sigh as she listened to the woman's footsteps fade out and then return. She reached out and pulled his badge close to her eyes, then finally she opened the door.

"There are so many sick people around here, they'll even steal from an old lady." She was still suspicious of them.

"I know. But we're harmless," Jacob said. "We'd just like to ask you a few questions about your daughter."

They followed her into a small, dim living room with brown rugs. The TV was on, a quiz show. The host looked worn out. The living room had no plants, and it smelled like cheroots.

"I don't have a daughter," she said. "Would you like some coffee?"

"No, thanks, I had plenty at the station today," Jacob said.

"Same here," Lisa said.

"Well then." Her hands shook as she poured herself a cup. Lisa guessed she would have liked to add a shot of schnapps from the bottle hidden under the table. The woman was younger than she'd first thought, probably not over sixty. Her bent back and saggy skin made her look older. It was difficult to imagine what she'd looked like when she was younger.

"You don't have a daughter, you say?" Lisa said.

"I did once. A long time ago."

"What happened to her?"

"She moved away."

"To a foster home?"

"No, she moved out on her own. She didn't want anything to do with me; I never saw her again. She just came home one day, picked up all her stuff, and left. That was right after my husband disappeared."

"How old was she then?"

"Fourteen."

"That's early to move away from home. How could that happen?"

Mary Nielsen hid her face in her hands. For a moment, Lisa thought she was crying, so she spoke softly. "I understand it's hard to talk about this."

"No. There was something wrong with her. I don't know how these things can happen."

"What do you mean, exactly?"

"She was evil. You have to respect your parents, that ought to be natural. My daughter was a nasty person. It's so hard to believe...she killed her own kitten. I went into the bathroom, and she'd smashed it against the floor and crushed its head. It peed in her school bag, she told me. My husband was an officer, he tried all sorts of ways to make a decent person out of her. She was his princess. She was an only child; I couldn't have more."

"We understand that your husband drowned."

"He disappeared August fifth, seventeen years ago. They never found his body or the boat; finally, they declared him dead."

"Was he out sailing alone?"

"Yeah, and he fished a lot. But he was a good sailor. Sometimes he took Isa along, just not that day. Why are you asking all these questions? Is she dead too? Is that why you're here?"

"No, your daughter's in good health."

"I see. But like I told you, I haven't heard from her all these years. And honestly, I don't want to. I'd rather not even know anything about her."

"We'll respect that," Jacob said.

After a few moments of silence, Lisa said, "What did the authorities say about her living alone at the age of fourteen? Didn't they get involved?"

"They'd have had to know about it. So, no. I knew where she lived for several years, the apartment was in my name. I put some money in her account every month until she was eighteen, so she could pay rent and eat. I had my husband's life insurance, I could afford it. Whatever else she did to get by, I have no idea, but she's always found a way. She was like that even when she was little. She never asked. Found out about things herself."

"How did she get along with her father?" Jacob said.

"Like I said, she was a nasty person, but he adored her. He bought dresses for her all the time."

The woman's eyes blurred, and Lisa looked at her watch. It was late, there wasn't much else they could do that evening. Who was this woman, this Isa? A young, popular sociologist? Or the devil her mother made her out to be?

Chapter Fifty-Three

JUST AS TROKIC HAD HOPED, a light was on in the old whitewashed house set back from the street. The neighborhood was exclusive; small round bushes stood like small dwarfs along the sidewalk leading up to the pathologist's house, where he'd lived all the years Trokic had known him. He'd inherited both the house and his profession from his father and grandfather. It was more like a family religion than a matter of acquired knowledge.

"Have a seat," Bach said, after showing him into the large living room. He didn't seem the least bit surprised to see Trokic, though it was almost midnight. A stack of papers on a small table indicated that he'd been busy with a scientific report on ballistics. "What happened to your head?"

"Long story. First, I have some questions."

"I'm assuming you want to talk about the hand? I've only been home a half hour or so. I was going to call early tomorrow morning, but now you're here. Cognac?"

Bach opened a cabinet and brought out two glasses without waiting for an answer.

"I need to know where it comes from," Trokic said.

"It's an unusual specimen."

"Can you say how old it is?"

"Not precisely. It's possible a taxidermist can."

Trokic leaned back in his chair and stretched out his legs. "Okay, what else can you tell me?"

"I checked it for gunshot residue, just on a whim. It tested positive."

Trokic's thoughts swirled. Was there a third body lying somewhere? The area around the two bodies had been searched thoroughly; could it be buried in some hidden place?

The pathologist spoke as if he were reading Trokic's thoughts. "I found several grains of sand under the nails. Not that it necessarily means anything other than whoever the hand belongs to was around sand—"

"A beach," Trokic murmured. "And the residue? Did this person fire a weapon?"

"Definitely. There was enough left to see the pattern."

"A fight, then. There must have been a fight somewhere."

"You can't be sure of that. Lots of people shoot at gun ranges. Or they use guns in their line of work. Like you, for example."

"True enough."

Trokic thought about the forest. The quiet forest. What significance did it hold for the killer? Was it just somewhere off the beaten path? Hardly. Something told him there was a connection. Right in front of his nose.

"You know what?" Bach said. "I just remembered, I know someone who might be able to help us. He's an archaeologist, he wrote his thesis on conservation. He knows all about these things. I'll find his number and send it to you."

"Thanks, that would be great."

They sat for a few moments, letting their cognac warm up. "Have you been back to Croatia lately?" Bach said.

"Not since Spring. I'm spending Christmas down there with my cousin and her husband."

Bach stared at the wall. "Don't know if you knew, but I was down there with several other forensic pathologists, to identify bodies in some of the mass graves?"

Trokic was surprised. "No, I didn't know."

"It was only a few weeks. I felt like it was my duty. I don't know why, really. Maybe because there aren't many of us doing this work, and it means so much to the families left behind."

They chatted a while longer until Trokic realized he was tired. "I have to get some sleep, I'm dead tired. Thanks."

Bach smiled. "Glad to help, you know."

Chapter Fifty-Four

HER EYES stung from the many hours in the dry air and cold light of the office. They needed to go home soon and sleep. Her fingers raced over the silver-gray keyboard; Agersund wanted to read her report about the newest interviews tomorrow, and she was almost finished. The door behind her opened, and she heard the steps of the man she cared about more than she had about anyone for a long, long time.

"Coffee." He set the mug on the desk. "You still haven't gotten hold of Trokic?"

She shook her head. "I can't believe that damn phone of his. Why doesn't he get a new one? We can't sit here working on something this important without him knowing about it. I imagine we'll catch hell for not telling him. We can't stay here all night, either."

"I know. But that father who drowned, I'd like to see the report."

"I'll find it for you while you write. Hopefully, it's in the database, so we don't have to wait until tomorrow for one of the office girls to find a copy."

The room felt cooler when he left, and she kneaded her sore muscles. Moments later, she was a million miles away, and the letters on the screen began to fade out. The phone in Trokic's office rang at ten minutes to midnight. Who would be calling his office this late? She punched eight and took the call herself. "Yes?"

"I know it's late."

She recognized the deep, assertive voice. Hanishka.

"I don't think Palle took his own life," he said.

Lisa's stomach sank, her muscles tightened, and she more or less knew what he was going to say. That despite everything, Palle was innocent. Just like Søren Mikkelsen. They'd been blind to have focused so much on the semen.

"I think you should stop by early in the morning. He knew who killed Anna Kiehl. And when you read his diary, you might know who did, too."

Chapter Fifty-Five

SUNDAY, September 28

LISA WOKE up and stared at the man asleep beside her. The morning light shone softly on him. It had been a long time since she'd had a man in her bed. She had tumbled around with faceless men in strange beds the past few years, but she'd always left before dawn. That was the safest way to avoid rejection. This man, however, warmed her bed and showered her with his wonderful scent. Had she finally found her man?

He'd located the case about the drowned officer, but her conversation with Hanishka took center stage. They'd gone home together, neither one of them able to sleep. Hyper from the many hours of work. Finally, they'd made out-of-their-minds love.

She turned off the alarm on her clock beside the bed and got up. Jacob mumbled contentedly in his sleep. She thought about making breakfast—sausage, scrambled eggs, thick slices of bacon—but they didn't have time. They'd have to grab something on the way. She let Jacob sleep fifteen minutes longer while she read the report on the disappearance of Isa Nielsen's father.

THE LETTUCE in the sandwich wasn't exactly crisp. The tomatoes were mealy and had soaked the white bread, turning the whole sandwich into a soggy affair. So much for breakfast. Jacob drove as she guided him through the streets to the sect's house. They had tried to call Trokic again, but all they got was his answering service. Again. She could barely sit still at the thought of telling him everything they'd found out. It worried her that he might be driving around alone, which he should not be doing in his weakened condition. Had something happened to him? To top it all off, Agersund had called that morning and wondered aloud if she knew where he was but wasn't telling him, which annoyed her to no end.

She punched a number in on her phone and pointed toward Dalgas Avenue. "That way."

The lieutenant answered, and she introduced herself and apologized for calling so early.

"You sound young," he said.

She heard the scraping of plates and silverware in the background. Breakfast? "Just my voice, I'm afraid." She smiled.

"I'm retired, myself."

"I thought you were. We're seeking information on one of your officers who disappeared seventeen years ago, Konrad Nielsen. Your name is in the case files."

"I remember Nielsen well, yes. He served with us in Vordingborg for over ten years. We had a lot in common, he liked to fish."

She could hear him smile.

"We spent most of our off-duty time fishing, in fact. We became good friends over the years. He was a fanatic, even built his own jolly. Fiberglass. Painted blue. It may not have looked like much, but he was really proud of it. We took it out fishing a lot. We kept in contact after he was transferred to Jutland."

"When was that?"

"When was he transferred? That would've been in the late 70s. The year we had one of our worst winters. The sea froze. I remember because we celebrated New Year's together, right before he left. He and his wife and me and my deceased wife. They had an argument that evening, and we went home. I never understood why people discuss their relationship around other people. It's embarrassing."

"What did they argue about?" Lisa said.

"I don't recall."

"What was he like?"

"He was organized. And…very disciplined. Good qualities for a career in the military. A man of few words. He met his wife in London, he worked over there for a while when he was young. She was a maid for a British major, one of Konrad's friends. Later on, they visited them every summer."

"What about their daughter?"

"What about her?"

"What was she like?"

"We didn't see her much. Usually, she was in her room when we were there."

"Did he talk about her?"

"No, he didn't talk much about his family. Just vaguely now and then. But he adored her, I know that."

Lisa laid her hand on Jacob's thigh. "Did you happen to notice any change in his behavior, the year he disappeared?"

"No. But we didn't see each other much by then. The rumor was that he took his own life."

"What about that? Do you think he did?"

The lieutenant growled. "Absolutely not."

"What do you think happened then?"

"I think he took the jolly out that day, drank too much, lost his balance, fell out, and drowned. Which wasn't the worst way for him to go. He was in his element."

"Did he fish alone?"

"Normally, he'd take a friend out with him. Or his daughter. Apparently, not that day, though. That's all I know. I never talked to his family after that. And I don't think there's anything else I can tell you."

She thanked him for his help just as Jacob parked at the curb in front of the rundown house.

Chapter Fifty-Six

SHE HADN'T BEEN to work for a week now. In fact, she hadn't been outside her apartment for almost that long. It was more difficult for her to concentrate on trifling things when a more interesting and vital project ahead required her attention.

Her time here was coming to an end. This filthy, disgraceful city she'd wanted out of for so long. She still dreamt about him. Christoffer. They had talked about London. She knew a place in the suburbs with broad streets, rows of beautiful houses, teeming with life every day of the week. She had remodeled one of the houses for them on paper, and he had admitted it might be the right place for them. With a beautiful garden. Maybe even children. And he could have made it all possible if he had wanted, if he hadn't met her. She had grieved for the both of them.

But it wasn't too late for her. She would find her house and settle down there. It was still possible. She laughed to herself at the thought of the small, black attache case with the envelope.

SHE MISSED the odor of her bedroom. Several times that day, she had deeply regretted displaying her trophy. It had been a spur-of-the-moment

225

act that she hadn't been able to suppress. In some way or other, it had completed the circle, signified her break with the past. The absence of the trophy, however, had made it difficult for her to fall asleep, and she considered whether there was some way to get it back. Impossible. Finally, she stood up and wandered around among the many boxes in which she'd stuffed her possessions. The bare walls felt cold, and she shivered.

Three couples had looked at the apartment that day, and she was almost convinced that the last couple, a very pregnant red-haired journalist and her slim, unremarkable husband, would buy what had been her home for the past five years. She'd already sold most of the furniture, at a quite favorable price. But that was nothing compared to what she would have. Soon. In a few short hours, she would be leaving this place forever. Only one task remained. She stared at the yellow fur slowly rising and falling in a corner of the living room.

Chapter Fifty-Seven

HANISHKA OPENED the door a crack and looked at her. "Come inside, and please take off your shoes."

He seemed meek, yet uneasy. She had the impression everyone was tiptoeing around barefoot, trying not to make noise.

"So, you hadn't found anything new concerning Palle?" he said.

Jacob brought him up to date on the investigation and how Palle fit in. "We're assuming he took his own life."

"I don't believe that's true. In fact, I'm sure he didn't. To begin with, as we told you, Palle came to us several months ago."

"Did he ever tell you anything about himself?"

"At first, he didn't say anything about why he felt so bad. It took him a long time, maybe because he was so weak. But it came out that a woman had broken his heart, so badly that it almost drove him insane. No matter what anyone thinks about your world, it was a strange story because he'd been an excellent student up to then. One of the best, he explained. Before he cracked. God helped him get back on his feet though."

One psychosis replacing another, Lisa thought. But she fought back a smile; as it stood now, these people had done nothing wrong.

"But why did you call?" She felt a bit queasy.

Hanishka fingered the symbol hanging from his neck. "I was cleaning up in the basement today, and I stumbled onto a box that belongs to Palle. There are diaries about his ex-girlfriend. He was obviously frightened to death of her."

He stared directly at Lisa. "He suspected her of having done something horrible. He's the one who called you. And I think that's why he's dead."

Chapter Fifty-Eight

SHE SENSED they were on her trail, and she had the nagging fear that someone would get in the way of her future. She began to sweat, which shifted her highly analytic brain into another gear. Everything had been proceeding smoothly until that crazy Palle had called and said he knew what had happened. How dare he do that. Once, she had liked him, his groveling admiration for her, and she had enjoyed having him follow her around, but it didn't take long for her to tire of his unintelligent comments and the constant stream of questions she had to answer. Not to mention that he brayed like a billy goat when he released his secretions inside her.

All in all, though, he had been quite nice, and at times she actually had missed his constant worshiping presence. Until recently, it would have been unthinkable that he would turn against her, and with all his blather about God and the imminent kingdom, it hadn't been without a certain measure of amusement that she lured him into drinking the hemlock.

In any case, she was glad it was over. Death had proven to be quite different from what she had imagined, and every time it had surprised her how much truth there was in "ashes to ashes, dust to dust," because the body swiftly becomes a waste product when life deserts it. She didn't care for all these unpleasant events, but they would soon be replaced by something else: her eudaimonia. She picked up her large suitcases and carried them out to her car.

Chapter Fifty-Nine

LISA RETURNED Hanishka's intense stare. "But he must have invited her in."

"Maybe he wanted to share God's light with her," he said.

"I don't understand."

He tilted his head. "Perhaps, someday, you'll also wish that someone showed you compassion. Maybe he wanted to find forgiveness for her."

"We'd like to see those diaries," Jacob said, impatient now.

"That's why I called." Hanishka stood up demonstrably. "Follow me."

They walked toward the back of the house, and suddenly she shivered. The unheated rooms were obviously seldom used; cobwebs grazed her face. Hanishka opened a trap door in the floor and pointed. "They're down here. The box in the corner. His name is on the front of the diaries, there are two of them. I'll turn the lights on for you."

They descended the ladder backward, and Lisa almost

knocked her head against the naked light bulb dangling from the ceiling. The stench of mold surrounded them. A basket of rotten apples stood on the floor to her right. She found the box in the corner and plucked out one of the tattered books. The handwriting was neat and clear.

Hanishka called down to them. "Everything okay?"

"Yeah," Jacob said.

Lisa nodded to herself. Only moments after opening the first book, a sense of horror began rising inside her. "My God. Let's take them into the office."

IT TOOK them a little over an hour to skim the diaries. Jacob picked them up. "Let's bring her in. I'll leave a message on Trokic's answering service. He'll blow up when he hears about this."

Chapter Sixty

THE FRONT DOOR of the apartment building stood open, and a cat hissed as it ran by Lisa and Jacob when they stepped inside. Lisa froze mid-step on the stairway. "I just remembered—the lieutenant said the jolly was blue. But the report described it as red."

"What?"

"According to the report, Isa's father took his boat out fishing, and they searched for it in the nearby sea and along the beach when he didn't come home. The report said his daughter had described it as a red jolly. But the lieutenant said he built the jolly himself. And that it was blue."

"What does it mean?"

They stared at each other. Lisa felt the coldness of the stairway. All sympathy vanished for the child who'd lost her father at sea. "I think Isa liked to tell stories even back then. She sent the police out to look for the wrong jolly. I'd say she didn't want her father's boat to be found. Or her father."

"It sounds incredible, but I can see it, yeah. Maybe she can explain it. Can we arrest her?"

"Let's try to get her to the station first, so she doesn't clam up on us. Maybe tell her we just want to talk about Palle."

But there was no name on the fifth-floor door; the nameplate had been removed, leaving only two small screw holes. Lisa rang the doorbell, then she tried the door. Locked.

"The pretty woman's gone."

The thin voice startled Lisa. She turned to a boy about five years old, sitting on the steps behind them. "When?"

"A few hours ago."

"Do you know where she went?"

He shook his head. "She had candy. She always gave me some. Them with the red and white paper."

"And what's your name?"

"Milton."

"Okay, Milton. Can you show us where the trash is?"

"Are you garbage men?"

Lisa looked over; Jacob was biting his lip, holding back a laugh. "Something like that," she said. They followed the young boy down the stairs.

She hoped that Isa Nielsen had cleaned up before moving and had thrown out a lot of interesting things. But the green dumpster was empty except for two black plastic sacks filled with what smelled like lark branches.

"When do they pick up the trash?" Jacob said.

"I don't know. I can ask my mom."

"Forget it. Thanks for helping us."

Something glittered in a corner of the dumpster behind one of the sacks. "Can you find a stick for us, Milton?" Jacob said.

A moment later, he handed Jacob a long branch. They were disappointed when he fished up the object, a soft, brown leather strap with metal studs on the outside.

"It's the yellow dog's collar," Milton said. He frowned deeply. "But she said it ran away."

Chapter Sixty-One

HE WAS STILL a bit woozy as he drove out of town. An hour ago, he'd woken up wide awake on the sofa. He could still see the sneering rabbits, gray gaunt creatures from a village near Goriă. Rabbits someone had raised by the hundreds on a small secluded farm, rabbits the Serbian Army had starved to death by not letting them out when they killed their owners. He could still see them. He'd slept for nine hours. Almost ten. More a state of unconsciousness than sleep. He woke up burning with fever, and he'd found a few aspirin in the bathroom and thrown cold water on his face. He'd get by.

He tried to turn on his phone, but it was dead. He found the charger to plug into the car's cigarette lighter and stuck it in his pocket. He'd answer any calls when the phone was alive again; anything important would just have to wait until later when he reached the office.

"YOU SHOULD KNOW, I don't have much experience with this type of thing. Primarily, I work with bodies several thousand years old. But there's no doubt it's been preserved without any common preparations, formalin for example. This is very unique."

Trokic had taken Bach's suggestion to look up the archaeologist. He lived in a small, thatched-roof house not far from the prehistoric museum where he worked. A nerdy young man, late twenties, Trokic thought, and if Bach hadn't said that he'd written his thesis on the conservation of grave relics, he wouldn't have trusted him. His long ponytail and silver necklace of marijuana leaves didn't exactly inspire confidence.

"Normally, it would have rotted away, but because it's mostly lean tissue, bone, and skin, it avoided that fate."

He poured two cups of coffee and eyed the hand with interest.

"Thanks," Trokic said, as he slid the coffee in front of him. The mug was enormous, no way he could drink that much. He looked around; posters covered the walls, some of them ads for films, others from the museum. He studied a woman with Indian features and a colorful sarong, leaning her head against a gray wall. "Best in Bombay," in orange letters. He had the impression that the archaeologist spent most of his time in this living room. The view was a dug-up yard with an old shed; fields of stubble lay behind the hedge.

"Can you explain exactly why it hasn't rotted?"

"Most likely it's been dried. Something like people do with meat, if you'll excuse the comparison. The most important thing here was to avoid bacteria and to hold the biochemical processes in check. The bodies found in our bogs were preserved that way, plant life produced so much acid that bacteria couldn't live."

"But—"

"So, a natural conservation takes place. But that's not

the only factor. The body also has to be thrown into the bog while it's cold. Otherwise, the inner organs will rot before the acid penetrates the body, and it can   "

"But how old would you guess the hand is?" Trokic wasn't there for a lecture on bog people. He was very well aware of what bacteria and heat did to bodies after two summers in a country at war. "Is it even from this millennium?"

The archaeologist played with his ponytail in a personal way that bothered Trokic. "I can't say precisely..."

"Oh, come on, just a guess. I have to have something to go on."

"Between fifteen and twenty years. But don't quote me on that."

Trokic shook his head. "How can an entire body dry up that way?"

"Well, it wasn't cut off from the body recently, definitely not. It happened soon after the person died. Or even before. I'm absolutely sure of that. May I ask where you got it?"

"Sorry, but no, you may not."

On the way back to town, Trokic felt he'd learned very little. His phone was almost charged up. For now, anyway. He turned it on and noticed his phone message icon blinking. Before he could call in to hear them, the phone rang. The number wasn't familiar, but the voice was. The sociologist.

"I'm calling about the hand you found. I've been thinking quite a bit about it."

"It's interesting, yes. I want to clear everything up in this case, and I think that hand is important."

"I see. In what way?"

"We know how old it is now. That makes it easier to find out where it comes from."

"How did you find out?"

"I talked to an archaeologist who specializes in conservation," Trokic said.

"Okay. Did you take the hand along?"

"Yes."

"So, you have it with you?"

"Yes. I'm taking it back to Forensics now, in fact."

"I was wondering if you had time for a chat? There's something I'd like to show you, down on the beach."

"What?"

"You'll see. You'll find a blue jolly just south of Eagle's Nest. It's white inside. An old one, it hasn't been used in years. I think you'll find it interesting."

"Listen, I'm really busy tying up all the loose ends up, so this has to be relevant. I can't justify—"

"Believe me, it is. Meet me there in a half hour and I'll tell you about the hand."

Trokic remembered the sand under the hand's fingernails. Did she know something from before the hand's preservation? He wanted to ask, but there was something childish in her voice, like she had a surprise for him, a gift, and she wanted to keep him in suspense for a while.

"Okay, I'll meet you there." He shut off his phone and turned around. He wasn't all that far from Eagle's Nest, just a few minutes away. He thought about calling Lisa or Jacob, but something stopped him. It was what Agersund referred to when he told him "no one-man show": his preference to dig deeper into a case alone. They could manage without him a little while longer. He sighed. If he hurried, he could grab a hot dog on the way and still be there in a half hour. Then he'd see what she had to show him.

Chapter Sixty-Two

THE DOOR to the Institute wasn't locked, but the building was quiet. Lisa and Jacob walked around aimlessly until she found a male student engrossed in a book. They startled him, and he slammed the book shut.

"We're looking for Isa Nielsen, do you happen to know if she's in today?" Jacob said.

"You're too late. She just stopped by to pick up her things. Not more than half an hour ago. She doesn't work here anymore."

"Why not?"

"She quit," he said. "New challenges. It really surprised us, the ones who've had her for several years. Too damn bad. She was really popular."

"Did she say where she was going?" Lisa said.

"Right now? No."

"Did she say anything about a new job? Where it might be?"

"No," the student said, "she didn't know yet. Only that it wasn't going to be in Denmark. There's not so much happening in sociology here."

"Is there a photo of her somewhere around?"

"You don't even know what she looks like?"

"No."

He sighed and stood up. "Wait here; I'll find one for you."

A moment later, they were holding a photocopy.

"This is the photo on the back flap of the textbook she wrote. I hope it's okay for you."

"It's perfect, thank you."

Lisa frowned as she studied the blonde woman in the photo. Her smile was friendly but reserved. Could they be wrong? Was she really this horrible person Palle had described in his diaries? A perverted creature who enjoyed humiliating him sexually. Who in several ways had said too much because she wanted him to be a spectator and had misjudged him, thought he was harmless? And could she really have killed these people? The semen on Anna Kiehl's body, Palle's role. How exactly did it all fit together?

THEY HEADED BACK to the station. She absolutely had to get hold of Trokic so they could fill each other in on developments and discuss what to do. Everything seemed to be moving fast. She sat up straight; she was worried about him, he'd taken quite a blow to the head, and she doubted he was following the doctor's orders about resting and how to treat the wound. Where the hell was he? Jacob sat beside her, reading what was written about Isa Nielsen on the flap underneath her photo.

"We could put out an APB," Jacob said.

"Let's hear what Trokic has to say."

She punched his number in for the fifth time that day. It rang. Finally.

Chapter Sixty-Three

HE PARKED the car at one of the small rest areas leading down to the shore. The wind had picked up, millions of leaves were rustling, and he clenched his teeth when the cold air ripped through the thin bandage and stung his infected wound. He felt his cheeks and scalp reddening, a sign of fever coming on.

The area was deserted except for a small blue Toyota that backed in, turned around, and headed down the gravel road. Was it her car? He glanced around but saw nothing to be nervous about, so he followed the narrow steps snaking down the steep slope to the bay. Clouds were gathering, a drizzle hampered visibility. He could barely make out the painted jollies far below, their hulls green with algae. Somewhere around a hundred of them lined this stretch of beach. Isa had fished here as a child, she'd said. He was on the lookout for a blue fiberglass boat, white inside, as she had described.

His head was pounding, and he felt nauseous from pain, but he was too close to clearing up this business about the hand to stop now.

The tide had almost reached the jollies when he stepped onto the shore. The air stank of rotten seaweed washed up by whitecaps. He started when a figure in a dark green rain jacket appeared from behind a bluff, but it was just a woman walking her dog.

"Quite the weather," she said as she approached. His appearance frightened her, however, when she passed by next to him. She pulled her boxer closer in. Trokic jogged as he scanned the jollies. Where was she?

He hopped up on the meter-high stone dike and walked into the bushes to answer the call of nature when he noticed more jollies hidden behind bushes and trees. Maybe this was where she was talking about. It all felt hopeless, and soon the fading twilight would make it impossible to tell one boat from the next. He took care of his business, and as he turned to head back north, the form of something blue by a wild rose bush caught his eye.

He struggled to drag the boat out, almost fainting at one point. Anyone strolling by would definitely suspect he was up to no good, standing in the rain with a thin bandage around his head, pulling on a blue jolly. Finally, the boat was free of the thorny bushes, though he'd cut his hands. The depression where the boat had rested looked empty.

He turned it over. It was a simple, primitive fiberglass boat with two seats. The filthy bottom smelled faintly rotten; apparently, it hadn't been used for many years. And that was it. An old boat. Disappointed, he tapped out a cigarette and mulled over what he had. Why hadn't she shown up? He couldn't know if this was the right jolly, or even if there was any point to all this. He decided to pull it back in, go home, get some sleep, and then get briefed by his colleagues.

It was nearly dark when the boat was finally back into the bushes. He almost tripped on a small mound. A corner of black plastic was sticking up right beside his shoe. He tugged on it cautiously, but it didn't budge. Then he realized it was a sack. Of course he couldn't pull it up, he was standing on it! He stepped aside and pulled again. This time the ground loosened, and the black plastic sack appeared. Trokic's mouth was dry as he glanced around the windblown edge of the forest and opened it.

The rotten stench knocked his head back and nearly caused him to vomit. He pulled open the edges of the sack to let some of the stench rise and drift away with the sea breeze.

The smell made him think the sack contained decomposing human remains, but if anything, his disgust deepened as he exposed what was inside. He felt drained of strength.

He fished around in his pockets and found a pen and a small miniature flashlight to help take stock of what he'd found. What was going on here? His brain raced to make sense of it all.

His phone rang. Lisa. It must be important, the way she kept calling.

"Yes?"

"Where are you?"

"At Eagle's Nest."

"What the hell are you doing there?"

"I got a tip about the hand."

The total silence that followed made him think the phone had gone dead. When she finally spoke, she sounded assertive, insistent. Not like Lisa at all.

"Who gave you the tip?"

He shone the light on his find. The fleece blanket in the sack was soaked in what once had been fresh blood but now was simply a stinking mess. Maybe Christoffer Holm had been wrapped in it when he was moved to the pond, he thought. He also noticed a small ax inside.

"The woman from the running group," he said. "The sociologist. Isa Nielsen."

A vague thought began forming in his head. He heard the faint crack of a branch in the forest nearby. Quickly, he closed the sack and peered around, but the forest was silent again.

"And you're alone?"

"Yes."

"Get out of there, now."

"What?"

"Right now."

Another voice joined in from behind. "You wouldn't think there's so much inside them."

He froze. The hand. The sand. The phone slipped out of his fingers and rolled down the slope behind him. He turned to the woman.

Chapter Sixty-Four

IT TOOK Lisa a few moments to realize what was happening. She was certain that, for whatever reason, the woman was after Trokic. Why else lure him there? She stared out from behind the wheel at the pouring rain. "*Oh my God!*" she yelled. "She's a psycho, what's she planning on doing?"

She switched lanes and hit the blue lights and siren.

"DID you see the writing on the hand?" she said, her gun pointed directly at his heart. Her voice was calm, though with a hint of childishness, as if she were demanding attention. He thought back to the reconstruction of events. *She* was the one who had moved Christoffer in this blanket and dumped his body in the pond.

Isa Nielsen was wearing a dark rain suit, and her blonde hair was only slightly visible from under her hat. Dark, as camouflage? Or rainwear, easily washed off? He was close enough to her to see the lunacy in her eyes. Why hadn't he noticed it before?

Trokic nodded and recalled the shrunken hand and all

the speculation it had spawned. For some reason, she wanted it. It was still in the car.

She smiled. "Good." She stepped forward and opened his jacket, then she pulled out his gun. His heart sank as she glanced at it and stuck it in her jacket pocket.

Now he knew where the hand came from.

"Where's your father, Isa?"

"Underneath us, in a hole under the bush. I dug for six months before he was to die."

She paused a moment. A very chilly moment. "He was the first."

He already knew that. "Why?"

"It's the same old story. A man with a drunk for a wife, she can't satisfy his needs in bed. So, he started in on me."

There was no self-pity in her voice. Just the bare facts. "The hand, that was a good one, wasn't it?"

She'd felt so confident, he could see that now. Overconfident, after leading the police around by the nose for so long. The lack of physical evidence, their search for a motive, the investigation leading nowhere had bored her. Her cryptic, ambiguous clues had been planted solely for her own amusement. And in her eyes, despite giving them all these extra leads, they were incompetent. He sensed that not only did she disapprove of them, but she gave herself credit for the progress they *had* made. A conclusive sign of her superiority.

He answered her question with one of his own. "What happened to Christoffer, Isa?"

"I did have feelings for him, of course. I didn't mean for it to end the way it did…at least not with him. He was a good person, it was just…an accident. He was my ticket out of here. His research and the profits from it." She sighed. "Surely, you don't think I'd want to stay in this…in this hole for decades. We had dreams, he and I…we were going to live…get away from this small-minded mentality, all the petty Danes…well, now I'll just have to do it by myself."

"So, then he met Anna?"

She grimaced, then a smile spread across her thin lips. "At first, he didn't want to tell me…said it had nothing to do with me, he just wanted some time alone. I found her panties under the bed. Men are so very, very primitive."

Her voice turned thoughtful. "I called him when he was in Montréal and insisted on picking him up in Copenhagen, where I had a meeting. I told him it was important. At first, he refused. He'd rather take another flight than drive home with me, can you believe it? After we were together for several months?" She shook her head. "When I told him I was thinking about talking to Søren Mikkelsen about his research, he changed his mind. On the way home from Copenhagen, I tried to convince him he was making a grave mistake. We argued. He was very angry, and it turned violent. I couldn't concentrate on driving, and we…we had an accident. He wasn't wearing a safety belt."

"The splinters of glass— "

"Precisely. His face was…smashed up. He would have blamed me. And that's when I realized I'd lost."

Trokic was disgusted. "Really, you had little choice, you practically had to kill him with an ax."

"Shut up," she shrieked. She lifted her gun and aimed at him again, then she took her hood off to reveal her long blonde hair. "I knew where he usually kept his reports. After he was dead, I went to his apartment to get them. No reason to let money go to waste, is there? But the report with the new research results was gone."

He remembered what Lisa had told him. "You found it at his sister's?"

"It was obvious. He was close to his sister; he confided in her."

She tossed her head back slightly. Her laughter sounded like small, delicate bubbles. "Procticon has offered me one point two million for the report."

"That's not much when you think about what—"

"Pounds, my dear detective lieutenant. All Christoffer's noble intentions and ambitions about medical criticism—complete hogwash. So what if weak people become addicted to that type of pill...it's their choice, isn't it? If I don't profit from it, someone else will. It's only a matter of time."

"But Anna. There was no reason to get rid of her too, was there? She was pregnant, Isa. Did you know that? And she had a young son."

She seemed to reflect on that for a moment, then she feigned guilt. "Yes, it was bad of me, wasn't it? But, you have to understand, she was suspicious. Out of the blue one day, she called me at my office and said she had a copy of all his research reports. Just as a precaution, she said. She claimed to know about my contact with Procticon. I thought she might have been bluffing, but I couldn't take that chance. I called her from a telephone booth and asked her to meet me somewhere, said I could pick her up. By then, I knew what I had to do. She said she was on her way out the door for a run, so I told her I'd meet her there in the forest. You know the rest. She cried when she realized what was going to happen. She kneeled down and begged, pleaded with me. When I finished up, I grabbed her key and searched her apartment for the copy she said she had. I looked everywhere, but it wasn't there. She'd only been threatening me. A stupid thing to do."

Trokic remembered how Anna Kiehl had been found in the forest. Near the man she'd loved. Isa must have savored the irony of them ending up together, two treacherous conspirators—to her, anyway. Illustrated physically by the sprig of hemlock. The blood-like red splotches on its stem, as well as its use in executions in ancient Greece, only added to the symbolism for her.

"And Palle? Did he get in your way, too?"

"He played a very minor part. He was one of my students for a time. Usually, he was completely infatuated with me. Some people…" She sighed. "Serve a purpose. It's as simple as that. And he served his. He was easy to arouse. He couldn't forget me even after he joined the sect. And I got the DNA I needed. That bit with the hemlock was amusing, wasn't it?"

Her facial expression changed, and for a moment she looked wistful. "It's going to be okay again," she said, nearly whispering now.

"You can get help," he said.

Instantly, the vengeful Isa returned. "Help to what? To become part of this mind-warping mediocrity, this third-rate society? There is no society, didn't you know that?"

He realized this was part of her method, the depersonalization of those around her, a military technique used to justify destroying an enemy. It had turned Palle into a psychotic empty shell into which a religious sect could stuff new truths. Trokic was tired and nervous about being dizzy. He wasn't sure some of the sounds he was hearing were real. Fever and lack of sleep were catching up to him. He badly needed to lie down, or at least sit for a while, rest his legs. But none of that mattered; from what she'd said, he knew she wasn't going to let him leave here alive.

Chapter Sixty-Five

"DAMMIT."

Lisa was in a rage; she knew the area and had taken the wheel, but the heavy traffic had slowed to a crawl. They were being professional and correct toward each other again, yet she could smell his soft, immaculate skin, which churned up the butterflies in her stomach. But mostly, she was in doubt. What if the situation became tense and Isa Nielsen fought them? Indeed, why would the woman surrender peacefully? Did Lisa have what it takes to stand up to a pure psycho who wouldn't hesitate to kill? Could she back up her colleagues? She'd wanted to work in Homicide, and now she had her wish, but she'd never expected to be facing a serial killer with an agenda they could only guess at. Her heart pounded; the steering wheel was covered with sweat. Jacob sat beside her, fidgeting in his seat.

"Jump the curb." He pointed out through what had become a downpour. The windshield wipers screeched. She shifted gears, checked her rearview mirror, and deftly drove up onto the bike lane and sidewalk. They passed a line of cars and buses, and finally, they were free of the traffic.

"You're one hell of a driver. How much longer before we're there?"

"Five minutes, if we don't get caught in traffic again." She was in the coast road's middle lane and had passed every slower vehicle.

"Five minutes is a long time if he's in danger," he said, frantic now. "I'm calling for backup."

"Okay, yeah, tell them to send another car out there, no sirens or lights, but quick. Give them her description. We don't know what she's planning on doing, but at least we'll be on the safe side if something goes wrong."

Chapter Sixty-Six

HER FACE WAS BARELY visible in the dying light reflected off the shoreline. He estimated how much time had passed since he'd spoken with Lisa. The woman facing him was beginning to feel she had the upper hand in this game, where not even Goffman or any game theorists could help him. Where the least sign of deceit or lack of character would be punished.

"You're right," he said, his voice firm and unwavering, yet with a measure of resignation meant to stymie her. "But I need to know, Isa, it's…it's really the most important part of all this to me. How did you get him all the way from the rest area to the pond?"

She smiled brilliantly but briefly, the way she would had he been a student who asked an intelligent question. "Daniel, Daniel, I thought you had that figured out. Now that you've found the blanket. We dragged him down the trail."

"We? Who's we?"

"Europa and I. It was the most difficult part of all, in

fact, because she was whimpering so much of the time. She didn't like the smell of blood."

"Where's Europa now, Isa?"

"Like me, she's on a long journey. She couldn't come along on mine. Everyone I care about seems to die…"

The forest around Trokic was fading out. He stood erect in an awkward position, close to blacking out. Was the hissing in his ears from the wind or the blood pumping wildly through his veins? He reached for the tree beside him for support. He had to distract her, disarm her.

"You're sick," she said as if she were a child who had found a wounded animal. "I hit you too hard back in the apartment," she added, blaming herself. "But I know you realize it was necessary."

She fell silent. For a moment, she again seemed lost in thought, until he noticed the focus in her eyes. She was listening. He strained to hear through the hissing sound, and finally, he picked up something faint from high over the steep slope: the blessed sound of a car approaching.

"Seems that it's time we were saying goodbye," she said.

Chapter Sixty-Seven

"THERE'S HIS CAR!" Lisa yelled. And it was his car, parked not far from them, beside a blue Toyota—hers? "We're too late."

"Which way?" Jacob said. His voice was flinty now, focused.

She pointed at the steps to the left. They would be visible, vulnerable, but there was no other way down the slope. Lisa's lavender jacket felt like a neon sign, and she took it off and threw it on the landing, despite the howling wind and rain. She peered down at the hundred or so steps, then further at the strip of woods separating them from the shoreline and foaming sea. Tall bushes lining both sides of the steps bowed to the gusts of wind.

"Be careful, the steps are slick," Jacob said. Slowly, he led the way down the old wooden planks.

There was no warning, nothing other than a short gasp when Jacob slipped in front of her. She screamed and ran down the final steps to the bottom, where he lay crumpled up. Only when she leaned over him did she see why he fell

—a splotch of blood had soaked through his thin jacket, in the middle of his chest.

"Get down," he snapped, obviously in pain. He breathed rapidly as he struggled to hold his head up and spot the nearby shooter. Lisa was dizzy and insanely frightened for him, for *them*.

"Where?" she said.

He pointed southeast, not toward the shore but to a row of trees closest to the water. She heard a whistling sound, the plunk of another bullet in the bush behind her. This time she'd heard the shot faintly, and she whirled to grab her gun. She would have to leave him.

"Be careful, Lisa," he said.

He lay beside her with his hand pressing hard against the wound, but the blood kept dribbling out. She let out an agonized scream, threw herself to the ground, and called for an ambulance but would they make it in time? For a second, she couldn't decide; safety was their first priority, helping a colleague, and there was nothing she'd rather do, but they were exposed. Isa was surely on her way to her car, and Lisa had to stop her. She hunched over and ran to an old tree she instinctively believed could shield her, given where the shot had come from. She had no idea if Trokic was still alive somewhere in the area. The rain felt like a waterfall; her clothes were soaked, her hair stuck to her face. She leaned her head against the beech tree's rough bark and plotted how to get to the next tree, four meters ahead and to the right.

Another bullet smacked into the tree a few centimeters from her. This time, though, she saw Isa's sharp silhouette against the clearing in the woods, moving toward the only way up from the beach: the steps. Lisa crouched further down and aimed at the woman; if she found Jacob, which she would, she'd kill him. The thought that he might already be fatally wounded was like a knife in her gut.

Chapter Sixty-Eight

HE HEARD the thunder far away, though something sounded wrong. Too muffled, dull, and it startled him when he came to and realized it wasn't a natural sound. Rain poured down through the treetops. Trokic rubbed his face and squeezed the rainwater out of his eyes. For a moment, he thought she'd left until he spotted her in the woods. He tried to sit up and get to his feet by hanging onto the tree he'd been leaning against. There wasn't much time; he had to maneuver around in front of her. But she noticed him moving before he stood up, and she headed northeast. She'd passed up her second chance to kill him as he lay helpless. Why? Did she want an audience? For him to admire her?

The thought drove him to his feet as he tried to antici- pate her next move. Several other places along the beach had steps up the steep slope, but without her car, she'd be on foot and vulnerable. Another shot rang out through the rain, this time from farther in the woods. *Lisa.*

Isa was vaguely visible to him as she ran out to the beach and down the rocky shoreline. He reached the end of the dark woods, and his colleague stepped out from the trees.

"Are you okay?" Lisa said.

"Yeah."

They watched the fleeing woman. She was in good physical form, and Trokic was much too weak to even consider following her.

"Take care of Jacob, he's up by the steps, he's been shot, and I called for an ambulance."

Lisa sounded desperate, and he nodded. "Did you call for backup too?"

"Yes, they should show up any time now."

She took off to follow Isa Nielsen; after a few seconds, she vanished. He shivered at the thought of how close he'd been to death as he struggled through the underbrush over to Jacob. He ran the last few meters when he saw Jacob was unconscious and badly hurt. Even in the hard rain, it was obvious he'd lost a lot of blood. Trokic bent over the motionless man in front of him.

Chapter Sixty-Nine

LISA COULD ONLY MAKE out the silhouettes of the large rocks that sectioned off the beach every hundred meters. She ran under cover of the stone dike separating the beach and the woods.

In the short time Lisa had spoken with Trokic, the woman had gotten a sizable head start. Lisa was nervous when she couldn't spot her on the broad beach; she felt certain the killer would try to get to her car at the rest area since she knew she couldn't get far on foot.

She reached a break in the dike where a short, wispy path led back into the woods. Without thinking, she followed it.

HE NOTICED A MOVEMENT, which in his half-numb state of anxiety was enough to make him duck and cover Jacob's body with his own. But it was only a bird, a jay scurrying under a nearby bush. Alert now, he realized the steps were the best way to get to the cars above them. He glanced around; he wanted to move, they were too exposed, and Isa might return at any time. But Jacob's condition meant that moving him could be just as dangerous. His face was pale gray, his breathing weak and irregular. The jay rustled around in the bush. Trokic pressed hard against Jacob's chest to slow the bleeding.

HE KNEW who was pressing lightly against his back before he turned around.

"You keep getting in my way, Daniel."

Her hand trembled slightly. "You can see my problem, can't you? I need to get up the steps, and before long, your colleague will discover I backtracked, so I'm in a bit of a rush. And I can't turn my back to you. I'm sorry, but I have to do this."

The woman behind him pulled the trigger, and he fell.

Chapter Seventy

LISA SPRINTED the final stretch to the two fallen men as soon as she heard the sirens approaching. Backup arriving. Maybe the ambulance too? A single glance at Jacob told her that the next few minutes would be crucial. She held back her sobbing and checked Trokic. He moaned slightly when she touched his arm, then he sat up and spoke through clenched teeth.

"It's not serious, I'll be okay. We can't let her get away; I have to go after her. Stay with Jacob."

Lisa heard a car starting in the distance. Thinking about Jacob almost made her faint, plus she saw how Trokic's anger ignited him. He gasped for breath and felt around on the ground.

"My car keys."

"Here." She handed them to him. "I think she has a blue Toyota."

"Call in, tell them to set up a roadblock at the end of the forest, if they can."

She nodded. In a burst of energy, he ran up the steps.

HE THREW himself into his Peugeot, shoved it into first gear, and peeled out of the rest area, sending up a shower of muddy rainwater and gravel behind him. It was a seven-minute drive into town on the winding road. With luck, a patrol car would have her blocked off in the other direction.

Trokic floored it. Though the windshield wipers were on full blast, rain still blurred the windshield. A third of the way through the forest, he slowed down and pulled off on the shoulder. The hectic driving had stunted his rage, and his brain kicked in again. Isa wouldn't dare drive all the way back to town. She'd try to avoid the open city and any road-blocks. He checked his rearview mirror; how many rest areas and forest roads had he passed? Three at the most. Immediately, he turned around and drove back, slower this time. He rolled down the window and peered into the dark forest for some sign of her vehicle. Every second meant she was farther away. He drove by a narrow road leading into the forest, but it was blocked by a barrier, and there was no sign of the car. He felt dizzy, and the bullet wound hurt like hell. At least the bleeding was minimal.

Doubts nagged at him. If Isa had headed to town anyway, she could have taken the first road southwest and blended in with the evening traffic. With a little bit of luck, she could already be on her way. And she could easily vanish into the crowd when she got rid of the car. In his mind, he saw Jacob's pale face again and a jolt of pain shot through his stomach. He passed the next road on his right, also blocked by a barrier. How far back had he driven? Halfway? He stomped on the brakes when he glimpsed something blue. Or was it just a road sign? He backed up slowly to the small road and peered into the darkness. Then he saw it. Not far from the highway, the forest road split off in two directions. He maneuvered around the barrier and took the narrow road to the left. A few seconds later, he was stuck in a puddle of mud and rotting leaves.

"Damn!"

He gunned the engine, but two noisy attempts and a stinking cloud of gasoline later, he gave up. It was hopeless. He killed the engine and turned off all the lights. Two patrol cars screamed past out on the highway, followed by an ambulance.

He was in total darkness. A minor waterfall hit him when he opened the door. At least he was outside. He could barely make out the trail in front of him. The blue Toyota was parked fifty meters ahead. Instinctively, he crouched down, but before he reached the car, his eyes had adjusted to the darkness well enough to see it was empty. He shivered as he stared straight ahead. The forest was unfamiliar to him and he had only a vague sense of the trail's direction. Isa, on the other hand, probably knew every twist, every branch. Most likely, she'd already found a main trail leading into the city and was gone for good. He hesitated before opening the car door; she might have heard him coming. The handle felt sticky, and when the interior light came on, he saw a reddish-brown splotch on the driver's seat, close to the gearshift.

"Good shot, Lisa," he mumbled to himself.

Chapter Seventy-One

SHE'D HEARD the car fly past out on the highway, and she'd heard when it returned. It amazed her that the attractive lieutenant detective, who had drilled her with questions from the moment they'd met, knew so much about the hand and her motives. And now he was horribly close. The pain in her thigh no longer bothered her, it was only an isolated pounding somewhere underneath her, but she knew she'd lost blood. And now the Peugeot blocking her escape enraged her. Before long, the whole area would be illuminated, with barking, slobbering hounds on her trail. And she had only so much strength left. There were noises all around her. Familiar sounds of the forest that suddenly had become threatening, treacherous. Voices.

You look great in those clothes! Kill it, Isa. Kill the fish. Why are you crying?

Isa stepped off the narrow trail and behind several large tree trunks, then she laid her weapon down to press both hands against the wound in her thigh. She was starting to feel weak, drowsy. The old man sat down beside her and took a swig from the metal flask. She could smell the liquor on his breath. A stump of an arm pointed at her.

Why did you do it, Isa? Why? My little girl.

Because you asked me to.

What are you talking about?

May lightning strike me down if I'm lying, you said. And it did, old man. The lightning hit you that day in the forest, didn't it? You lied. You said you wouldn't hurt me. You bastard!

She jerked; she'd shouted that last sentence, and for a moment her head cleared and she peeked up over the tallest stump. The trail was deserted. Where was he, the policeman? Isa laughed to herself. The wind blew through the trees above her, a sweet, inviting rustling of leaves. It was Saturday; her grandmother had given her five kroner to buy an ice cream cone down on the corner. She was freezing and wanted to throw the ice cream away, but the cold seeped in and took over her stomach; her muscles stiffened. She sat up and peered again at the trail. To her right, about thirty meters away, she sensed a quick movement. Isa smiled. She could still make it.

Chapter Seventy-Two

TROKIC TOOK off his sneakers and socks. The forest floor was wet under his feet, and icy cold, muddy. Filled with things he didn't want to know about. Despite all that, he had a better sense of where he was stepping, while making less noise. Yet he sensed that now he was the hunted. That crazy woman wouldn't get far in her condition, she would know that, and she would turn against him one last time. He could make out the larger shapes around him. His rage surged again. He noticed several tree stumps ahead, and he stopped mid-step. The forest whispered, the smaller trees swayed, leaves swirled up around him. Slowly, he walked down the trail, waiting for the bullet he was sure would hit him at any moment. Five meters short of the stumps, he saw the hand sticking out on the ground. He sprang forward, zigzagging until he reached the stump and glanced behind it. The woman lay motionless, curled up holding her thigh, and for a moment he thought she was about to die. Then he realized she was staring at him, her face contorted in a grimace. He stepped forward and snatched the pistol she'd laid down so she could press on her wound. Trokic's muscles twitched, and a wave of hate and nausea washed through him as he recalled Jacob's cool skin under his fingers. With both hands on the gun, he aimed at her. His feet were almost numb.

"Stand up!" he said.

A plan began taking shape. It would be self-defense. Two shots in her liver, painful. With the blood she'd already lost, she would be dead before the ambulance arrived. The woman stood up. She was only slightly shorter than he was, and despite her condition, she looked agile, cat-like. Trokic raised the gun and aimed at her again, but he hesitated. This wasn't for him to do. Others would handle her. He breathed out, felt his strength returning, streaming through his body. He stuck his hand in his pocket. "I don't know what time it is, but you're under arrest."

He was about to handcuff her, when Isa let out a deep guttural sound and threw herself at him, smacked into him like a dead weight. He fell back with her on top. A split second later, he pulled the trigger, and the woman's blood began streaming onto his pants, soaking them. He shoved her aside and stood up. She was still alive, her hand moved, but his fear had vanished. And there was nothing more he could do. He stepped back and picked up the handcuffs, then he watched the life slowly ebb out of her. The sirens still wailed in the distance.

Chapter Seventy-Three

IT WAS an ending as well as a beginning, and they'd agreed to have a beer together at Buddy Holly's. Even though it was barely past noon, the Friday crowd flowed in and out. The bar buzzed cheerfully in the background. He could see she was still affected by what had happened. They both were. It all still felt so close. But the most important thing was that Jacob had pulled through. He'd guessed that Lisa and Jacob had something going, even before she told him. He lifted his glass to her, and immediately the chest muscles around his wound tightened painfully. But he was alive. It had only taken a few days to get on his feet again, in fact. They touched glasses.

"Welcome to Department A. I heard you have the office just beside mine."

"Really? So, I'm not homeless anymore?"

He laughed and shook his head. "Did you deliver the documents to the psychiatric ward?"

She nodded. They'd found Christoffer Holm's contribution to neurochemical research in an envelope in Isa Nielsen's car.

"I hope they'll use it wisely," he said.

"I talked to the head doctor out there. He strikes me as an ethical man. I don't think he'll just publicize Christoffer's research."

"Why not?"

"I read all the material myself, you know. And, of course, the doctor has too. Christoffer didn't want his results to be misused by the pharmaceutical industry, so he must have had very mixed feelings, must have thought a lot about it, what the implications might be. His colleague told Jacob and me that antidepressants without side effects would cause problems. It would be too easy."

"What do you mean?"

"Well, Christoffer was afraid it would affect society. It's more complicated than you might think. And I can understand it. What if no one complained about stress that leads to depression, simply because there was a solution to the problem? With no side effects whatsoever? It's important that people stand up and fight against how everything is supposed to go faster and faster."

"It's food for thought, for sure," Trokic said.

"Yeah, no one can really know the consequences."

Trokic emptied his glass and raised his hand to get a waiter's attention. "You want another beer?"

Lisa smiled. "What the hell."

"But what happens now? Will his research be thrown out?"

"The doctor said he'd try to find a way to gain better control over things. That he would meet with the National Health Authority."

"So, time will tell."

"Something like that."

The waiter set two glasses of beer on the table. Trokic's phone rang. It was impossible to hear anything in there, so he walked outside. He could see Lisa through the plate glass window. She looked sad; of course, she was still thinking about Jacob, but she would be okay. She was tough, he knew that much about her now.

It was Agersund. "Am I disturbing something?"

"Aren't you always?"

Agersund grunted. "A patrol car was out checking a field, not far from Smedegården. A rider found something strange there, several pieces of a broken mirror. A hell of a mess."

Trokic shifted his weight from one foot to the other. "And?"

He was off work. It was Friday, and he'd already planned his culinary ritual.

"Can you go out there now?"

"Monday."

Silence. Trokic watched as a group of people approached. A stag party. The groom was wearing a rooster's comb and fangs hung from his mouth. Agersund was breathing heavily in the phone.

"All right then. Monday."

THE END

Afterword

Dear Reader,

Thank you for purchasing *Dark September*. I hope you enjoyed it.

This was the first mystery I wrote. It all started back in 2006 when I was a single mother living close to the forest on the outskirts of Aarhus. Anna Kiehl's apartment was my apartment, and several times a week, I would take a long walk in the forest. Then one night I forgot about the time, and I was afraid I would get lost in the dark. I started imagining a young woman, a single mother like myself, lying on a bed of leaves with her throat cut. When I got home, I couldn't stop thinking about her. So I created Daniel Trokic so that he could help me find out what had happened to her.

At the same time, I was being treated for major depression with antidepressants, and I was very interested in the research revolving these chemicals. During my research, I visited the scientific facilities in the basement under Risskov Psychiatric Hospital. They did experiments with antidepressants on rats similar to those described in the book. I saw the rats, and a scientist showed me how they did their tests.

The next year, I won the Danish Crime Academy's debut award for this book. So, somehow, all my darkest hours turned into something positive. Something you just read.

Today, I again live next to this forest, close to the sea. This is where I breathe and heal. You can see pictures from my beautiful neighborhood on my Instagram profile. https://www.instagram.com/ingerwolf/ or Facebook-profile https://www.facebook.com/ingerwolfauthor/

Thank you for all your support. Don't forget to leave a review, it means so much to me.

Take care,
    Inger

About the Author

Inspired by the Darkness

Inger Wolf is an International Bestselling Danish mystery and thriller writer.

Her first mystery novel, Dark Summer, for which she was awarded the Danish Crime Academy's debut prize, was published in 2006. Since then, her bestselling books have been translated into several languages.

She loves to travel and get inspiration to her books from all over the world, but lives in the outskirts of the town of Aarhus, the second largest city in Denmark, close to the forest and the sea. In this beautiful place, she got a degree in English and worked as a translator for many years.

Today, Inger Wolf works as a full-time author. The household also includes a dog called Harry Hole, named after one of her favorite detectives, and a cat called Mis (Kitty).

Connect with me here:

www.ingerwolf.com/us
contact@ingerwolf.com

Books by the Author

- On the Side (Danish)
- Dark Summer (Danish, Norwegian, Swedish, German, Dutch, French, Spanish)
- Frost and Ashes (Danish, Norwegian, German, Dutch, Spanish)
- The Song Bird (Danish, Dutch)
- The Wasp Nest (Danish, French)
- Evil Water (Danish, French)
- Under a Black Sky (Danish, English)
- Dark September (Danish, English)
- The Perfect Place to Die (Danish)
- Burned Souls (Danish)
- The Crow Man (Danish)

Under The Black Sky - excerpt

For a special sneak peak of Inger Wolf's Bestselling mystery novel **Under The Black Sky**, turn to the next page.

Prologue

Asger Vad woke up because he wanted an apple. He lay quietly under his comforter for a while, listening to his wife's shallow breathing. Why an apple? Not the most filling of foods, to say the least. And did he really feel like getting out of bed? But suddenly it was very important to get something to eat.

At least that's what he thought because when he finally got up and went downstairs, he heard Zenna growling softly in her laundry room basket. Maybe that was what woke him up. He stopped for a moment and listened, but since there was no other sound, he headed for the kitchen and the basket of fruit on the kitchen counter. The snow swirled in large flakes outside the window; the streetlight threw fluttery shadows around the chairs and table. Winter had dug in and Asger Vad had no problems with that. If you don't like a little snow, don't live in a subarctic climate.

His stomach suddenly cramped up painfully at the

thought of the message he'd received the day before. How could he have forgotten it? It was as if sleep and a blanket of sheer darkness had shooed reality away for a moment, and an apple had become important. As if his unconscious had put his brain on standby, in a sort of survival mode where it didn't need to deal with the big questions in life. Before long, everything would change, his life would be in ruins. There was nothing to do about it. He felt powerless, angry. Terribly angry. Suddenly, he wasn't sure he wanted the apple. Or anything at all.

His heart heavy now, he walked around the corner to the kitchen and stopped abruptly. Something lay on the kitchen table; he could just make out its form in the darkness. Something square and solid. His right hand felt around on the wall for the light switch, and a moment later the room was brightly lit.

It was a dollhouse. He squinted at the unexpected sight. It was big, made from some sort of dark hardwood, varnished. And it looked expensive. Even at a distance, he could see it was of exceptional quality; someone had spent ages on every tiny detail. Asger Vad had never seen it before. It certainly hadn't been there when he made the rounds and locked all the doors before midnight. It was a gift for Marie, it must be. But why? Christmas wasn't on the horizon, and she'd just received an ungodly number of presents for her birthday. He frowned. In light of the circumstances and the brutal message from the day before, it was wrong, so wrong, to buy her this.

He leaned over and peered through the open windows of the dollhouse. His heart began beating wildly at the sight of four dolls sitting around a dining table inside. Two adults, two children. A family. Well-dressed. And in the middle of the table, a tiny mound of ashes. He pulled back. Ashes? What was that all about? He heard Zenna breathing heavily in the washroom; the dog was getting old, and sometimes it sounded like a locomotive chugging. Tonight it was bad, though. Unusually bad.

He stiffened. Something was moving in the shadows. Something that had nothing to do with the streetlight outside. Thoughts about unlocked doors raced through his head. Then the figure stepped out of the darkness, and Asger swallowed hard, his mouth dry as a bone; suddenly he felt weak, powerless. How had this man in front of him managed to get inside the house? Why hadn't Zenna barked? Something was horribly wrong.

"What are you doing here?" His voice sounded much too shrill in his own ears.

The man didn't answer. He smiled weakly and shook his head, as if he were apologizing. And suddenly, Asger knew who had placed the dollhouse on the table. And why.

Chapter One

ANGIE JOHNSON COULD STILL RECALL the volcanic ash scratching her throat. That was her first thought as she approached the house, the crime scene, in the murky morning darkness, the snow crackling under her feet. Several years ago, the ash had gathered in a threatening mushroom cloud above Mount Redoubt and drifted over Anchorage, falling on the town, spreading a black film over the snow outside. The sulfuric air irritated everyone's throat and eyes. The birds perched silently in the trees, all air traffic ground to a halt, and a great deal of the state's population sat glued to television screens, following what was happening. A gigantic river of mud had flowed down the mountain in the Drift River Valley in the direction of an oil terminal, and everyone held their breath while much of the six million gallons of oil was driven away as quickly as possible. They had breathed a sigh of relief when a dike prevented the rest from causing a still-greater natural catastrophe.

That was the first time she'd seen the Danish volcanologist, Asger Vad. He had towered above everyone at the round table in the television studio, and his deep voice and gruff expression behind his round glasses had calmed the newscaster and the Alaskan population. The catastrophe had been avoided, the volcanic ash cloud would soon pass, the health hazard was practically non-existent, and air traffic would soon resume.

Angie had believed him. Fifteen years as a researcher. Employed at the Anchorage Volcano Observatory. One of the world's foremost experts, it had been said. And the town was back to normal after weeks of volcanic bubbling. It wasn't easy being a neighbor to an entire chain of slumbering volcanoes.

Now he was behind this door, inside his house. And not just him. His whole family was there, all of them dead. One of the two officers standing guard at the driveway, a stout man in his fifties, wiped the snow off his blank face and nodded at her. "I just don't know what to tell you." He pulled his hat further down over his ears. "You better take a deep breath. Did you hear about the dollhouse?"

She shook her head. "No, what about it?"

His eyes darted around and his voice sounded a bit shaky. "It's sitting there on the table. It's really sick."

"I can handle it," she mumbled.

She swallowed heavily, fastened a hair tie around her long black hair, and put on a hairnet and mask. It was in the lower 20s with a light wind; snow from two cars parked in the driveway swirled into her face. A short time earlier, while drinking her morning coffee, she'd been called in by Sergeant Mark Smith. He'd told her she would be heading up the investigation on this case, and she had a serious case of butterflies.

The two-story wooden house was painted an off-white. Round bushes lined the wall in front of a small, snow-covered lawn, and someone had made an eyeless snowman that faced the street. The small front porch was made of dark-stained wood, and the two steps up to it creaked. The front door was halfway open, as it had been at four o'clock that morning when the neighbor was leaving for work. The family dog had been barking like crazy inside, too, so she had called 911. Six techs had been hard at it since then.

Angie stomped the snow off her shoes on the mat in front of the door, then she slipped on a pair of shoe covers and gloves. She opened the door wide and walked inside the house, which was so cold that she could see her breath. It smelled of wood, food left over from the previous evening's meal, a hint of orange. And the ash. Harsh dust. It reminded her of the Mount Redoubt eruption. She thought of her people, the native legends of volcanoes. About eruptions that darkened the sky.

The moment she stepped into the open kitchen, she saw the family. Despite the officer's warning, she froze and gasped for air.

"Morning, Angie. Welcome to hell." The technician, Ian Brown, gave her a strained smile. "This is the main stage. We're almost finished inside, so enjoy the show."

Angie's eyes darted around the table as she tried to absorb the many details. The three members of the family, the dollhouse, the ash. She felt the blood draining from her head at the horrifying sight. Asger Vad sat at the end of the dark table, his arms, elbows, and hands resting flat on it. His close-set, slightly somber eyes were now empty, staring straight in front of him. At her, she thought at first; the dead, piercing eyes and downturned mouth startled her. But, in fact, he was looking straight at what lay on the table. He had visible marks on his throat and wrists. And a bullet hole in the middle of his forehead. Ian followed her eyes.

"There's gunpowder residue around the entrance

wound," he said. "All three of them were shot at close range. A straightforward execution."

The two other family members sat on each side of Asger. A woman in her mid-forties, wearing a red sweater, her hair set up in a bun. Two empty eyes above powdered high cheekbones, staring at the same thing as her husband. Her lipstick was smeared, which made her mouth look crooked, sneering.

And the boy. Angie guessed he was about ten years old, a young copy of his father, with the same empty stare directed toward the middle of the table. She shook her head and swallowed. He was just a child.

They all stared at the dollhouse. It was made of dark wood, with small, open windows and a white roof. Under normal circumstances, it would be considered beautiful; someone had taken great pains in building it. Now, though, it looked menacing.

"It's like they're supposed to see it, don't you think?"

She spun around. It was her boss, Mark Smith. His usual suit had been replaced by a pair of black pants and a green sweater, most likely the nearest clothes he could get his hands on that morning. He was a tall man, around fifty, and his easy-going presence immediately made her feel a bit better.

"Take a look inside," he said.

She leaned down and peered through one of the doll-house's windows at a tiny table with four chairs; on each chair sat a doll of plastic and cloth. Two adults, two children. They were well-dressed, with big smiles, and big eyebrows drawn on their faces. A small, peaked mound of ashes lay on the table. A teaspoonful.

"Christ," she mumbled. Quickly she raised up. "What's this supposed to mean? And there are four dolls, but only three people killed. How many were there in the family?"

"That's another problem," her boss said, frowning. "I've been told that one of them is missing."

Angie stared at him. "Missing? What do you mean?"

"They had an eleven-year-old daughter. Marie. She should have been home. The neighbor saw her outside yesterday evening with her brother, building a snowman. She thinks she remembers they were outside until around dinnertime."

Smith bit his lip and studied the scenario. "The question is, why isn't she here at the table? She's definitely not in the house. So, either she went to a friend's house for some unknown reason or else we're missing a body. Or he took her along with him. Which I really hope he didn't. This is enough. More than enough."

Angie nodded and turned to the tech, who was packing his gear in a bag. "Ian, you said this is the main stage. What did you mean?"

"Yeah, well, I meant that there's a backstage too." He blinked his eyes slowly. "It's upstairs, and it's not one goddamn bit pretty."

Chapter Two

SO, there was one missing. Had the daughter escaped, or was she in the hands of a totally insane killer? Angie didn't want to think that possibility through.

"They weren't shot here, then?" She heard how dry her voice was.

Smith shook his head and scratched his throat as best he could with gloves on. "No. It all happened upstairs. Come on, the techs are finished up there."

They walked through the kitchen with the light, glass door cabinets and into the television room. Dark wooden floor, big windows. A large set of antlers hung on one wall, together with two abstract paintings and a photo of a mountain. A volcano, Redoubt, if she wasn't mistaken. At one end of the room were two black leather sofas and a coffee table, flanked by a row of large potted plants. A long bookshelf was filled with books, and a standing lamp in the corner was turned on. Had they still been awake when the killer broke in, or did he turn it on to arrange the family around the dining room table? The Vad family's home looked nice, clean. At first glance, they seemed like a well-functioning family. Not like the usual victims in a homicide case.

"How long have they lived in Alaska?" she asked.

"I'm not sure yet," Smith said. "But I think for about fifteen years."

"So, both kids were born here?"

"I would think so, yes."

This home could just as well have been American. They might have lived here a long time, but the parents, at any rate, were Danish citizens.

"It doesn't look like anything happened here," Angie said.

"No, it happened upstairs, like Ian said."

They walked up the winding stairway. "No blood here," she said. "Did the killer wash the victims before dragging them downstairs? Or wasn't there much blood?"

"He did what he could to avoid too much blood. He wanted them to look good at the table."

On the second floor, they went inside a bedroom. The sight nearly knocked the breath out of her. Once it had been a showcase bedroom. White walls, parquet floor, salmon-colored bedding, two large plants, and a green dresser with a mirror above. Now there was blood practically everywhere. She shivered. While she had been sleeping in her own little place at the other end of town, her TV on in the background, a family had been put through the worst possible suffering. The story was right in front of her.

"Christ." She shook herself.

Smith walked around the room. "According to the techs, it went down something like this: the killer broke in by cutting a pane of glass at the back of the house. Most likely early last night. That got him into the pantry next to the washroom, which leads to the living room."

"They don't have an alarm system?"

"No, they probably relied on the dog. It's a big Bernese."

"So, what about the dog? It must have been barking like crazy."

"Yeah, we don't understand it either. Maybe it knew the killer, or maybe he sedated it. It's at a vet clinic, they'll keep it for the time being and take a blood test."

"Okay, so what do the techs think happened then?"

"They say the killer overpowered Asger Vad first. They're not sure where, but at any rate, he was tied to the chair over in the corner there."

He pointed. "Then the wife was shot, here in bed."

"And what about the boy?"

"They think he was dragged in here because it looks like he'd been asleep in his bed. It was unmade."

"So, the boy was shot in here too?"

"Yeah, up in bed. And either before or after, we're not sure when, he stuffed ashes into Vad's throat. As you can see, that made a mess. It's clear that Vad was supposed to see and hear his wife and son die."

He shook his head. "Watch his family being killed. For God's sake. Anyway, the killer took care of Vad while he was in the chair. We'll get a bloodstain pattern analysis, that might shed some light on what happened. Ian's pretty sure about the order of the killings. Not a hundred percent sure, but close."

"But had they gone to bed?" Angie asked. "Because they're all dressed downstairs at the table."

"The killer dressed them when he was finished up here. There's blood on their underclothes, and the techs found a bunch of bloody night clothes, so that must be how it happened. Then he either dragged or carried them all downstairs and arranged them at the table. For his amusement or for some other reason we don't understand."

Angie shook her head. "Whoever did this must be

crazier than I can imagine. The dollhouse tells me we're dealing with a totally warped sense of reality."

"Yeah. We've contacted the psychiatric hospital. We'll need information on all former patients who could be dangerous enough to do this, or who have something going on inside their heads about dolls or dollhouses."

Smith's light blue eyes were now dark against his pale face. But he was always pale. Angie looked out the window. A spot between a few tall pines in the yard showed a faint pink dawning. A new day was coming and she'd hardly slept. "The weapon?"

"Probably a high-caliber pistol. Something powerful anyway, all the victims show a large exit wound in the back of the head. But he took all the bullets with him, it's going to be hard to pin it down precisely."

She noticed a gray stuffed rabbit halfway under the bed. There was blood on its fluffy tail. For a moment, she imagined the boy trying to hide under the bed. Hoping he wouldn't be discovered.

"Could it be a break-in that got out of hand?"

"I think we can eliminate that for the time being. Asger's wallet is still down on the kitchen counter, and none of the drawers have been touched. The killer doesn't seem to have been interested in money. It looks like something very personal. Not necessarily aimed at Asger and his family, but certainly personal in the killer's head. And it must have been planned to some extent. It could be he just picked out a family at random, kept them under surveillance for quite a while. It's impossible to say at the moment."

"Or he could've seen Asger on TV."

"Possibly."

She inspected the bloody bedding. It was already turning dark, and she noticed small clumps of tissue and bone fragments here and there. She felt nauseous. *Clumps of people*. In a way, this was worse than the bodies downstairs. This was a story about pain. So many lives ended in such a short time, in such a small space. And the chair where Asger Vad had sat, now covered in blood, where he had watched his family being killed one by one. Heard them scream, beg, plead for their lives, draw their last breath and wait for death. Had he finally wanted to die himself, just to end the pain? She breathed out heavily.

"There's quite a bit of ash here. Is it from a volcano?"

"We don't know," he said. "Who the hell knows. Maybe you're right, maybe it's some crazy obsessed with volcanos, and he saw Vad on TV. In any case, we'll send the ash to the Volcano Observatory. Our techs have no idea if it can be pinned down to any specific place."

"But why the ash in Vad's throat?" she wondered aloud.

Smith shrugged. He seemed to be taking this better than she was; after twenty years in Homicide, he'd seen plenty. "Only the killer knows. I don't, that's for sure."

"So, there's nothing that points to the daughter being in here? Marie?"

"No. Not in here. But it looks like she'd been asleep, and there are four plates and glasses and silverware in the dishwasher, so right now we're assuming she ate dinner here. She's not here, though. She might have been sleeping over with a friend, we have a few people checking on that. I hope so, but I'm not optimistic. She'd been seen making the snowman before dinner. If we are that lucky, I hope we find her before she sees the news. The media is going to be all over this."

"Imagine waking up to this," Angie said. "Your whole family dead."

He looked over at her, concern written on his face. "Yeah, and knowing whoever did it is still out there. We have a briefing at ten o'clock, but Marie is our first priority right now. I want you to talk to her babysitter, she's the last person besides the neighbor who we're certain saw her alive. The neighbor said her name is Joanne, I found her number in an address book downstairs. She's a student at the university. I've already called her and said you were coming."

Angie zipped her coat up. "Okay, I'm on my way."

She took a final look around the bedroom. It was the worst thing she'd seen in her entire life. She noticed a picture of the kids on the dresser. There was blood on the frame, and for a moment she imagined the killer stopping to look at it. Marie was very young in the picture. Maybe five years old. Wearing a pink dress, looking into the camera with a shy smile. Her hair was short, and she had small, pointed ears and dimples.

If you're out there alive, I'll find you. She turned and left the room.

Chapter Three

DETECTIVE DANIEL TROKIC stretched his legs and leaned back in the chair facing Captain Karsten Andersen. He'd just been given the first details of a case halfway around the globe that his boss had apparently taken an interest in. Trokic had sensed something going on from the moment he was called into the office. Right before he was about to dive into a steak. And even worse, just before having a glass of the red wine he'd opened. And he had wondered. It wasn't like his boss to call him into a meeting without very good reason. In fact, it almost always meant something very bad had happened. He hadn't said much on the phone, and because Trokic hadn't heard of any homicide in their district that demanded his presence, he'd been completely in the dark until now.

The question was what this volcanologist's death had to do with him. And where exactly was Anchorage? He stared suspiciously across the large black desk. "A dollhouse, you say? In the middle of the table? What's that all about?"

Andersen shook his head. "I have no idea, but it looks

like one of their sicko serial killers. You know, there are always several of them on the loose."

Trokic was about to mention that they'd just finished a case with their own serial killer, whose insane use of leeches was still the talk of Århus. They weren't all that far behind the Americans. But Andersen was all worked up. "I got the news from the Copenhagen Chief of Police, who got it from the American Embassy, who got it from the consulate in Anchorage. The killings took place last night, local time, so we're talking about a matter of just a few hours since the victims were found. The consul was pretty upset. Especially about poor Marie, they haven't found her yet."

"But I don't understand why we're —"

"It's like this," Andersen said, trying to be patient with Trokic. "I know Asger Vad. Really well. We went to school together here in Århus a few centuries ago. Catholic school. If I remember right, he would've been fifty in a few months."

He stared off into space. "He was a good friend, and we've stayed in contact since he moved to Alaska fifteen years ago. When he came back to Denmark, he always stopped by for dinner and a game of backgammon. And he was damn good at what he did. He studied geology here in Århus, and he's worked in Iceland and then Alaska. Dammit anyway."

He swallowed the lump in his throat, plucked some lint from his blue cashmere sweater, and looked away. Trokic fidgeted in his chair; he wasn't used to his boss being so emotional.

"Sounds like a tragic case, but why are you telling me all this?" Trokic gazed at an October-red tree just outside the captain's window.

"I'd think it's obvious." Andersen sighed and stared

straight at Trokic. "I want somebody over there to follow the developments."

"Okay. And?"

"And now that law and order has once again been established in our fair city, I was thinking this might be something for you. A little trip over the Atlantic to join our American colleagues. The last time we spoke, you were wanting to take a step down the ladder. You were sick of paperwork, remember? So, here's your shot at some of that action you obviously want. Plus, you speak English fluently; you're the perfect candidate. The Danish police often send officers out into the big wide world, and now it's your turn."

"But why don't   "

Andersen waved him off. "I can't possibly go myself. I'm too busy here, and besides, I'm too involved personally. I'd shoot the bastard on sight if I ever found him. In fact, I'd like to shoot somebody right now."

Trokic stared at him. Alaska? It was cold as the North Pole and full of bears of all sizes and crazy trigger-happy Americans. Not long ago, he'd seen a documentary series from National Geographic; the state seemed to love guns and illegal substances. And maybe it really was incredibly beautiful there, but if he was going to barge into an investigation, he wouldn't have time to see much. At first glance, it didn't seem all that appealing. On the other hand, he really was tired of all the paperwork, and Andersen had yet to find a replacement for him.

"I'm really sorry about your friend," Trokic said. "But why do you think they'd want a Danish cop in on the investigation? Can you imagine having a Russian running around here?"

Andersen wiped his forehead and clenched his teeth. "I'll take care of that. After all, we're talking about four Danish citizens, at least I think so. I'm not sure about the kids. They don't have any more family over there, so if Marie shows up alive…and honestly, I doubt she will, but we'd need somebody to bring her back to her family. And besides," he plucked a nail file out of a drawer, "they can only be happy to have another skilled investigator on the case, and you are one of the best we have. And I won't mention anything about your issues with authority, or any other problems you've caused. You'll have to try to fit in."

Trokic scratched his black hair and shifted in his chair. Tried to look skeptical. Something like this could drag out. On the other hand, there wasn't much holding him back. He hadn't seen Christiane for a month, since telling her he didn't want children, that he preferred living alone. Maybe it would do him good to have something else to think about, and his neighbor could take care of the cat, now that he had trimmed her hedge for the second time this year.

"Why am I sitting here discussing this like you had a choice," Andersen mumbled, "when it's actually an order?"

They glared at each other. Despite having worked together for several years, they weren't friends. That Andersen, in fact, did have a friend was possibly the most personal thing Trokic had heard about him in all that time.

"What exactly did he do over there?" he asked. He was trying to understand why a Dane would move to a colder climate.

"He taught and did research the first several years. But then he had an accident up in the mountains, or the wilderness, or whatever the hell they have over there, on a hunting trip with a friend. He hurt his leg and he couldn't stand up for very long at a time. That made it hard for him to teach. So, the last two years he's worked as an advisor at the university, and he had something to do with a volcano observatory. And he wrote, too."

Andersen sounded proud. "In fact, he's written three

books about volcanoes. As I understand it, he did well for himself. Not rich, but he wasn't hurting. They had no plans to come back to Denmark. Anyway, not the last time I talked to him."

"And what about the family?"

"As far as I know, his wife worked as a secretary for an engineering firm owned by a Dane in Anchorage. The kids went to a private international school."

"And the daughter, Marie?" Trokic asked. "She didn't just disappear into thin air?"

"There's no sign of her whatsoever. They're afraid the killer took her with him, is what I've heard. Either he's holding her prisoner or else he's killed her. It's horrible. Asger brought her along to dinner one evening when she was a lot younger. She was such a pretty little girl, pigtails, carrying a teddy bear. She sat at the coffee table and drew, just jabbered away. My own daughter is only a few years older, and they had fun playing together."

He slumped as his eyes lost focus. "It's almost unbearable to think she's in the hands of such a gruesome person. Or was."

"What about the police in Alaska, what do they know?"

"More or less nothing, just what they found at the crime scene. The only thing I could get out of them was that the three members of the family were shot, that Asger's throat had been stuffed with ashes, and that it was a damn slaughterhouse. And then there's the dollhouse, of course."

A sense of horror rose up inside Trokic. His throat stuffed with ashes? "Sounds like a very disturbed person, someone who had something to say. Like that case with the Waspman, who cut off lips. It must mean something."

Andersen laid down his nail file, then he grabbed a cigar from the box on the table and sniffed it. He laid it back down reluctantly. "I agree. And I want to know what.

Anyway, they're ten hours behind us over there, and the trip takes about twenty hours. So, if you leave early tomorrow, you'll be over there in the afternoon, local time. Maybe earlier if we can find a good connection."

Trokic let out a breath. It looked like it was time to bring out his winter clothes, whether he wanted to or not. "I'll do what I can." He stood up.

"Thanks. And don't piss them off over there. That lone wolf attitude of yours isn't going to work. And watch out for the bears. I've heard they're man-eaters."

Chapter Four

THE STUDENT DORMS were on the outskirts of the university campus, across from the town's hospital, Providence. Angie parked her black Ford in a half-filled parking lot, got out, and stuck her long, black ponytail under the collar of her black coat. She pulled up her gray leg warmers. The heat from inside the car vanished immediately as crisp, cold air surrounded her.

Several officers had called around to every conceivable place Marie could have been, but there was still no sign of her. And Angie's thoughts kept running in circles. Had she escaped in the middle of the killings and hid? If so, where? In somebody's shed? The search of the area had turned up nothing so far.

Once more, Angie looked at the unframed photo taken from the Vad family's living room. It was newer than the one in the bedroom. Marie had grown into a pretty young girl with long blonde hair, delicate features, and shy blue eyes. Something about the girl moved Angie deeply. Marie could be her own daughter. She stuck the photo back in her inside pocket and looked around. If you wanted to hide out in Anchorage, there were plenty of places to do so, but had she really done that?

The university, the state's largest, was in the middle of town, surrounded by small green sections of thick under- brush with small pines, thin birches, and an extensive system of paths. It consisted of a long row of buildings of various architectural styles, some more attractive than others, and if you didn't know where you were going, it could take a long time to find your way. About a thousand students were on campus, strolling and walking and bustling along with their faces underneath thick stocking caps. It wasn't far from the police station and the Scientific Crime Detection Laboratory.

Snow had fallen that morning, and most cars in the parking lot had at least some snow on their roofs and front windshields. A young guy in a sweatshirt, his hair wet from the flakes, stared first at her then at her car, as if she were a foreigner among all the young people. Then he hurried over to the university.

She walked down a narrow path and soon reached the dorm building where Marie's babysitter, Joanne, lived. That morning the police had called all the teachers and students at Marie's school, and several of them had mentioned Joanne, who often picked Marie up after school. Angie's stomach felt leaden when she pushed the dorm door open. She found Joanne's room and knocked.

The pale girl who opened the door had red, swollen eyes from crying. Her long, dull black hair was unbrushed, her matchstick arms stuck out of an oversized light orange sweater. She looked tiny, fragile, like an anorexic. The faint odor of marijuana hung in the air, but she didn't look stoned. Angie decided to let that go for the moment.

"Come in," the girl said, opening the door wide. The room had two unmade beds, a desk, and a small flat screen

TV hanging from the ceiling. A report from the local television station was blaring, and Joanne grabbed the remote and shut it off. "I can't stand to hear the news anyway."

She pointed to the office chair. "Sit down if you want."

"That's okay, I'll stand." Angie fished her notepad out of her shirt pocket. "You're aware that we're investigating Asger Vad's death and the disappearance of his daughter. You babysat her and her brother often, isn't that right?"

"That's right. Mostly Marie, though. I've known the family a few years. I don't understand; did the killer take her after murdering the rest of the family?"

"We don't know," Angie said. An honest answer.

"Marie is so sweet. I can't stand thinking about it."

Angie grimaced and silently cursed the media, which all morning had been obsessed with theories about the deaths of the volcanologist and his family, as well as the disappearance of the daughter. "We don't know yet," she repeated. "We're trying to establish where she was yesterday, and I was hoping you might know something. As we understand it, you picked her up after school, is that right?"

Joanne nodded. "Right, but I really don't know very much. I picked her up at three; I do that three times a week. We hung out here and read Harry Potter, and I helped her with her math. She had to go home at five."

"How did she get home?"

"Her mom stopped by around that time. She was almost always the one who picked her up. Her dad did it once in a while."

Angie thought about the two cars parked in the Vad's driveway. Nothing had seemed unusual. They hadn't yet established whose winter clothes were hanging in the hall, which was why they didn't know if Marie had left the house dead or alive, wearing her coat. "Do you know which coat she had on when she left here?"

"Yeah, she had on her thick down coat. Light purple. I don't remember the brand. She loved it; it was fairly new and she wore it all the time."

"What about the rest of her clothes?"

"A light-colored pair of jeans and a sweater. I think maybe it was a purple fleece. Purple was her favorite color. I can hardly stand thinking about it. I mean, God, what if she's being tortured?" She sniffed and dried more tears off her cheek.

Angie swallowed the lump in her throat. "What's she like?"

Joanne thought that over for a moment. "She's wonderful, I just love that kid. Some people might think she's a bit introverted and odd, but that's only until you get to know her. Really, she's great. Fun to be with. Even though we've had a few ups and downs."

"What do you mean?"

"Sometimes she tells so many stories that I don't know if she's lying or not. Nothing serious, but it's enough that I've had to straighten her out when she's tried to lead me on. It can be a bad habit."

Angie frowned. "What about other people? Does she talk about her school, her girlfriends, her teachers?"

"Some. She really likes the school. Sometimes there's some girlfriend stuff that goes on, catty stuff, but that's normal for her age. She gets along with her teachers, too. Even though she thinks her English teacher is a little bit too rough on her."

Angie looked over at several Take That stickers on the desk. Wasn't Joanne a little bit too young to be a fan? Maybe it was someone else's desk? "Has she mentioned anything lately about any new people in her life? Someone bothering her or trying to make friends with her?"

"You're thinking about a pedophile or something like that?"

"I'm just trying to cover every possibility."

Joanne shook her head. "Nothing like that. I think maybe she would've told me, she's always talking to me when I pick her up. It's like she has to tell me everything that happens to her that day. So, no, I don't think she met anybody on the street that tried something with her."

"What about here?"

"Here?"

"Yes, have any of the other students talked to her or shown any interest in her?"

"No, not at all."

"Okay. I'd like for you to make a list of everyone she's talked about, in any way, bad or good, so I can get a picture of who she's been around. We're going to have to talk with all of them."

Joanne raised an eyebrow. "It won't be a very long list. It's mostly her classmates, like that."

"Just write them all down. Anyone you can think of. Is there anything else you can tell me about her?"

Joanne began crying again, and Angie paused for a moment before finding a Kleenex in her bag and handing it to her. She repeated her question.

"She likes animals. She has Zenna, you know, their dog, and she talks a lot about it. And she says she wants more dogs and a cat as soon as she moves away from home."

She smiled shortly. "As if she's about to do that. We've also walked a lot of trails around here, she's always wanting to spot squirrels. Even though she's lived here all her life, it's like her fascination with nature is new somehow. It's all animals, animals, animals."

Joanne frowned and looked down at her hands. Her nails were short and badly manicured.

"Those stories she tells," Angie said. "Could you count on her telling the truth about things that happened to her during the day? Were there times when she'd say something, just to make her life sound interesting?"

Joanne ran a hand through her dark hair and picked at a small scratch on her cheek. She looked uncomfortable. Finally, she said, "I admit I've had my doubts once in a while. I don't mean that in a bad way. I don't mean she was all the time lying to get out of something. It's more like… like her imagination runs away with her."

"You mean, she's not a compulsive liar?"

"No. That's an ugly label, and it doesn't fit her at all."

"Did you know her parents well, Asger and Mette?"

Joanne hugged herself tightly. "Yeah, because sometimes I babysat both of the kids at their place, and they let me borrow their computer equipment for my schoolwork. They have a color printer and a scanner. And if I was around at dinner time, I ate with them. They were really nice that way."

"What did you think of them?"

"I never really thought that much about them. They were friendly. The dad was a little formal. But he was polite. I liked the mom. Mette. She was pretty cool."

"Cool, what do you mean?"

"Like she was helpful, intelligent. She taught the kids a lot about Alaska and nature. How the native tribes lived, how people survived under tough conditions. I know because Marie talked a lot about it. Mette was really interested in the country around here. I liked that."

"What about her relationship to her children?"

Joanne shrugged. "I never saw anything to criticize her for. They were always well-dressed and had warm clothes. She didn't just buy clothes that looked good, she bought stuff that could stand the cold. Like Marie's light purple coat. Asger was more like he was living in his own world. But it seemed to me he treated the kids good."

"What about their relationship. Did they seem to get along?"

"The parents?"

"Yes."

"I don't know. Sometimes it was like there was something in the air. You know, you're sitting there at the dinner table and they only speak really shortly to each other. Like, one syllable words. One time Marie said they'd argued about money her mom had spent, and she was scared they were going to split up. But it was just that one time."

Angie stuck her notepad and pen back in her pocket, brought out a card, and handed it to the young woman. "If you think of something else, call me. And one last thing. Yesterday, when you picked her up, what kind of mood was she in?"

"Really good. Happier than usual." Joanne frowned. "In fact, I commented on it when she left. I said she was in a really good mood."

"And what did she say?"

"She said she was getting a new pair of boots."

Chapter Five

HOMICIDE WAS AN OPEN-SPACE OFFICE
ENVIRONMENT, each officer with their own territory. A
long table marked a conference area. The wall behind the
table was covered by a large whiteboard and short shelf
with a stack of files, a small American flag, and a green
plastic crocodile that no one claimed to know anything
about. Angie nodded at her fellow officers and sat down
with a cup of coffee. The warm, comfortable room had
come to feel like a second home to her.

The interview with Joanne was swirling in her head.
Marie's family seemed to be normal. If the killer had taken
her, why? Why her? Were they looking for a pedophile the
family had walked in on as he was kidnapping her? She
hoped not; it didn't feel right, either.

Today, Smith wore a gray suit with a green tie; he stood
by the table in front of the whiteboard, scratching his thick
salt-and-pepper hair and looking soberly at the many faces
as they settled in their chairs. The unusual silence was
awkward. Also, he looked at her a bit oddly, as if he had
something up his sleeve.

It had been business as usual the day before. Everyone was paired up and had their job to do. One team had been on a case involving a drunk criminal who had died accidentally during an arrest. Another had been investigating a man who had called and turned himself in after shooting his wife. And she had been finishing up a case involving the shooting of a pusher. Killers were identified quickly in practically every case, and their percentage of solved cases was very high. For the most part, Smith's close-knit unit worked well together. Everyone had their strengths, and Angie couldn't imagine a better place in the world to work.

"All right," Smith said. "We're all here, I believe."

Everyone focused on him. Cases such as this were rare in Alaska, and the state was already in an uproar. The phone had been ringing all morning, and she'd heard that Smith had been at his desk, trying his best to reassure the press and several people who had known the family. He began by summarizing what they'd found that morning.

"Angie is leading the investigation," he continued. "I'll get to who will be assisting her in a moment."

He stared at her and she narrowed her eyes and stared back, suspicious now. She'd known him for several years, and she could always see when he was about to pull something on her.

He moved on. "There are a lot of aspects to this case we need to deal with; we're going to have to find the resources. Asger and Mette Vad's life and circle of friends, the murder weapon, the ashes, the dollhouse, their daughter Marie who is missing."

He rubbed his eyes, tried to blink away their weariness. "The latter is our first priority, Marie might still be alive. Several troopers are searching around Anchorage, Matsu Valley, and down towards Seward and the Kenai Peninsula. They've been told to look everywhere. Empty buildings, abandoned houses, anywhere at all she could have been taken, and to talk to any witnesses who could have seen her with someone. If we find her, we'll probably find our killer."

"We're almost sure she was home," Angie added. "But we can't be absolutely sure she was there when the killer broke in."

"And," Smith said, "according to the babysitter Angie spoke with, Marie was wearing a light purple down coat. The techs say it's not on the premises."

"So, she might actually be sleeping over at some girl-friend's house," a young officer said, his voice hopeful.

Smith looked skeptical. "That's unrealistic. By now the whole town knows she's missing; the news has spread fast. The media has been on the story for two hours now, and already some students have printed up posters with her face and stuck them up over half the town. She would have gotten ahold of us somehow if she could or wanted to. She's vanished into thin air."

"Maybe she got scared and ran away when the guy broke in," suggested Danny, a stocky officer in his late 30s. "She might be hiding somewhere."

"But there are four people inside the dollhouse," Angie said. "Four of them were supposed to die. Why isn't she dead too? It doesn't add up, not at all."

The sergeant paced a few moments with his hand in his gray pants pocket. "Exactly. And that brings us to the doll-house. Somebody built it. The techs have looked at it and they say it's made of small pieces of varnished oak. Looks like professional work. It could be a cabinet maker or some other sort of craftsman. Maybe the killer made it, maybe not. I don't want any information about the dollhouse getting out; the public would be scared out of their wits. But a few of you are going to have to check this out. Maybe this type of dollhouse is sold somewhere. With or without the dolls."

Smith pointed to the next line on the board. "We don't know much about the weapon yet. We might not be able to pin it down. No bullets or casings have been found at the crime scene; the killer knew what he was doing and he covered his tracks. But Danny, maybe you can check reports of stolen weapons. We can only hope it'll show up in some bushes or something."

He knew it was a very long shot. He took a sip of coffee; his cup had "Hero" printed on it. "As most of you have seen, we're already bringing in all the neighbors for questioning. That's going to take most of the day."

"But then there are the ashes," Angie said.

Smith nodded. "That must be in connection with Asger Vad. It could be a co-worker he humiliated or some volcano-obsessed lunatic. There's no doubt it has some sort of significance. We're looking into it. Angie, we'll need to talk to the people he worked with at the university and observatory, and other people who knew him."

"So, who's going to be with Angie?" said Linda, an investigator. She sounded hopeful.

Smith frowned and glanced over at Angie. "It's a little complicated," he said through clenched teeth. "The thing is, the Danish police are sending one of their investigators over, and since we'll be talking to several Danes who knew the family, he'll be assisting us."

Angie gasped. "What? That's lousy."

"Angie!"

"Why do I get stuck with him? Why can't he just hang around, be an observer? I don't have to haul him around in the car with me, do I?"

Smith narrowed his blue eyes. "Look. There's nothing we can do; the decision was made higher up."

"So what? Since when did we start sucking up to them? Surely the decision can be unmade."

"They assured us he's extremely competent. Presumably, he's an experienced detective lieutenant."

"Really?" Angie said. "Like that's a big deal. He's probably some snob Viking asshole who's not going to do us any good at all."

"We're going to make him welcome. That's who we are. As I said, he could be very useful to us because the victims were Danish. He'll be arriving tomorrow around noon, and you can pick him up at the hotel later. I don't want to hear any crap about this."

"Yeah," Linda said. She swiped a lock of her hair behind her ear. "He'll probably be so jet-lagged that he'll just snooze in the car. Or else he'll stare at all the magnificent scenery and babble about whales and bears. If you're lucky, he'll go skiing and you'll never see him again."

Angie scowled. She was used to driving alone, taking care of herself; she didn't like having anyone else in the car. Especially some Danish stranger who knew nothing about their town or criminal justice system.

Smith smiled. "Make sure he's issued a weapon and that you both make the best of the situation."

Angie held back a sigh and mumbled something ugly under her breath. It seldom paid to discuss things with her boss.

"And while you're waiting ..." He held a dramatic pause, "you can watch the autopsies. All the victims were brought in this morning, and Jane Lohan, the forensic pathologist, has already started on them."

He glanced at his watch. "Good thing it's close by."

Chapter Six

FROM THE PLANE, Trokic looked down on the mountainous landscape below and wondered if some of them were volcanoes. He shuddered at the thought of a sudden eruption, ashes being spewed out into the atmosphere. Ashes with tiny rock particles that would fly into jet engines, melt, and shut the engines down.

The plane was filled up, partly by an entire national hockey team planning to spend the winter in Anchorage, the passenger next to him had explained. Shortly after takeoff from Seattle, the pilot had announced it was snowing in Anchorage, with temperatures in the lower 20s. Half the passengers had applauded this news, which Trokic thought was bizarre. What had they been expecting? And was snow really something to clap for?

He wondered how his American colleagues would receive him. Presumably, they'd told Captain Andersen that a Danish investigator was more than welcome. But really, was he? Would he enjoy having a foreign detective following him around? He hoped they'd be able to work together without any problems. Otherwise, the next several days were going to be awfully long.

He had slept quite a bit on the way over, but now it was time to do some reading in Asger Vad's books, research articles, and interviews, which the captain had been kind enough to loan him. He tried to ignore the stewardesses banging around in the galley. Could the key to the family's murder lay in any of this? Was Asger the intended victim? Had he stepped on someone's toes? The volcanologist had written three books, all in English. One, "On the Edge of Hell," described the inner processes of a volcano. Dry reading about cracks in the earth, continental plates, magma, lava, and ashes. The various types of volcano were covered, and the book was full of illustrations, graphs, and boring black-and-white photos. Trokic emptied another glass of red wine from Alaska Airlines' dubious selection, skimmed through the book, and stuck it back in his carry-on. The second book, "The World's Volcanoes," was a reference work about the largest and most significant volcanoes, active and inactive. Hekla on Iceland, Etna in Italy, Colima in Mexico, Kilimanjaro in Tanzania, Mauna Loa in Hawaii, and a number of others Trokic had never heard of. Apparently, Asger had been to all of them; he'd written a short travel story to accompany each volcano. The writing was easily understandable and enthusiastic, and at least the photos were in color.

The last book was dedicated to Mount Redoubt, an active stratovolcano southwest of Anchorage that Trokic had never heard of. Asger apparently had a thorough and unique knowledge of it. The book had several photos of the snowy, slightly asymmetrical, cone-shaped volcano. Its latest activity had taken place in 2009, the book said. Not all that long ago. It had erupted several times during a two-week period before finally calming down.

Three hundred miles later, Trokic had reached the interviews. Captain Andersen had known Asger Vad well, and he'd had only good things to say about him. And because they were good friends, he had cut out newspaper articles about the volcanologist. One feature article in a Danish daily, *Jyllands Posten*, dealt with his leaving Denmark and devoting his life to a rare branch of science. Asger Vad was both witty and thoughtful, it seemed. He liked Alaska, one of the most beautiful places on Earth, and he and his family had adjusted well to American life. Americans were open and warmhearted, though there were also people who at times were limited in their world-view, and also a bit too religious, in his opinion. But for the most part he enjoyed his life there; he was an advisor for students writing their theses, he wrote books and studied Alaska's volcanoes, and along with his colleagues he kept an eye out for volcanic activity.

Simply put, he came off as a serious and likable man with respect for nature, and none of the reading material gave the slightest hint as to why he was lying in the town's morgue, his throat stuffed with ashes, the victim of a mass murderer.

Chapter Seven

THE SCIENTIFIC CRIME DETECTION LABORATORY was located on Martin Luther King Jr. Avenue, not far from the police station. It was relatively new and tastefully decorated with white walls and a large glass mosaic gracing the lobby. It looked nice. That is until you opened the heavy doors and walked into the heart of the laboratory, where reality set in. The autopsy facilities were divided into what Angie thought of as the good and the bad section. The latter was closed off with a separate ventilation system; it was exclusively for seriously decomposed corpses that smelled horrible and whose flies and maggots needed to be held in check. The former handled new corpses without such problems. Due to Alaska's short summers, most autopsies were fortunately performed in the good section. The laboratory often received bones from distant parts of Alaska, where people stumbled onto the remains of humans and wanted them identified. Most were from old gravesites, but once in a while, a person showed up who had been buried underneath the snow and had gone missing for several years.

Things were hectic at the laboratory. Office girls were

busy at their computers when Angie signed in. Some
mumbled a hello as she walked past, adding that people
were apparently dying like flies at the moment. Angie
walked into the autopsy room.

The pathologist, Jane Lohan, was leaning over a corpse
on the steel table in front of her. She straightened up when
she saw Angie. "Have you found Marie Vad?"

Angie shook her head. "No. But we're doing absolutely
everything we can. The whole town is on the lookout, we're
turning over every rock."

"I can't bear to think about it," Jane said. "It hasn't been
the best of mornings here. You're just in time for the grand
finale. The main character, so to speak."

The room was spacious enough to perform four autopsies simultaneously. For a moment, Angie had imagined the
entire Vad family would be lying there, each on a separate
table. But Lohan had apparently decided to take them one
at a time.

Angie dried her sweaty palms on her black pants and
stared down at the body of Asger Vad. There was surpris-
ingly little blood, and had it not been for the small entry
wound on his forehead, he looked as if he might have died
of natural causes. *Someone must really have been angry*, she
thought.

Jane carefully cut the victim's clothes off and put them
in a numbered bag, to be sent to the lab for analysis. She
was in her late forties, with a small, angular face, clear green
eyes, and dark brown hair in a ponytail. Her face seemed
frozen in a worried expression, and Angie was always
surprised when her face cleared up and she suddenly
smiled.

She raised an eyebrow in Angie's direction. "I've been
busy all morning and I've just about had it. I've seen a lot in
my time, but this…I think this beats everything. I'm sorry I

didn't have time to talk to you earlier; it would've been good for us both. But it was important to get them in here as quickly as possible and get started."

"I was more or less in shock myself," Angie confessed. "The crime scene. It spoke for itself, way too much."

The pathologist nodded. She lived within walking distance of Angie, and occasionally they had a cup of coffee together. Even though they seldom talked about anything other than work, Angie considered her a friend, one who knew her deepest secret and had once saved her from going off the deep end and losing her job. A friend she could trust, whose abilities she had the greatest respect for.

"Anyway, it's time for the last man," Jane said. "Like I said, the main character, the one it's possibly all about. And everything he was supposed to see. But we'll get to that later."

That didn't sound good to Angie. "What do you mean?"

"Let's look at him first, then I'll explain."

Angie studied her; she was hiding something, and that made Angie nervous. But Jane liked to work systematically. She would talk about it when she was good and ready.

"He was dressed in these clothes postmortem, no doubt about that. The same goes for the other two."

"Yeah. That had to have been difficult. Some of the clothes might not have fit them all that well."

"It *is* difficult to put clothes on a lifeless person," Jane acknowledged.

She worked slowly and in silence. Took samples, weighed organs, measured distances. Once in a while, she mumbled into a Dictaphone and wrote a note. Angie made an effort to endure the sound of the saw. The sight of blood and inner organs didn't bother her, nor did the smell, but the sounds were hard to handle; despite spending a lot of time at the lab, she'd never gotten used to them.

She glimpsed her own reflection in a mirror above a sink. Strands of black hair had loosened from her braid under her white knitted cap, and her nervous, brown almond eyes and angular cheekbones made her look like a frightened bird.

A raven, she thought. Her clan's animal.

"I can only confirm our theories up to this point," Jane said. "He was shot at close range. There's only a faint trace of gunshot residue, which means the gun was pressed against his forehead."

She measured the entrance wound. "I would say, forty caliber. The entrance wound is always a bit smaller when a shooting occurs at such close range because the skin stretches some and then contracts. And the exit wound on all three family members is bigger because the bullet hit the skull and tumbled before exiting from the back of the head. I would say from the trauma on all three that the weapon was a common handgun."

Angie licked her dry lips. The pathologist might as well have said that Asger Vad had been killed with a fork. It wouldn't be any more difficult to find the murder weapon, unless it was found in somebody's yard or some other place the killer had dumped it. Even if they stumbled onto it, proving it was, in fact, the murder weapon would be tough, since none of the bullets had been found. Gun permits weren't required in Alaska, where everyone had the right to defend themselves against the wildlife they encountered, whether at home or out in the country.

"I wouldn't count on being able to identify the murder weapon," Jane said. "It all seems very calculated to me. A crime of passion is possible, but if that's the case, he had the presence of mind to cover some of his tracks."

Jane pointed to Asger's wrist. "He'd also been tied up and tried to escape. Fought like a maniac. His skin is flayed in several places, there are wounds. That's not the case with the other victims."

Angie couldn't erase the image from her mind. "So Asger was tied up while the killer took care of the rest of the family? Is that how it happened?"

The pathologist pushed a stray hair back under her cap. "Yes. It was probably necessary. He was obviously a strong man, and I doubt it was easy to overpower him. But it also seems that he was supposed to watch it. The violation."

"What do you mean?"

The furrow between Jane's eyes deepened. "His wife was raped."

"No."

"Yes. He used a condom, and she was bitten repeatedly under her clothes. On her breasts, stomach, and thighs. And there was some bleeding around her vagina. Can you imagine? That he was forced to watch it? It's gruesome." She sighed. "But not as gruesome as watching your own son being killed. In a way, it's the sum of all these gruesome acts that makes this so thoroughly evil."

Angie felt wretched. Her braid was stuck to the back of her sweaty neck. A silence fell between them as they digested Jane's description of what happened. Someone in the building laughed loudly, and they heard a metallic sound, something being drug across a floor. What would the people of Anchorage think about this if all the details came out? The dollhouse, the rape, the violent deaths? The quiet town would panic. People would keep their children home from school. Everyone was used to dangerous animals, but nothing like this.

"All of this puzzles me," Jane finally said. "He rapes the mother, but then he takes the daughter with him. Maybe he knew the family, but Marie put up a fight, so he took her away and killed her somewhere else. Some of this doesn't make sense, anyway."

She looked worriedly at Angie and bit her lower lip. Then she walked over to the sink, pulled off her blue latex gloves, and washed her hands with her back to Angie. "I have to say, I'm pessimistic about Marie. You know how it is. Every hour that goes by, there's less chance we'll find her alive. It's almost unbearable to think about it. I'm thankful I don't have any daughters that age. Or any daughters at all."

Angie nodded and glanced at Asger one last time. What suffering had he gone through in the final minutes of his life? Who could possibly deserve that? His face gave her no answer.

"Maybe," Jane said, "the murderer got a kick out of Asger watching him rape his wife. Maybe you're hunting one of the worst sex offenders we've ever seen in Alaska. That's what bothers me. Not only that he has Marie, but that this family might not be the last."

Grab your copy today!

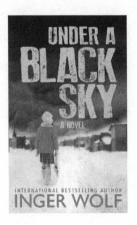

Go here to order:
https://www.amazon.com/dp/B071RTV2W6